The Inheritance

Heidi Hostetter

The Inheritance / Heidi Hostetter. —1st ed.
ISBN 978-0-9961337-0-8

For Hannah, who said I should,
For David, who knew I could,
and
For Emmett, who sat with me every day.

Chapter One

As the etched glass doors slid open, Lydia entered with authority, the snap of her heels echoing against the polished marble floor. As she walked the tiled pathway, she slipped the leather gloves from her fingers and unwound the silk scarf from her neck, tucking both into a lined pocket of her handbag, and focused on the business of shopping.

Striding past a bland display of shapeless winter boots in the shoe department, she glanced with satisfaction at her own boots: hunter green suede with a sharp stiletto heel, perfectly matched to the plaid in her new winter coat.

Rounding the corner to the cosmetic counter and the spicy winter perfumes, Lydia slowed to inhale the comforting scents of clove and cinnamon and felt the pressure uncoil from the base of her neck for the first time all day. Shopping always helped.

"Can I help you find something?"

Lydia glanced at a saleswoman wielding a perfume spray bottle, her eager smile showcasing a disturbing collection of crooked teeth. Not bothering to hide her disdain, Lydia frowned and walked on.

After a nasty work day, she needed something more than a bottle of perfume or shade of lipstick – something substantial, something that would make a difference.

Maybe a new spring coat.

Inspired, she cut through menswear and was about to step onto the elevator when she caught sight of the one place she couldn't go, the only place she ached to belong.

Tucked discreetly into a corner on the first floor was an oasis of privilege, framed with delicate curtains in layered shades of gray and white, the entrance guarded by a fierce receptionist whose sole purpose was to shield clients from customers, and Lydia badly wanted to be a part of the first group.

At her company Christmas lunch the year before, Lydia had successfully pried a stylist's name from the wife of one of the senior partners, and by spring, Lydia had saved enough money to buy something small. It was the experience of being pampered and appearing important that she wanted – she had no occasion to wear the clothes they sold. After waiting three weeks for an appointment, Lydia called into work sick and used the whole morning to get ready.

Arriving precisely on time for her appointment, she had been welcomed by an assistant wearing an elegant black linen sheath accessorized perfectly with a single sterling cuff, and had been guided beyond the curtains to a consultation room. She remembered trying to look unimpressed with such elegance, the matte-silver sconces, the leather club chair, and the small side table laid with champagne and fruit, but she hadn't been sure she was convincing, especially when she saw the pieces they had selected for her; the prices on a few of the dresses were more than her monthly paycheck.

Spanning the entire wall in the dressing room was much more than she had expected – lavish outfits with accessories and shoes instead of the classic, sensibly priced pieces she had hoped for. Evening dresses for benefits she would never attend were paired with delicate sandals and stunning jewelry that she would never wear. And although Lydia had dressed carefully for the appointment, she had known immediately she didn't belong. She wasn't a pampered wife living in a house that was too big, on a street with a clever name, making important wardrobe decisions, and hiring staff to entertain her husband's clients. She was just Lydia Meyer, an underpaid legal researcher with a husband she didn't like living in a house she couldn't afford.

Arriving late with breezy excuses, the senior stylist – Glenda was her name – entered the room with a plastic smile and a sharp eye. Skeletal and petite, she offered a perfunctory fingertip handshake and went to work immediately, uncovering the real Lydia. With every pointed question, Lydia felt the veneer she'd created seep away. Soon after the stylist was "unexpectedly" called away, leaving the assistant to attend Lydia, and Lydia felt her pretend life dissolve like snowflakes in the gutter.

Distracted by the memory of her appointment in the Personal Style department, Lydia was unprepared as the escalator separated into steps. She faltered, grabbing the rubber handrail for balance as her foot caught on the teeth of the stair, scuffing the suede of her new boots. Tamping down her frustration, she straightened her shoulders and entered the coat department.

The clutter and the chaos from the after-Christmas sales had been removed. The ugly red sale signs and tacky discounted rounders had been replaced with polished mirrors, soft lighting, and attentive salespeople.

Lydia inhaled and allowed herself to relax. The best part of shopping came before anything was selected. In that moment there was the magic of possibility. At this moment she could *be* anyone, shopping for anything, and able to afford whatever caught her attention.

"Can I help you find something?" The saleswoman's voice was jarring and overly-familiar, but Lydia was not there to make friends. She was there to be served.

Standing before her was a disheveled woman stuffed into a tight dark sweater, her cheap polyester skirt strained at the seams and her unnaturally dyed hair was pinned to the side of her head with tacky plastic clips.

This woman had nothing to offer, and Lydia dismissed her with a cool glance and a flick of her fingers. "No. Thank you. I'll look for now."

The manager of the department approached soon after. Lydia quickly assessed her appearance and decided to accept her help. She inhaled deeply and slowly as she pondered her vast choices. "I'm looking for a spring coat. Something lightweight but warm, cashmere probably. And in a pastel spring color..." she fluttered her fingers in the air as if the exact description eluded her, "...maybe blue."

A practiced smile slid into place, one so similar to Glenda's that Lydia's heart skipped a beat. "Of course. My name is Vivien." She inclined her head toward the same woman Lydia had rejected just moments before. "Nadia can show you to the dressing room while I find something for you."

The clerk led Lydia to the fitting room without a word. She unlocked the thin slatted door using the key tethered to her

4

wrist. The moment Lydia cleared the threshold, Nadia released the door and it slammed shut.

In a flash, Lydia spun around to open the door, her face burning. "Did you just *slam* that door?"

"No, I didn't." The woman's voice was cool, unconcerned, an insolent smile spread across her face. "These doors are sometimes not what they seem to be."

For a second too long she held Lydia's gaze, and it was in that moment Lydia decided to leave. This was not the experience she wanted. Just as she stepped from the dressing room, Vivian breezed down the hallway carrying a blue coat like a trophy. With a look of triumph, she offered it to Lydia. "It was delivered only this morning and hasn't even been moved to the display yet."

Light as a robin's egg and soft as a whisper, Lydia felt the silk lining slide over her arms and settle perfectly on her shoulders. Vivien fastened the contrasting belt and stepped back so they both could admire Lydia's reflection. She looked elegant. And important.

"No one else has this coat. You will be the first." Vivien draped a silk scarf in a slightly darker shade of blue around the lapels of the coat and the effect was so stunning that Lydia almost forgot to breathe.

As Lydia turned to congratulate Vivien for finding a garment so exquisite, she caught Nadia and Vivien in an unguarded moment. Nadia tilted her head slightly toward Lydia and rolled her eyes; Vivien returned her look with a curl of her lips.

Lydia's heart squeezed. They knew she was pretending, that

she had no use for a blue cashmere spring coat. But she refused to be pitied. Drawing herself to her full height, she shrugged off the coat and handed it back.

"Shall I box it up for you?" The mask settled back over Vivien's face so quickly that Lydia could almost believe her expression was real.

Almost.

"No." Lydia shook her head. "I don't want it."

As Lydia reached for her things and prepared to leave, Vivien tried again. "The cashmere is perfect for you, but I understand that carrying it with you while you shop might be uncomfortable. Might I suggest we have it delivered to your home? It's a service we offer only to select clients...." Her voice trailed off as she stood beside the door and waited.

Lydia understood she was being manipulated, but at that moment she didn't care. She'd spent her days alone in the law library researching minutia for attorneys who didn't appreciate her while rejecting lunch invitations from uneducated secretaries who were beneath her. She felt like the classic British governess: better than a servant, not quite family.

She followed the women to the register, watching the price tag flutter in their wake and trying to read the numbers. She hadn't planned to buy anything today. She didn't have money to buy. All she wanted was to be served.

Vivien slid behind the counter and removed a thick ivory notecard from a drawer. Uncapping a silver pen, she asked, "Where would you like this delivered?"

For the briefest moment, Lydia imagined she lived in one of the big houses in the neighborhood that her little house overlooked. She could pretend that someone would be at the house to sign for the package and whisk it upstairs to hang it in her cedar closet, and soon she would wear it to a charity luncheon. But in reality, if it were delivered and left on the doorstep of her house, it would be stolen.

"Actually, I have an event I can wear it to tomorrow, so I'd like to take it with me." The event was work, and no one would see her at all.

Both Vivien and Nadia pretended not to care that the cost of the coat had to be spread among three credit cards. Instead they complimented her good taste, describing places she could wear the coat and painting a picture Lydia wished were true.

On the way home, Lydia drove through the Short Hills neighborhood she *should* have lived in, the one she could have lived in, if the chance hadn't been stolen from her. Filled with doctors, lawyers, and executives, the houses were set back from the tree-lined street. Behind a wide front yard, the outside was architecturally perfect, the inside professionally decorated, with a lawn service, a live-in staff, and pair of potted evergreens flanking the front door.

But her house wasn't in this neighborhood.

Her house was in a neighborhood that bordered the one she wanted to live in. In her neighborhood, the streets were threaded with frost-cracks that were never repaired, the trees were spindly and neglected instead of arching gracefully over the street as they should, and the sidewalks were hastily poured concrete instead of carefully laid brick.

They had been able to afford their house only because it had been in foreclosure. Greg's salary, commission generated from managing client investment accounts, fluctuated wildly and the salary she was paid for her job as a researcher at a law firm was laughable. The first thing she had done after they had moved in was hire a lawn service – one of the big white trucks from the good neighborhood came to her house twice a month and parked where all the neighbors could see.

Today, in fact, in addition to spring clean-up – mowing, edging, and sweeping – the landscapers were supposed to plant spring flowers in the window boxes as well. Just in time for Easter.

But as she drove up to the house, the boxes were empty.

Instead, taped to the glass front of her storm door was a white business-sized envelope that could only be an invoice. If she could see the paper from the top of the driveway, the neighbors could, too. Tightening her grip on the steering wheel she knew the landscapers hadn't been paid since Thanksgiving, but she had hoped they would come anyway.

She would deal with the invoice but first she had to get past the mailbox. Pulling her car next to the hateful yellow brick, she opened the window, welcoming the cold evening breeze on her hot face. She knew what waited for her inside that mailbox, something she made a point to keep from Greg, but the stack grew bigger and more urgent every day, and keeping it from him was becoming more difficult.

Reaching in, she removed a bundle of letters rubber banded inside a glossy catalog and tossed it onto the passenger seat. As it hit the seat, the band broke and letters exploded onto the floor. She froze. Final notices and past due warnings scattered across her car like landmines; she had never seen so many.

Her breath caught in her throat and her heart pounded in her chest.

Greg could never see this. Most of the bills would have been paid with his January commission, but that was three months past due, and she refused to ask him for it. He would want to know why, and she couldn't tell him.

Entering the house quickly, she made sure Greg wasn't home before moving to the living room and spreading the pile on the hardwood floor. She pulled out a final foreclosure notice and set it aside to take care of in the morning, because it looked like they were serious this time. Gathering the rest she worked swiftly, triaging the bills into piles of urgency, one for utility terminations, another for NSF slips, a third for overdue credit card bills.

As she surveyed the piles, she swallowed, pushing down the acid that burned her throat.

This was Greg's fault.

Everything she had bought in the last five months had been put on credit in anticipation of his January commission. Hosting that stupid Thanksgiving Open House, Christmas gifts for his clients and managers, clothes and makeup for her. She might not have bought such extravagant gifts for her managers if she had known his check would be late.

She put the mortgage notice by the telephone to remind herself to call the moment the bank office opened and pushed everything else under the couch to join similar bills from yesterday's mail.

As she tossed the last catalog across the room and into the trash, the letter that would change her life fluttered from the pages. The envelope was heavy stock and ivory, her name and address handwritten. Sliding her finger under the flap, she pulled out a single sheet of watermarked stationery. She read the letter through twice before allowing a smile to spread across her face.

A way out had presented itself after all.

And best of all, the letter was addressed to her alone – not to her and Greg.

Chapter Two

Thumbing quickly through the screens on her cell phone, Tyra found the contact she needed and sent a quick text.

Project completed and ready to post. Pls advise location.

It was a stupid project – boring and easy to do – but the client, a tech start-up flush with a recent infusion of cash had promised her a bonus for immediate results, and she knew they were waiting.

The reply came almost immediately, and Tyra started the process. As soon as it posted, she could leave. Her car was packed, her apartment vacant, and there was nothing to keep her here.

This restaurant was quiet in the few hours before the lunch rush and it was the best time to work. The only customers were a scattering of snowbirds, retirees who wintered in the desert to get away from the snow and the cold in the north.

"More hot water?" Stale brown water sloshed in the stained carafe as the waitress clutched the orange plastic handle. "Not this water – this water is for customers who overstay their welcome and forget to tip." She side-eyed a table of three older men hunched over what looked like a cribbage board, and she leaned in, finishing with an exasperated whisper. "They stay for *hours.*"

Tyra pushed the teapot closer to the waitress. "Thank you, hot water would be great." She didn't want more, but she also didn't want to talk.

After the server left, Tyra watched the men playing cribbage. The tabletop was littered with twisted sugar packets, and wadded paper napkins, stubby pencils and scorecards. The men bent over their game with the concentration of generals overseeing a battlefield. There was no friendship in that game, no conversation, no laughing. Each man could have been sitting alone, and Tyra wondered what drew them together.

Her cell phone chirped, signaling a waiting text message, and Tyra flicked to it with her thumb.

Project received, thank you. Pls confirm bank routing for payment.

Tyra sent the information and waited for confirmation. She didn't like working this way; it seemed nefarious somehow to request payment as soon as the project was delivered. But startups were unpredictable and she couldn't wait.

Her trip had taken almost three years to plan, and she had dreamed about it for longer than that. A change of climate, a new address, a gamble, and a new start altogether.

The dining room buzzed with hushed conversation and the soft clink of utensils against plates as the few customers finished their meals. The front door opened letting a gust of hot desert air and bright sunshine into the small room. A pair of older women entered, their heads bent together in shared conversation. In unison they walked to a large booth near the wide picture window and settled in. One woman shrugged off her cardigan and draped it casually in the space next to her as the other settled into her seat and anchored her purse firmly in her lap. When their iced tea arrived, the cardigan woman lifted a pink sweetener packet from the box and offered it to her friend. It was accepted with a quick smile of thanks as if it were something routinely done, and Tyra wondered how long you would have to know someone before they knew what sugar you liked. How close you would have to let someone get? What secrets would they have to know? And keep?

The glass front door slammed open letting another rush of hot air into the air conditioned dining room. This time a troop of chattering women entered, herding their drippy toddlers in front of them. Claiming the big center table, they scattered the far end with an assortment of toys so vast it reminded Tyra of the Christmas charity boxes sent to the group home where she used to live.

A toddler's shriek ripped through the air and the noise hit Tyra's spine with the force of an explosion. At the same moment, something solid hit the table and skittered to the edge before falling to the floor.

Instinctively Tyra reached for a weapon. Her fingers scrabbled underneath the napkin for the butter knife – dull now, but strong and heavy, easily concealed and easily sharpened. Gathering her legs underneath her, ready to spring from the chair in any direction, she held the knife in her fist and waited.

The sound of someone speaking came to her as if she were underwater, blurry at first but becoming clearer as she focused.

"It's okay, honey. You're okay." Laying her fingers gently on Tyra's wrist, the server used her other hand to slide the butter knife from Tyra's fist. "It's nothing, just a plastic block."

The Inheritance

As her vision cleared, she began to recognize the restaurant. The floor was carpet, not concrete. There were no bars on the window, and she could leave when she wanted. Her heart pounded as she forced out the breath she had been holding.

The server pushed a glass of ice water toward her. "My husband does that sometimes, when something startles him. Either military or you've done time." While Tyra's heartbeat slowed, the server waited. "You got someone you want me call for you? Someone to come get you?"

Tyra shook her head. There was nobody she could call, nobody would come. The closest person she knew was twenty-five hundred miles away. Reaching for her water glass, she drank it all. "I'm fine now, thank you. I just need to go."

The waitress pulled a notepad from her apron, ripped a page and handed it to Tyra with a deep scowl. "I'd leave, too, if they'd let me."

They both watched as one of the mothers scattered cheerios across the table like chicken feed, and one of the boys smashed the pieces into dust with his plastic hammer.

"Can you imagine the mess they're going to leave for me?" She shoved her order pad back into her apron pocket and glared at them.

Tyra reached into her back pocket to withdraw a few bills and handed them to the waitress.

The woman unfolded them and eyed her warily. "You do know there is no place on earth where a pot of tea costs forty dollars, don't you?"

She pointed her chin at the bag at Tyra's feet. "Wherever you're going, I wish you luck. You're a good customer – you don't leave a mess and you tip way too much. I wish there were more like you." She touched the table top with her fingers. "Good luck."

As she walked away, Tyra glanced at the toddler table. Taking advantage of the server's absence, the mothers packed up quickly and rushed their children out the door, leaving devastation in their wake and no tip on the table.

Reaching into her pocket, Tyra removed a few more bills and left them for the waitress. No bars on the window didn't always mean free to leave.

As she left the dining room, she chose a path close to the fireplace and the two women who lingered over their early lunch. As the women chatted, they leaned in like school girls sharing a secret, and Tyra again wondered how that kind of friendship happened.

She passed the table, wishing she had the courage to smile at them and knowing at once she wouldn't.

Slipping her sunglasses on, she crossed the parking lot to her car. After starting the engine and turning on the air conditioning, she pushed speed dial for the first number on her cell phone. As she counted the rings, she directed the cool air to her face.

"Yeah?" His voice was burly and gruff, and she relaxed the instant she heard it.

"Uncle Mike?" Her voice sounded pathetically weak so she cleared her throat and tried again. "Hi, Uncle Mike, it's Tyra."

"Kit-Kat? Hold ona minute, lemme turn down the idiot box." In the background, she heard the sound of the television being turned down, then the muffled sound of him propping the phone on his shoulder and tilting his head toward it. "Everything okay?"

"I don't think I can do this, Uncle Mike."

There was a silence then she heard him draw a deep breath and let it out slowly. After a moment, he spoke. "I know. It's going to be hard, and you don't have to do this at all. But you've been talking about it for years and saving for years, and now it's time to take your shot." He hesitated, then asked, "That girl's mother talk to you yet?"

"Tressa Montgomery. Her daughter's name was Eileen. No, she still won't talk to me, but she sent me a letter. A little while ago."

"Oh yeah? That's good. What'd the letter say?"

Tyra glanced at her backpack. She kept the letter in a zippered pocket inside. It was never far from her. "She thanked me for paying her daughter's medical bills and gave me permission to go on with my own life. Not exactly forgiveness but–"

Tyra's voice trailed off and Uncle Mike finished for her. "– but maybe that's the best she can do. Her daughter wasn't exactly blameless you know. She understands that and as a mother it's got to be hard to work through."

"Yeah."

"Okay, Kit-Kat. Enough of this. You weren't the only one, and you've paid for your part in this already. Let's start moving forward. Now when are you leaving?"

"I'm on my way out of town now."

"Oh yeah? You got enough dough?"

Tyra laughed. "Yes, Uncle Mike. I've got enough money."

Uncle Mike drove a forklift in a lumberyard in Bayonne, New Jersey, and Aunt Patty waitressed at a diner nearby. Every day for thirty years, he walked two blocks to the diner where she worked so she could make him a hot lunch and sit with him while he ate. After her release, Tyra stayed with Uncle Mike and Aunt Patty until she figured out what she wanted to do. She decided that what she wanted were her sisters.

"All right, then." Uncle Mike paused. "So what're ya waiting for?"

"Okay, I'm going. Give Aunt Patty my best."

"I will, Kit. And remember, you've worked hard for this, but that don't mean it'll be easy. Maureen has her own family and that seems to be all she wants. You might have a better shot with her though, than you do with Lydia." He scoffed. "Lydia's just like her mother. And I can say that because your mother was my baby sister, may she rest in peace. Nothing was ever good enough for her. That's not bad if you're willing to work for it, but neither of them did." Uncle Mike's voice trailed off. "I dunno. I just don't want you to get your hopes up."

"I won't, Uncle Mike. And I know I can always come back to you and Aunt Patty." For an entire week before she left New Jersey, both Aunt Patty and Uncle Mike had practically followed her around the house, reminding her that she didn't have to leave, that she was welcome to stay with them as long as she wanted.

"You bet your ass you can." Uncle Mike's booming laugh traveled across the phone lines and enveloped her like a hug. "Just not today. Twenty-eight freakin' degrees out there with more snow tonight. It's not supposed to snow in March – it's almost Easter, for cryin out loud."

"Is that why you're at home?"

"Yeah. Too much snow in the lumberyard. Anyone stupid enough to buy lumber today has to load it themselves."

"Thanks, Uncle Mike."

"Anytime, Kit-Kat."

Chapter Three

At the bottom of the stairs three duffle bags slumped against the front door, lined up and ready for the camping trip to Echo Lake. Fourteen little girls, two Brownie troop leaders, and three volunteers with camping experience were leaving this morning for a three-night camping trip and would be back on Saturday afternoon, leaving them plenty of time to recover before school started again on Monday. At seven years old, Dilly was just old enough to join and Joe had agreed to chaperone. Excited since January when Maureen and Joe signed her up, Dilly had been packed and impatient to leave for more than a week.

School was out for Easter break and all of her children had plans. Joey, the oldest, was spending the week at a friend's house with the rest of the robotics team, working on their junior year project. Maureen offered to host the team and even provide meals for them, but Joey told her they were practically required to meet at the team captain's house. So she offered to chaperone Juliette's trip to Seattle. Her dance team was driving up from Portland to see two performances, tour a rehearsal space, and take several classes. Juliette had simply rolled her eyes when Maureen had offered to drive.

With Juliette rummaging in her closet upstairs, and Joe in the shower getting ready, Maureen descended the stairs to look for her youngest child. Moving slowly as she always did on the first trip down the stairs, one hand palming the railing while the other grazing the opposite wall as her knees worked out their overnight stiffness. The surgeon had said if she lost thirty pounds she might not need knee replacement after all. Apparently, her condition was borderline, so he gave her a diet to follow and booked another appointment for August. Maureen looked forward to neither.

When she reached the bottom, she leaned against the finial to rest and noticed a lumpy plastic bag tucked behind the duffels. Moving closer to examine it, she smiled, identifying Dilly's handiwork: handles tied together and the top of the bag taped shut with great swatches of blue painter's tape. Peering through the slits in the bag, she realized that Dilly would need to be reminded again not to bring anything crawly back from the lake because, clearly, her youngest daughter was planning to do just that. The bag was stacked with plastic boxes poked with air holes and Ziploc bags stuffed with handfuls of grass.

As Maureen straightened, she heard her daughter humming to herself. She rounded the corner to the kitchen and found Dilly perched on a stool watching the toaster.

"What are you doing, little bunny?"

Dilly answered without taking her eyes away from the toaster. "Making jelly toast for Daddy and me."

Maureen smoothed a dark curl from her daughter's face and kissed the top of her head. "Daddy's still in the shower, so maybe you should eat the first one yourself."

"Okay." Dilly nodded, without taking her eyes from the toaster.

Rounding the corner to the sink, Maureen pulled the carafe from the machine and filled it with water. After scooping grounds into the filter and closing the lid, she clicked the buttons for "bold" and "speed brew" because she wanted it to be ready when Joe came downstairs.

At the sound of metal clattering together, she turned to see Dilly rifling through the silverware drawer. Reaching over Dilly's shoulder, Maureen pulled out a wide plastic knife and offered it to her daughter.

"Dilly?"

"Yes, Mommy?"

"Do you remember me asking you not to bring back anything living – or *anything at all* – from Echo Lake?" Once Dilly had brought back a snail from a hike, explaining that it wasn't really alive because it was hibernating, which was more than sleeping. After that, Maureen had added "anything at all" as a safety measure.

"Yes, Mommy." Her daughter nodded solemnly, climbed onto the stool, and unscrewed the lid from the jar of strawberry preserves.

"Then why do you have a grocery bag filled with critter cups?"

"Oh." Dilly sighed deeply, as if the answer were obvious. "Well, I was just getting ready in case any of them *wanted* to come home with me."

The toaster popped and Dilly pulled on an oven mitt, snatched the bread, and tossed it onto the paper towel in front of her. After plopping a knife full of jelly onto the center of the toast, she carefully spread it to the edges, turning the toast as she worked.

Dilly's concentration was absolute, and Maureen watched until Joe came around the corner into the kitchen. His short hair was still damp from the shower, and he smelled like the spiced soap Juliette had given him for Christmas. Resting a warm hand on Maureen's shoulder he leaned in to kiss her. He tasted like spearmint toothpaste.

"Good morning, ladies."

"Hi, Daddy," Dilly answered as she crunched her toast.

"Hello, Piglet. Are you ready for your big trip?" He rested his hand gently on Dilly's shoulder.

She nodded and stuck another slice of bread into the toaster.

Joe turned to Maureen. "You sure you don't want to go with us? We could always use another chaperone."

Maureen shook her head. This was supposed to be a daddy-daughter trip. "No, you go ahead. I've got plenty to keep me busy around here."

Joe looked dubious but conceded. "Okay, if you're sure." He grabbed a yogurt from the refrigerator, a spoon from the drawer and went to the kitchen table to eat.

He pointed to the newspaper puzzle, already solved and tucked under a yellow placemat on the kitchen table. After Juliette and Dilly were asleep, Maureen kept herself busy as she waited for Joe to come home. "You're finished already." He pointed his spoon at the folded newspaper. "I've never met anyone who loves puzzles more than you do."

"That was from last night; it's yesterday's paper." The coffee machine beeped signaling the end of the cycle. Maureen filled

Joe's travel mug and thermos and added cream to both.

She glanced at Joe, irritated that he had worked so late last night. He caught her eye and flashed a smile, diffusing her anger. After seventeen years of marriage, her husband still made the back of her knees quiver.

The toaster popped a second time, and Dilly slipped on her oven mitts. "I'm making toast for you, Daddy. I already tested it out." She brought her offering, thickly smeared with strawberry preserves and balanced precariously on a saggy paper towel.

Putting his yogurt container on the table, Joe took the toast with both hands. With Dilly carefully watching his reaction, he took an enormous first bite and made an exaggerated display of satisfaction. "Mmmmm. Strawberry is my favorite, Dilly. And the jelly is all the way to the edges exactly the way I like it." After another large bite, he swiped the crumbs from his lips with the back of his hand. "Delicious."

He smiled at Dilly, and Maureen smiled at both of them.

Resting his hand on Dilly's shoulder, he said, "We have to get going Dilly-bar; the car's all loaded up and we have to pick up your friends."

"Okay, Daddy." Dilly hopped off the stool, leaving the knife in the jelly jar and sticky berry lumps on the countertop.

Maureen handed Joe the mug and tucked the thermos into the soft-sided lunch cooler. "You worked late last night." Her voice was reproachful, but she hadn't meant it to be.

Sighing, Joe rubbed the back of his neck. "I missed dinner, I know. I just wanted to make sure nothing came up while we were on the camping trip."

Moving toward the sink, Maureen pulled a dishtowel from the side drawer and ran cold water on it, choosing her words before she spoke. "I'll be here, you know. I can handle whatever comes up. I was right there with you, starting the restaurant. Equal partners, remember?"

Lately the only bone of contention between them was how much time Joe continued to spend at the restaurant, and she suspected the projects that demanded his attention were manufactured and the emergencies could be delegated.

After sixteen years, she was ready to step away from daily operations, let someone else do that part so they could spend time as a family before their children left home. Joey had already taken the SATs, and his score combined with his grades had interested colleges so much that they sent personalized recruiting letters. It broke her heart to know that he would be gone in a little over a year, and Juliette would soon follow. Joe finally had agreed to hire a manager for the restaurant and cut back his hours, but even though Josh had been hired three months ago, Joe still went to work every day.

"I was trying to give you some extra time, too. You need a rest as much as I do." Joe drank deeply from his mug and set it on the counter with a sigh. "This is good, thank you."

As Maureen rinsed the dishtowel to wipe the counter, Joe moved toward the jar of preserves, scraping Dilly's dull plastic knife against the mouth of the jar before dropping it into the dishwasher.

"Josh seems to have everything under control. I don't think he'll call this weekend." Popping the last corner of the toast into his mouth, he dragged the back of his hand across his lips. "This is good. Is this the sample they left for the restaurant?"

Maureen nodded. "One of them. I thought we'd try one at home, and I left another jar for the baking crew."

"It's good. The strawberries were ripe, and I think they mixed in a bit of coriander." Turning to leave the kitchen, Joe called over his shoulder, "Can you save it for me? I'd like to work with it a bit when we get back on Monday."

Biting back a reply, Maureen screwed the top on the jar and slid it into the refrigerator, then poured a cup of coffee. As she swallowed the first sip and felt the warmth in her chest, she closed her eyes in bliss.

After another sip she wondered what she could do with an empty house and a free week. At the sound of light footfalls padding down the hallway, Maureen turned to see Juliette enter the kitchen, head bent over her cell phone, ponytail swaying as she walked. Tall and lean, Juliette moved with the grace of a dancer.

Juliette spoke without looking up, her voice dripping with disdain. "I need my team suit. They're on their way." Her fingers tapped her screen.

Maureen waited, reminding herself that this was the daughter she brought to the Nutcracker matinee every year since she was six years old. The same daughter who loved building pillow forts, stories about fairies, and pretend tea parties. This daughter who couldn't bear to look at Maureen when she spoke.

After a long moment, Juliette looked up from her phone and fixed Maureen with a look of deep irritation. "Mother."

Every conversation with Juliette had become a chess game,

a test of wills with moves and countermoves. It was exhausting and Maureen hated it.

"Yes?" Maureen moved to the sink and leaned against the counter.

Juliette sighed but stopped short of rolling her eyes. "Mother. I need my team suit. Bridget's mother doesn't like to wait."

Maureen noted the irony of Juliette wanting to be ready for her friends while saving her venom for her own mother and Maureen's patience crumbled like a sandcastle in the tide. After hooking the damp dishtowel over the faucet to dry, she turned to leave the kitchen but kept her voice carefully neutral. "I hope you find it soon, especially if Bridget's mother doesn't like to wait."

Maureen left Juliette in the kitchen, knowing her daughter was glaring holes in her back. Maureen's relationship with Juliette, the toddler in pink tights and tiny ballet slippers who used to line up an audience of stuffed animals and dance for them on the tiled floor of the kitchen, had become fragile and heart-wrenching in the last two years. Not a day went by that Maureen didn't wish their relationship was different.

Twenty minutes later, the team suit recovered from the floor of her closet, Juliette ran down the driveway, smiling and waving at the minivan full of her friends. Maureen would have liked to at least have driven some of the girls up to Seattle, but Juliette absolutely forbid her mother's involvement – not to help drive and absolutely not to chaperone.

Maureen watched her daughter tumble into the van and close the door behind her. Bridget's mother waved cheerfully through the windshield before backing out of the driveway and pulling away. Almost immediately after Juliette had left, Joe and Dilly grabbed the rest of their gear and headed for the truck, and Maureen waved them off as well. When the taillights of Joe's truck melted into the early morning traffic, she closed the door and wandered back to the kitchen.

Inside the house was empty and quiet. The snap of the second hand on the wall clock echoed in the empty kitchen, and for the second time that morning, Maureen wondered what to do with her week. Pulling her cell phone from the charger, she dialed the number to the restaurant. By now the overnight baking crew should be clearing out, and Josh should be settling in.

He answered on the second ring. "Kauffman's Portland, this is Josh."

The name of their restaurant always made Maureen smile. Seventeen years ago both of them dropped out of college after realizing a formal education had nothing to offer them. They withdrew after a single semester and found jobs in a small restaurant in the Pearl District of Portland near the railroad station. Joe wanted to be a cook, and Maureen wanted to be with Joe. After a particularly rainy year, the owners decided to sell the restaurant and move somewhere they could see the sun. When the owners offered to finance the loan, she and Joe accepted. While Maureen remodeled the dining room, adding more tables and a take-out service, Joe overhauled the menu to include local ingredients and an on-site bakery. When it was all finished, Joe changed the name, adding the city in case their restaurant became a chain.

Married by then, Maureen had stayed home with two-year-old Joey and newborn Juliette, placing orders, calculating payroll, and paying taxes while Joe worked in the kitchen. At night, the children slept in the restaurant's office while she supervised the front of the house and Joe cooked. It was a staggering amount of work, but Joe loved it. Maureen didn't.

"Hi, Josh. This is Maureen."

In the awkward silence that followed, Maureen immediately regretted calling. To her, checking in was automatic, part of her day. Every morning after seeing the kids off to school, she called Joe to see if he needed anything before she drove to the restaurant herself. But Josh was newly hired, and to him a boss was calling to check up on him on the heels of another boss working late the night before. He had to feel confined.

"Things are settled over here. The produce delivery is unloaded and stacked in the walk-in; bread and pastries are displayed in the case. And we open for take-out in fifteen minutes."

His voice was too energetic, too upbeat, like someone trying too hard to prove himself and it was painful to hear. She didn't want him to doubt himself; he was doing a great job. She ended the call as soon as she politely could and would not call again. "Okay then. Call me if you need me."

After hanging up, she turned toward the bay window near the kitchen table. Outside a brown bird pecked at the peanut butter pine cone Dilly had made in school. The driveway and patio were silvered with dew and a quick glance at the sky revealed a low ceiling of layered dark clouds. According to the calendar, spring was supposed to officially start later this month, but in Portland the winter rains continued, and the sun wouldn't be out full-time for several more months. Maureen hoped Joe had remembered to pack the rain fly for the tent, and that Dilly would find and wear the extra clothes Maureen had stuffed into her daughter's duffle. At seven years old, Dilly was known to dress for imaginary weather.

Stacking the last of the scattered breakfast dishes into the dishwasher, Maureen thought how she could easily stay home and waste several days puttering around the house, but this time she wanted something better. What did most women do with an unexpected long weekend? All her friendships originated from the restaurant or the kids' schools and it was a little unnerving to realize she didn't have a single person to call who wouldn't be busy today. She used to have her own friends, but she had let them melt away as she focused her energy on the chaos of a new restaurant and parenting a growing family.

On a last sweep through the kitchen putting things away, she noticed a section of the newspaper tucked near the restaurant's recipe book: the business section, commercial real estate. Joe had mentioned wanting to open a second location, but she hadn't realized he was actively searching. Refolding the newspaper, she walked to the recycle bin and stuffed it in with more energy than was necessary. In the resulting puff of air, a letter she had received a few days ago fluttered to the ground. Maureen retrieved it and was about to put it back into the bin when she decided to read it again.

The letter, hand addressed to her alone and printed on ivory stationery, was from an attorney in Inlet Beach, a small town along the coast of Oregon about two hours' drive from her house.

She and Joe had been there once before Dilly was born. It was an easy drive. They had left after breakfast and arrived with plenty of time to let the kids run on the hard-packed sandy beach before deciding to spend the night. Maureen remembered how beautiful everything had been, and she wondered why they couldn't have made the trip more often.

Maureen brought the letter to the kitchen table to give it her full attention. Apparently a relative named Jensen had bequeathed property at Inlet Beach to Maureen and her sisters equally. But that was what made the letter unbelievable: Maureen didn't have a relative at Inlet Beach. With both of her parents gone, Maureen had only her sisters, Lydia and Tyra, and Uncle Mike and Aunt Patty in New Jersey. She would have known if a relative close enough to leave her an inheritance had lived two hours away.

A whisper of doubt crept toward her like a fog. It might be possible she had a relative in Inlet Beach – she wasn't close to either of her sisters. It had been years since she'd spoken to Lydia, and Maureen didn't even know where Tyra lived.

Tyra was the baby of the family, four years younger than Lydia, and eight years younger than Maureen. When she was younger, Tyra was happy and smart, friends with everyone and interested in everything. But a routine standardized test in sixth grade had changed everything. Her scores had been flagged as unusually high and more testing had labeled her gifted. Despite her protests, Tyra was pulled from a public school she loved and placed in an academically aggressive private school just before seventh grade. The school administrators had said it was the best environment for her – that she was lucky and would flourish in her new environment. But she hadn't.

Tyra had just turned fourteen when she was arrested for selling drugs in school, and it had shocked everyone. The drugs she'd sold were tainted, causing the death of one child and the hospitalization and eventual death of another. Her parents were devastated and sold everything they could to pay lawyers and experts who vowed to keep Tyra out of jail. But after a long trial, Tyra had been found guilty of manslaughter and sentenced to juvenile detention.

To her shame, Maureen hadn't been at the trial because a tiny bit of her had believed Tyra was getting what she deserved. But she hadn't counted on a guilty verdict.

None of them had.

Crumpling the letter and the envelope, she turned to throw them away when she noticed a detail in the last paragraph.

"...I would be pleased if you could attend a meeting at 11:30 a.m. in my office to discuss the details of the bequest on Thursday, March 3..."

Thursday was tomorrow. Maybe her sisters might be there. She hadn't seen either one of them in years, and lately she found herself searching the internet for information about where they were and what they were doing. Maybe this meeting could be a small first step in bringing them together.

After calling the number on the letterhead and leaving a message for the attorney to confirm, Maureen turned her attention to the puzzle of who the Jensens were. It took a bit of digging, but she found Uncle Mike's cell number and called him.

"Mike Franzelli."

The rumble of heavy machinery in the background made it

difficult to hear and she instantly regretted calling during a work day. She hesitated, hoping she wouldn't have to explain who she was. She hadn't spoken to him in years; contact with him and Aunt Patty was sporadic, down to a Christmas card and an occasional school picture of the kids and she regretted that, too. She wished she had made more time for them.

"Hi, Uncle Mike. This is Maureen Kauffman."

She held her breath and waited.

"Maureen. Hello. How are you?" Uncle Mike's voice stretched across the phone line and a picture of him flashed before her – round-faced with a wide smile and a full beard that she and her sisters tugged when they were younger just to see if it was real. He lived for ice hockey and campaigned hard to persuade each of his nieces that the NY Rangers were the only team worth cheering for.

After asking about Aunt Patty and telling him about Joe and the kids, she steered the conversation toward the inheritance.

"Uncle Mike, do we have any relatives named Jensen?"

"Jensen?"

"Elizabeth and Lloyd Jensen. They would have lived in Inlet Beach in Oregon."

Uncle Mike blew a puff of air. "Lemme think..... No one related to me or to your mother, but I remember something about the Jensens being related to your father. Through his mother, I think. We met them once a long time ago, but I don't remember exactly when. We don't get out that way much."

"They lived in Inlet Beach?"

"Yeah, something like that. Along the Oregon coast, if I remember."

"It seems odd that I've never heard of them. Did you know they left us a house?"

"Left who a house? You and Joe?"

"No, Tyra, Lydia and me. I don't even remember them, and they've left us a beach house."

"Interesting. What are you going to do with it?"

"I'm on my way to go see it."

"By yourself?"

The question struck Maureen as odd, but she answered anyway. "Yes. Joe is camping with Dilly, and Juliette and Joey are gone for the rest of the week."

"Good." The phone muffled as Uncle Mike called to someone in the distance over the sound of heavy machinery. And when he came back on the line, he was apologetic. "Sorry, but I gotta go, Maureen – they're waiting for this order. Have fun down there and call us once in a while. I know your Aunt Patty would like to hear from you."

And he hung up before she could ask why he thought it was good that she was going alone to Inlet Beach.

She used the rest of the day to clean the house, wash some clothes, and make sure her children knew she wouldn't be home. She reminded them to use their own house keys, but she shouldn't have bothered. Joey was busy with his group, and Juliette wasn't listening.

In the morning, she threw some clothes into a suitcase and grabbed a handful of cash from the coffee can under the sink.

After locking the doors and checking every window, she was on her way.

She drove in silence for a while, letting her mind wander over memories of her family. Both of her parents had died a few months after Tyra's sentence in a car accident that had seemed avoidable. Maureen didn't know where Tyra was now, and the last time she had seen her sister Lydia had been at her parents' funeral, but that was a memory Maureen would rather not have.

After her parents' death, Maureen traveled back to Ohio. She paid bills. Closed accounts. Cleaned the house. Sorted a lifetime of memories from closets and drawers. When she had scrubbed every surface, vacuumed every rug, mopped every floor, and agonized over what to send to charity, her sister Lydia arrived asking very specific questions about remaining assets. It wasn't until Maureen showed her sister proof -- bank statements, personal loan agreements, and mortgages documents that Lydia final accepted there was nothing left in their parents' estate. Everything had been spent on Tyra's defense. The bills for lawyers and fees for expert witnesses had been staggering.

On the last night Maureen would ever spend at her parents' house, she stood at the sink washing dishes using the last drops of her mother's favorite lavender dish soap. With nothing left to do but leave the keys for the estate agent in the morning, Maureen looked forward to finally collapsing and surrendering to unconsciousness. It was then that Lydia had chosen to stride into the kitchen flashing a stack of sample wedding invitations, expecting to discuss each in detail.

Maureen hadn't known Lydia was engaged and at that

moment didn't care. What happened next was a mistake. Maureen remembered screeching at her sister about the appropriateness of bringing wedding invitations to a funeral, accusing her of coming home only because she smelled money. It was the last time they had spoken. If they had been closer to begin with, maybe they would have worked things out, but neither of them tried.

The rest stop along the highway gave Maureen a good excuse to pull off the highway and stretch her legs. Years of waiting tables at the restaurant, pulling stock from the walk-in, and rushing about had taken a toll on her knees and made her feel old.

When she got back in the car, she sat for a minute before starting the engine and thought back to the conversation with Uncle Mike. Besides the tug of guilt she felt for not calling Aunt Patty more often, the quickness of his answer nagged at her. The Jensens knew enough about her and her sisters to leave them a substantial property, yet Maureen had no memory of them and Uncle Mike's did? How was that possible?

Turning her attention back to the car, she started the engine, but before pulling back onto the highway, she programmed the property address into her GPS. She was early for the attorney's appointment and maybe if she went to the house, she would remember the people who left it to her.

As she drove, the misty rain turned to heavy drizzle, her wipers slapping across the windshield, and she reached to poke the defrost button. She passed the first beach exit as her GPS insisted and clicked her blinker for the second. Once off the highway, she caught glimpses between the trees of a churning gray ocean stretching all the way to the horizon and wanted to stop the car to look, but the road was a narrow two-lane and the hill was steep.

Her GPS smugly proclaimed that she had reached her destination, but there was no house along this road. The only turn off was a muddy dirt road that disappeared through a grove of twisted hemlock trees. After driving past it twice, she took the turn and hoped for the best.

When she cleared the hemlock trees, the muddy path changed to chunky gravel before opening up to a larger courtyard.

To the right was the main house, a stately three-story Victorian with a gabled roofline and three dormer windows that lined up neatly across the top. The house was set back from the driveway and positioned so the back faced the bluff instead of aligning with the street, as if defying convention.

Wrapping the entire first floor was a deep porch accented with rounded columns and outlined with a crumbling milled railing. The first floor was built entirely from stone, roughhewn and carefully layered in wintery shades of black and gray from the foundation to the top of tall windows along the porch. From the second floor to the roofline were wide cedar shingles, most of the paint had peeled away but what remained was a gently weathered silver. On the third floor, the windows were different – wider than those on the other floors and with a rounded top and accented in stone. Though she couldn't be completely sure, it seemed the back corner of the house just might be a turret.

Maureen gaped at the house through the windshield. She would have remembered something this beautiful. No matter how old she had been when she visited, she would have remembered. It would have been breathtakingly beautiful in its prime, but now much of the house was badly in need of repair. Great patches of cedar shingles were missing, possibly blown away during a winter storm, and had been replaced with plywood sheeting. Each of the first floor windows was covered from the inside with plywood, and the stonework on the bottom steps leading to the porch had crumbled almost to dust.

The grounds were badly neglected as well.

What appeared to be a matching stone wall running along the length of the house was covered with a thick net of blackberry vines, its tendrils reaching between the stones and crumbling the wall. And the driveway was patched with coarse construction gravel; only a bit of the original crushed oyster shells remained near the little house and at the far edge of the driveway.

Maureen pulled the car near the smaller building: one-story, cedar shingled, with a stone foundation and a large awning spanning the length. Too big to be a garage or storage shed, it looked like it might be a small guest house, although the windows were boarded with plywood and the front door was bolted.

After pulling the car into park, Maureen unhooked her seatbelt to get out and was welcomed with a gust of briny ocean air and a soft rumble of ocean waves in the distance. Closing her eyes to feel the mist on her face, she breathed deeply. The air smelled like pine trees and wood smoke, ocean salt and seaweed, but hiding within that was a faint scent of flowers, unexpected at the beach.

Curious, she opened her eyes, and tracked the scent to a tiny garden behind the little house. At the center stood a tall plum tree, its branches covered with delicate purple flowers, and on the ground, slender green tulips and dense clusters of bluebells flowered despite the choke of weeds.

The garden was badly overgrown, and Maureen stepped into it to pull a thread of morning glory vine from the branches. As she pulled, a shower of purple blossoms fell gently to the ground. Maureen thought immediately that Dilly would love this garden and imagined her constructing houses for the fairies who lived there.

It would take only a few days and the most basic garden tools to bring this space back to life, and although Maureen hadn't gardened in years, she might like a chance to try. Although it was very unlikely, maybe Juliette, Joey, and Dilly would want to help, and Maureen would have a project with her children.

Maureen turned her attention toward the big house wanting a closer look before her appointment with the attorney. It could easily fit all of her sisters and each of their families. Had the sisters been closer, it might have been fun but they weren't. If the inheritance was real the property would need to be sold, and maybe she and Joe could buy something small for their family with the proceeds.

The driveway looped between the two buildings, filled with potholes and slick with mud. The grounds beyond were choked with weeds and tall grass, trampled in places and littered with beer cans and garbage. Further still, scorched tree stumps and plastic milk crates circled a burned campfire. And beyond all of that was the horizon.

She picked her way across the driveway toward the main house. Parked off to the side, at the corner of the smaller building, was a brown work truck with a toolbox mounted behind the cab and a ladder tethered to the side. At that moment, Maureen wondered about the sanity of wandering around an obviously abandoned house by herself. Pushing her hand deep into her pocket, she curled her fingers around the remote for her car. It wasn't much of a weapon, but she could activate the car alarm if she had to.

Maybe someone would hear.

Just one more look and she would leave. It really was one of the most beautiful houses she'd ever seen, and it looked like a house with secrets.

In the best stories, creaky houses with three floors and dormer windows always had secret passageways and hidden treasures. Maureen wondered about the people who used to live in this house; it seemed old enough to be passed through at least one generation. She wondered if they'd had children, and parties, and spent time together as a family. She imagined beach towels damp from the ocean, draped over the railing of the back deck and drying in the summer sun. Beach pails and shovels lining the back stairs and sandy feet running across the courtyard as children chased each other down to the shore.

As she stood beside the house, she reached around the blackberry vines and grazed the stone with her fingertips. Flecks of mica glinted in the weak morning sun, and she wondered about the person who had taken such care to stack the rocks, arranging the colors to look exactly like a winter sky. All of the tall windows that lined the front porch were shattered, the plywood fastened from the inside, maybe to protect the shingles or to keep people out.

A cold gust of wind blew across the yard carrying mist from the ocean, biting through her fleece jacket and making her shiver. She would have liked to have seen the inside of the house, but it seemed a storm was approaching, and she didn't want to get caught in it. A cup of steaming coffee and a warm muffin was just the thing to warm her up before her meeting.

She turned to walk back to the car choosing a path beside the crumbling garden fence. As she picked her way over crumpled beer cans and broken glass around to the back of the house, the feel of the path under her feet changed. Instead of soft mud and matted grass, it felt solid somehow. Poking a weed with her foot, she pushed aside the debris and uncovered a corner of a flat stone, smooth with wear and dotted with moss.

"This whole courtyard used to be Elizabeth's garden."

With a start Maureen whirled around to see an older man in a brown construction coat, some distance away but walking toward her, his collar turned up against the gathering storm. Underneath a faded baseball cap was a kind, open face and a wide smile. His cheeks and nose were red from the cold, and it occurred to Maureen that if his hat was felted and pointy, he would look exactly like a garden gnome.

After slipping his metal tape measure into his pocket and tucking his clipboard neatly under his arm, he offered Maureen a handshake. "Charlie Gimball's the name. Pleased to meet you."

Maureen liked him immediately and met his hand with her own. "Good morning, Mr. Gimball –"

He cut her off with a quick shake of his head. "Please, call me Charlie. More than seven decades on this earth and I still turn around expecting my father when anyone says, "Mr. Gimball."

Maureen smiled. "Charlie, it is. I'm Maureen Kauffman –"

Another gust of wind, stronger than the first, blew across the yard, scattering raindrops and yard debris in its wake. She turned away to draw her jacket tighter against her neck.

She turned back to see Charlie shaking his head. "This is not the weather to welcome you to Inlet Beach. I wish we could have given you better, especially to see Elizabeth's house for the first time."

"I don't understand – were you expecting me?"

"Of course. We were hoping you'd come to the meeting, but we didn't know for sure. This house has been vacant for quite a while, and I do what I can to look after her so I know about the letter the estate attorney, Steven Arshay, sent and the meeting you have with him later this morning." Charlie's blue eyes twinkled with mischief. "You will find in a town as small as this, there isn't much to do in the off-season but gossip and eat." He paused to give his Santa Claus belly a tap. "I'll almost be happy to see the tourists this year."

"You're a caretaker?" Maureen tried to piece everything together. If he was a caretaker, it meant someone – the estate probably – was paying him, and she didn't have any relatives with that kind of money.

Charlie held up his hand and shook his head. "Oh no,

nothing formal like that. I just do what I can."

He peered toward the sky, gray clouds gathering and turning to black. "We might want to get out of this weather for a bit. I can show you the first floor of the house if you'd like. Steven asked me to open up the house in case you and your sisters wanted to look at it after the meeting."

Charlie reached to straighten a crooked board on the fence and it crumbled to mulch in his hand. He let the pieces fall through his fingers, and they were swept away in the wind. "The old girl's been neglected. She deserves better than this."

After brushing his hands on the leg of his brown work pants, he rummaged through big outer pockets; he pulled out a flashlight and a disposable face mask, offering both to Maureen. As she took them, he raised his finger in warning. "The first floor only, mind. We need more safety equipment to get upstairs to the other floors."

A little unnerved about the reason she might need the mask, she asked, "Is there lead paint inside?"

"Oh no, nothing like that." Charlie waved his hand dismissing the idea. "They checked that before they cleared the house for seasonal rental. This is for the smell."

Maureen was silent as they continued on the path, wondering what kind of mess awaited them. As they approached the front door, all the reasons for not climbing into an abandoned house with a stranger came to her at once, and she recognized the absurdity of what she was about to do. She reached into her pocket again for her remote key chain.

As he slipped a key into the padlock securing the front door, she thought he might know something about the people that had owned this house. "Did you know the Jensens?"

As he nodded, his expression softened, and she saw memories cloud his eyes. "I did. Elizabeth and Lloyd Jensen were the finest people I ever knew. This was their summer house, and when they were in town, I practically lived here. Along with everyone else. Lloyd showed me how to bring a piece of wood to life, and Elizabeth held everything together. Her backyard parties were legend."

"Their summer house?"

Charlie smiled wide. "Yes. The Jensens were from Portland originally; they had a big house on the edge of town overlooking the Willamette River. I've never been, but that's what they tell me. He was a brilliant stone mason, Lloyd was."

Charlie patted the side of the house. "Elizabeth summered somewhere out East when she was a girl and fell in love with this style of house. Shingled Victorian or some such." He waved his hand through the air as if details didn't matter. "And this – this is the only house in Inlet Beach framed entirely in stone, built in 1944 when this town was only a stop on the way to somewhere else."

Maureen would realize later that Charlie Gimball loved nothing more than a long story and an attentive listener. He seemed oblivious to the patter of raindrops against the canvas of his work coat as his eyes danced.

"The story goes that Lloyd bought a plot of land in town as a wedding present for Elizabeth, intending to build her a modest summer house near everyone else. But on the way to see it, their car broke down on that very hill over there." He pointed and shrugged. "Couldn't quite make it up, I guess. As they waited for help to come, they took a look around. Well, as soon as Elizabeth saw the views from the bluff back there . . ." He gestured to the area beyond the back yard, then corrected himself. "Actually, as soon as *Lloyd* saw Elizabeth's face looking at the view, he scrapped plans for the house in town and bought this exact parcel of land."

Maureen considered all the stonework on the house, the slate on the path, and the wide plank siding. "This material had to be brought in, didn't it? You can't find this kind of stone around here, can you? How did they haul all this construction material up this hill?"

Mr. Gimball chuckled. "That's another thing. When Elizabeth found the plans Lloyd had drawn up for what he thought would be a modest summer house – with two front rooms, a kitchen, and a bath – what he assumed would be a fine vacation home, she had other ideas. She and Lloyd wanted a big family, you see, so she decided two rooms wouldn't be near enough. She remembered some of the houses in Newport –" Charlie smacked his leg with his brown work gloves. "Newport – that's it. Newport, Rhode Island. Anyway, in the end she got five bedrooms spread across three floors, along with a nursery and servant quarters in the eaves." Charlie shook his head. "Lloyd never knew what hit him."

They continued down the path and around the corner of the house to the front door, a tangle of fat brambles threading the holes of the metal fence erected to block it. Folding back a corner of the fence, Charlie gestured for Maureen to step over. "Watch that bottom step. Make sure you stay in the middle."

The front of the house was clean, with only three steps

leading to a shallow front porch, and it didn't seem to match the rest of the house.

Maureen looked for signs of demolition. "Did there used to be something else here?"

Charlie shook his head. "Right now, this is the safest way in. But when the house was built, the front door was a formal entrance for company. Friends wandered through the back." He pointed toward the bluff. "All the living happened in the back and within a year or two, this entrance was just forgotten."

The key slid into the lock but wouldn't catch in the tumbler, and Charlie's face clouded with concern as he pulled the door handle to align the assembly with the plate.

Relief flooded his face as the bolt popped. He pushed the heavy front door, and it opened with a groan, damp wood creaking loudly on rusted hinges. Charlie took a step back to let Maureen enter first, then stopped, brows creased with concern. "Before you go inside, remember this house has been vacant for two years and was a summer rental before that. You'll have to look hard to see how beautiful it was and know that it will take work to bring it back. But it's worth the effort."

As Charlie stepped back, the first thing to hit her was the stench of stale beer, old cigarette smoke, and mildew. After giving her eyes a moment to adjust to the dim light, Maureen was shocked at the destruction inside.

Carefully placing her feet, she stepped over smashed chair frames and around an overturned sofa. Thick chunks of plaster lay mixed with sodden mounds of wallpaper on the floor, both torn from the wall leaving gaping holes exposing wooden slats underneath. Wide swatches of graffiti covered most of the remaining wall, angry splatters of dark colors.

Charlie removed his cap and scrubbed his fingers over his head. Taking a deep breath, he exhaled loudly. "I haven't been inside in quite some time. I didn't realize anyone got in."

Shaking his head he replaced his cap, pulling the brim low over his brows. "I just didn't know."

The carpet squished when Maureen walked over it toward the open window. "They came in through here." She pointed to a splinted wood piece wedged into the sill, holding the window open.

Pulling the wood out and sliding the window gently closed, Charlie turned away. Without looking at her, he pointed to the carpet, matted with mud and covered with burn marks. "Underneath this...." His voice cracked. He cleared his throat and began again. "Underneath this carpet are the original floors, and I hope they're still good." His voice trailed away. Maureen laid her hand on his arm. "Let's go, Charlie. I've seen enough."

After he brushed his face with a gloved hand, Charlie shook his head. "No, you've got to see the rest before you decide."

"Decide what, Charlie?"

"About the house. You can't judge this house by this room. It was beautiful once, and you should know that." Stepping around a mound of crushed beer cans, he walked toward the back of the house. "Back here is the kitchen."

Maureen had seen her share of kitchens good and bad, and she admired the design in this one. Stretching the width of the house, it could accommodate a large group without affecting the work flow. Now it housed a collection of mismatched appliances and cheap fixtures, but it looked like it could be brought back to life.

Charlie continued through the kitchen to the skeleton of a room with a plywood floor and no windows. "This used to be glassed-in and heated with a wood stove over there." Charlie pointed to a hole in the wainscot ceiling patched with a slab of plywood. He turned to her with a twinkle in his eye. "I saved the original stove. And underneath this plywood are gray flagstones, perfectly cut and matched." Facing the bluff, he pointed toward the horizon. "This room is the perfect place to watch a winter storm. Wood stove burning, wrapped in quilts, with plenty of hot chocolate and popcorn. There is no better show."

Maureen imagined all of the kids piled into this room and felt a smile. She turned to see Charlie nodding slowly, a satisfied smile on his face. "You're getting it."

"You have time for one more thing before your meeting."

Startled a bit that Charlie knew about her meeting, she followed him anyway, back through the kitchen and over to the left. The room was small and divided with cheap drywall, some of it crumbling at the edges and scattered with nail pops. "The original walls in the living room are plaster; why did they switch here to drywall?"

Charlie's lips pursed and he spit the word from his mouth. "Kenny."

"Who's Kenny?"

Charlie's eyes narrowed. "Kenny." Crossing his arms in front of his body, he continued. "Kenny was a sneaky little kid who grew to be a weak and selfish man." He paused to gather his thoughts. "The Jensens had seven children all told, and one of the middle daughters, Joanie, married a man who couldn't hold his liquor." Charlie held up his palm. "No shame in that, but he never should have touched the stuff in the first place because it made him mean. So she started to send the children to her mother when things got bad. Kenny was young then, maybe two or three."

Maureen brushed her fingertips lightly over the wall, considering what Charlie said. "It sounds to me like Kenny has a stronger claim to the house than my sisters and I do, especially if he lived here. I'm not even sure how we're related to the Jensens. Do you know?"

The color rose on Charlie's cheeks as he looked away and mumbled his reply. "I'm sorry, I couldn't tell you that."

"No, of course you can't. I apologize for asking." Maureen pushed her hand in her jacket pocket and changed the subject. Although Charlie's reaction to her question was odd, she realized that it was better posed to the attorney. "So what did Kenny do to the house?"

Charlie pointed to the cracks in the wall and the rusty nails popping from it. "Kenny divided the dining room into three smaller bedrooms to attract more renters." He held his hand out. "Drywall can be easily removed. What you need to know is that this dining room was the most important room in the house, after the kitchen." He cocked his head and frowned. He reached to touch the doorframe. "The best Sunday dinners I've ever had were in this house. Everyone gathered here – in the off-season pretty much everyone could fit around the dining room table."

Charlie spread his arms wide. "A big table in the center of

the room set to overflowing with peas, asparagus, potatoes, and salads from fern shoots the neighborhood kids and I collected. Her Easter ham graced the head of the table, and she made the best hot cross buns I've had before or since."

His cheeks flushed as his eyes danced with memory. "During the summer was even better. You could never tell from one week to the next who would show up to Sunday dinners. Some days every level surface would be stacked with plates and platters of food." He paused and rubbed his chin. "Sometimes families would bring a pie or a salad and sometimes they didn't – or couldn't. Elizabeth never reproached anyone who came empty-handed. She just sent one of us kids running to the garden for whatever was ripe or to the chicken coop for whatever eggs we could grab." Charlie waved his hand in the air. "You know, to stretch the meal."

Maureen couldn't remember the last time her family had dinner together. Something at the restaurant always needed their attention, and it never escaped her notice that she and Joe made a living serving dinners to families other than their own.

Something occurred to her, and she turned to Charlie. "You watch over this house, don't you, Charlie? Despite what Kenny's done to it?"

Charlie lifted one shoulder in a half-shrug. "It's the right thing to do. The Jensen family has done a lot for this community. I think Elizabeth would be happy that her house is in good hands again."

"To be honest with you, Charlie, all of this is very strange. My husband and I – my family – have lived only two hours from Inlet Beach for a long time. It's hard to understand how relatives

I don't remember would leave us something this big. I don't see how I can accept this property from people I don't know."

Charlie's shoved both hands in his front pockets and started toward the front door, motioning Maureen to follow. "A quick walk through town will tell you who they are."

"That's only part of it, Charlie. I don't know who they are to me – to my sisters and me."

Crossing the threshold as Charlie held the door, Maureen breathed deeply of pine needles and wood smoke. A low gray mist had settled into the yard, coating everything in a heavy dew.

The lock scraped closed, and Charlie turned, flipping up his collar. "Remember the plot of land I told you Lloyd bought for Elizabeth? The one he bought first before she came up here and saw the view?"

Maureen nodded.

"Well, they didn't sell that. Lloyd donated seeds and material to start a victory garden for the people who couldn't make the trip up the hill to the house. Then they built a library and stocked it with books from Elizabeth's father's private library."

"They sound like wonderful people."

Charlie nodded. "They were. They were that." He turned to her. "When it was finished, the library built and stocked, the garden in full bloom, they donated the whole thing to the town. Both of those things kept this town alive for years."

After flipping her wristwatch to check the time, Maureen started to thank Charlie for the tour before heading down the hill and into town for her meeting.

But Charlie held up his hand. "Just one more minute. If you leave now, you'll miss the best part: the whole reason Elizabeth insisted on this plot of land instead of the one Lloyd already bought in town." He cocked his head ever so slightly. "Then you can go to your meeting and decide whether you're in or out."

That was the second time Charlie had referenced a meeting that she hadn't even known she was going to attend until just this morning. Was this town really so small that everyone knew your business before you did? Opening her mouth to ask how he knew, she snapped it shut when she saw he was almost completely across the yard and hurried to catch up.

Following his path, she rushed through a labyrinth of beer cans and garbage, avoiding tree stumps and driftwood around the camp fire burned into the grass. She couldn't imagine this area cleared and nice enough to ever host a party.

Waiting for her at the edge of the bluff, Charlie pointed to a thicket of blackberry vines just before the trail down the hill to the shore. "Before these invaded the grounds, you could see the horizon from the kitchen and the waves from the second floor. Now you have to come all the way out here to see anything."

Maureen stood for a minute; the cold gusts of wind had melted into a gentler breeze, bringing with it a salty seaweed smell from the ocean. Seagulls danced in the breeze offshore, calling to each other. She approached the ledge and looked across.

Below was the ocean.

To the left and the right as far as she could see were miles and miles of rocky coastline, scattered with tall pine trees trying their best to grow straight against a constant wind. Enormous rocks were dropped randomly into the water, rising up like mountains in the middle of the surf. The beach below was wide and flat, littered with massive logs of driftwood that had weathered to a silver gray.

The ocean was vast and flat to the horizon, broken only by long shallow waves reaching for the shore. The view was different from here, more grand somehow, and Maureen immediately understood why Elizabeth had been captivated. It looked like the ocean went on forever; the only sound was the rumble of the waves below and the faint call of the seagulls as they circled the rocks offshore.

She had never seen anything more breathtaking.

Closing her eyes, she let the sounds and the smells of the ocean fill her soul.

She opened her eyes to see a satisfied smirk on Charlie's face, although he pretended to be watching the ocean with his hands inside his coat pocket. "The blackberries and junipers weren't meant to be this overgrown. They block the summer breeze and the sound of the ocean. You should pull them out before the summer starts when the ground is damp and the roots will pull away easily." He turned toward her, his lips pressed together to hold back a smile. "I can show you where Elizabeth set out the tables. For summer parties." He stopped fighting the smile and it spread across his face with joy.

"Whatever you decide, I'd like to thank you for allowing me to show you Elizabeth's house. It means a lot to me." He inclined his head and Maureen smiled.

"It is a beautiful house, Charlie."

"If you don't mind, I'd like to enjoy the view a bit more. I don't usually get this far out, and I've got memories that I'd like to give some attention to."

After thanking him again for the tour, Maureen turned and walked toward the house, this time imagining how it must have looked when Elizabeth had lived there. Instead of plywood and broken windows, she saw sun shining on weathered gray cedar, windows outfitted with white shutters and black latches, and a front door painted bright blue with a pot of daisies to welcome you home.

She imagined the screen door to the yard slammed as children ran in and out, chasing each other to the beach. Wet towels draped over the banister while sandy flip-flops lined the stairs. Adirondack chairs positioned near a fire pit to get the best sunset view. Plastic shovels and pails tangled up in the yard, waiting to be dragged to the beach and used to make sandcastles with bridges made from shells and deep moats filled with sea water. Maureen smiled; it must have been magical.

Passing the side of the house, she imagined bouquets of summer flowers: black eyed susans, deep purple lavender, and tall yellow sunflowers scattered around the yard. A climbing rosebush with hundreds of tiny pink flowers running the length of a freshly painted white fence and spilling over the side. The mud from the garden path cleared and the broken slate from the courtyard repaired, allowing banks of pink foxgloves to grow tall against the stone walls. And finally, Elizabeth's vegetable garden restored, the harvest served during a backyard summer cookout, and everyone coming for dinner. Everyone cooking, everyone helping. Tea lights plunked inside mason jars, lit and glowing as the summer sun set.

As she slid behind the wheel of her car, she remembered their last family vacation. She and Joe, exhausted and desperate for a break from the chaos of opening their first restaurant, tossed bikes, luggage, kids, and coolers packed with food – they were restaurant people after all – into the station wagon and drove to the beach. The only goal had been to spend time together as a family. They didn't count on almost everything being closed for the winter and in the end, they spent the weekend in a small cottage with a wood burning stove but Maureen would welcome the chance to have everyone together again.

Smiling, she drove toward her meeting and decided to at least keep an open mind.

Chapter Four

Lydia woke to the sound of drawers banging in the dressing room. Squinting against the blue numbers of the clock on the nightstand, she recognized the first digit as a number four before the bright neon forced her to close her eyes. No one should be awake this early. She buried her head deeper into her pillow to muffle the noise and was on the blissful edge of sleep when Greg snapped on the bathroom radio, bouncing referee whistles and urgent commentary from a sports radio station against the tiled bathroom walls.

The door from the bathroom burst open throwing an explosion of light and sound into the bedroom, jolting her fully awake. Greg wandered in pushing a pair of sterling cufflinks through the holes of a new gray dress shirt. He liked his shirts custom made now, each one hand-stitched and perfectly tailored, which Greg insisted was an investment in his career and his future.

"Going off the playbook with light gray instead of white, but this weekend's offsite is important and a button down that's a little different from the rest is a good way to get noticed." Greg snapped the collar and looped the tie around his neck.

Gripping the duvet with clenched fists, Lydia buried her head deep into the down pillow, trying to erase the sound of her marriage.

"The tailor said nothing else is as good as hand-stitching, that people can tell the difference, and that it is an investment in my career because of the statement these shirts make. In fact, I might need to get rid of my old shirts so I can stock up on these."

Peeling away a corner of the duvet from her shoulders, Lydia thought to tell him they didn't have money to replace the shirts in his wardrobe. The growing pile of bills stuffed under the coach needed attention, and the mortgage company would not wait even one more week. At one hundred and five days past due, foreclosure had become a matter of "when" instead of "if." For the past two months she had been calling them almost every week, stalling the process with the promise of using Greg's bonus to pay the entire balance. She watched the mail and checked their accounts online, waiting for the long overdue deposit, but refused to ask Greg directly because it felt like begging.

In any event, her chance was lost because Greg had already left the room, leaving the door open, the light on, and the radio loud. She could see him from her place in the bed, leaning into his mirrored reflection above the sink, smiling and turning his head slightly so he could admire himself from different angles. Hooking his finger into his mouth, he pulled his lips from his teeth to examine them individually.

"It wasn't time to whiten my teeth again, but this weekend they're going to announce the new district manager, and I threw my hat in the ring. So I touched them up."

Lydia noticed them yesterday. Artificial and overly-bright, they were perfect for him.

Straightening, he buttoned the collar of his shirt, throwing his shoulders back and smoothing the fabric when he was finished. She watched him posing in front of the bathroom mirror, flexing and satisfied, a former coach's favorite who believed the spotlight followed him still.

"This cut makes me look good, doesn't it?" He slapped his belly with an open palm and smiled at his reflection. "Still got it. No way Harrison can compete with this."

Harrison was a new hire at Greg's office, a transfer from Wall Street, and Greg loathed him, insisting the sole reason Harrison had a larger client base was because he had gone to a fancy four-year college, that the clients actually preferred Greg's work ethic and practical advice. From a distance, Harrison seemed nice, and Lydia doubted he even knew Greg was competing, but Greg scuffled with everyone, ever watchful for anyone who got more than he did, like a bully in a schoolyard.

"Lydia, come and tell me how I look in this."

Lydia slid out of bed and into the chill of the room, knowing the sooner she complied, the sooner he would be on his way.

Goosebumps rose on her arms as she reached for her wool robe from the bottom of the bed and pulled it on. Tentatively she touched the heating vent with her bare foot, but the metal was still icy cold, the furnace yet to click over to daytime mode.

When she entered the dressing room, Greg's back was turned as he busied himself with something in the closet. Glancing over his shoulder at what he was doing, she saw the custom tie rack he bought at Christmas and her breath caught. Just three months ago it held every tie he owned, with room to spare. Now every cedar peg held a tie, and some held two.

"Greg. Where did all these ties come from?"

He turned with slightly different versions of the same red tie spread across his forearm, trying to decide between them. "I spent my bonus on myself this year."

The room got very still as a shiver moved across her body. "How much did you get?"

Greg pushed in front of her, moving from the dressing room toward the bathroom mirror, brows furrowed in concentration as he held each one against the gray of his shirt. "Twelve thousand."

Lydia dropped into the chair. Last year's bonus had been almost double that. Twelve thousand wasn't enough to satisfy the bank, but it might be enough to at least renegotiate the mortgage, possibly leaving enough to bring a card or two out of collection. Suddenly very cold, she pulled her robe tight against her throat and buried her hands in the folds of the shawl collar. "How much is left?"

"What?"

Irritated that he wasn't paying attention, she bit off each word and spit them at him one by one. "I said: how much is left?"

"Nothing, Lydia." His voice dripped with contempt. "I told you: I needed to update my wardrobe."

Lydia said nothing, stunned that Greg was able to continue his morning as if it were a normal day, as if they weren't financially ruined.

After deciding on a tie, Greg tossed the others through the

doorway of the dressing room, not bothering to see where they landed. "This is a very important time for me, Lydia. I told you yesterday the new district manager is coming today, and I have to make a good impression. The least you can do is help me out."

Picturing the eviction notice on their front door, bile rose from her stomach and she swallowed, the acid burning a trail in her throat. Lydia snapped. "You should have told me about the bonus, Greg."

Greg froze, his fingers arranging the tie around his collar, staring at her with the unblinking eyes of a snake. Beside him the radio blared, a referee whistle followed by incredulous commentary from the sports radio station she hated.

After leisurely smoothing his eyebrows with his fingers, he turned his attention to her and glared. "Between the two of us, Lydia, who has the college degree?"

She stared, unable to move and unwilling to give him the satisfaction of an answer.

Apparently satisfied with a non-answer, he tucked another shirt into his suitcase and snapped the lid closed. After pulling up the handle, he fired one final shot. "I do, Lydia. I do. Therefore, what I need and what I do will always be more important."

Turning on her heel she left the room through the bedroom and down the stairs. If she had been dressed, she would have walked to the garage, started the car, and left for work without another word. She'd done it before, several times, in fact.

Greg descended the steps soon after, dragging his suitcase behind him. Once in the kitchen, he lifted his work bag onto the top of his suitcase, arranging both so the logos were clearly visible.

Finally he looked at her, his lips thin with contempt. "I don't know what's going on with you right now, but you better get a handle on it before the party. Since you don't seem to be acting like yourself, I will remind you of my plans one last time. The corporate offsite is today through Sunday. It's invitation only, not everyone gets to go."

He threw her a look of triumph, which she ignored.

He smoothed his perfectly slicked hair and shot her an icy look. "I don't know why you refuse to remember things that are important to my career since it seems that I am the only one who has one. So I'll go over this one last time.

"I'm leaving for New Haven right now. Morning meeting starts at nine, but I need to get there before that so I can network over breakfast. Talking to the right people will guarantee my promotion." He jabbed a stubby finger in her direction. "You need to take the train –"

But Lydia cut him off. "Greg, the train from Millburn station to New Haven isn't direct. I'll have at least two transfers – it's so much longer than driving. Can't I just meet you there?"

Greg raised his palm almost the moment she opened her mouth to speak. "Managers appreciate a strong marriage, and it will give me an advantage if I let it be known that we drove up together."

If she had money, she would leave him. She remembered a time she had tried: four months ago, unable to face hosting another Thanksgiving open house for Greg's clients and colleagues, she spent two days looking for single housing close to her work, but every apartment, even the smallest one – the entire studio no bigger than the bedroom she had shared with Maureen when they were kids – required enormous deposits that were so far out of her reach as to be impossible. In the end, she returned to her ugly brick house in the suburbs and arranged a Thanksgiving reception for sixty potential clients, thoroughly defeated.

His eyes narrowed as he looked at her, his gaze traveling from her hair to her bare feet. When he was finished, his lips tightened. "You've let yourself go, Lydia. You're not the cute young wife you used to be and you need to make more of an effort." Nodding slowly as if he had arrived at a solution, he continued. "You have five days until you have to meet me on Sunday. See if you can use the time to fix yourself up."

Without waiting for a response, Greg turned and wheeled his suitcase toward the garage, leaving a trail of black smudges across her freshly waxed hardwood floor.

When she heard the motor for the garage door stop, Lydia headed for the bay window in the living room. She watched the Audi's taillights brake at the top of the driveway and disappear down the street. Only then did she sink into the window seat and take her first deep breath of the day.

Resting her head against the windowsill and closing her eyes, she released the breath she had been holding. She had gotten to the point where she could admit, if only to herself, that she married Greg only because she expected him to be successful, and it had been a mistake.

Almost a decade ago, waiting in line to register for night classes at the community college, her class schedule open and the one class she could afford to take circled in red.

Ahead of her in line, he had turned to ask what she was registering for, then had pretended to be horrified at her choice. She remembered thinking that his confidence was intoxicating; she'd never met anyone with such an unwavering belief in his own success. Now she knew it was slick veneer on a rotted foundation.

Within a year they were married, Greg persuading her that it made more sense for him attend classes full-time than it did for both of them work and attend classes at night. He quit his job the next week, and Lydia withdrew entirely and found a full-time job in data entry to pay for his tuition and their expenses. After graduation, Greg spent most of his paychecks funding his image – he needed new clothes, new shoes, and a leased car every two years because clients only sign with brokers who look successful.

A thump against the front door woke her with a start. She watched the newspaper delivery man back out of her driveway and heard his car rumble to the next stop. Outside the sky had lightened and the sensored lights guarding the top of every driveway in the neighborhood had clicked off. Another long day stretched out before her, and she couldn't bring herself to leave this seat to face it.

So she didn't.

Pulling open the drawer underneath the window seat, she felt for her favorite blanket. Cashmere, light as a whisper, in a soft buttery yellow, she buried her face in the material, breathing the scents of the cedar lining of the drawer she stored it in. If Greg had known about this blanket, and what it cost, it would have been on display, hanging prominently from the back of a chair during a client reception as a testament to his very good taste.

She draped the blanket across her legs and turned toward the window to watch the neighborhood come to life. A few wandered to retrieve their newspapers from the driveway. A bit later, some stretched on their front sidewalk before jogging off toward the rich neighborhood with the bigger trees and the wider sidewalks. Another man, dressed for work, walked his dog, scanning his cell phone as he wandered wherever the dog wanted to go. A mother held her son's hand as she walked him to the bus stop on the corner. Lydia wondered if all of these people did the same thing every day and if they took comfort in the sameness of it all. She wondered if their homes were happy: their spouses attentive, their children loved. When the last car turned at the end of the block, she pushed the blanket aside and went to find her laptop.

After emailing a quick note to work telling them she was taking a sick day, she filled the coffee pot with water and spooned enough grounds into the gold filter for an entire pot. She had just pushed the start button when her computer beeped, signaling an automated response from work, reminding her that she had up to three days to feel better; additional sick time would require permission.

The coffee maker beeped to signal the brewing complete; Lydia opened the door of the cabinet and pulled out the regulation white mug she used every day. Greg's taste, not hers. Turning it over in her hand, she decided she deserved better.

Pushing a kitchen chair directly under the top cabinet, Lydia climbed up to reach deep into the shelf that stored a few of their wedding presents. Bone china so delicate it was almost translucent, sterling serving platters padded and stored in felt bags to prevent tarnish. The sole purpose of all of these things, all of their wedding presents, was to impress potential clients enough that they signed their assets over to Greg to manage.

Sometimes when she was alone, she used the wedding china even though she wasn't supposed to, but she didn't have the energy for defiance today. Today, she just wanted different.

Reaching deep into the cabinet, her fingers touched the crinkly ridges of the plastic bubble wrap. Pulling it across the shelf, she cupped it in her palm and carefully unwrapped the packing tape. She remembered seeing the pattern, an achingly beautiful design of blue and white, and listing the entire set in the wedding register. With a significant invitation list and an upscale wedding, she had expected to receive the entire tea service, but all she had gotten was a single cup and saucer. She didn't remember who sent them, and she refused to write a thank you note for such a cheap gift.

After filling the teacup with coffee and adding cream, she was ready. Withdrawing the attorney's letter from deep inside her purse, she smoothed it on the table in front of her and read it through twice. It was the last paragraph that caught her attention:

"...I would be pleased if you could attend a meeting in my office to discuss the details of the bequest on Thursday, March 3..."

As she sipped her coffee, she planned. Research was what she did, and there was nobody better than she was. The first thing to do was investigate the attorney who sent the letter,

Steven Arshay of Inlet Beach, Oregon. A simple search on her laptop showed he was a general practice attorney and new to the area, but his credentials checked out, and she was satisfied that he was real.

However, she didn't remember a relative named Jensen. Her family wasn't exactly close. She hadn't spoken to Maureen in years and had no idea where Tyra might be, but if she was going to invest in a plane ticket to fly to Oregon, she needed to know the inheritance was real.

Aunt Patty would know. She was the only family connection Lydia had. Actually, Uncle Mike was the official relative, but Lydia didn't like him and suspected the feeling was mutual.

She dug out the photocopied "Season's Greetings From Bayonne" newsletter that Aunt Patty and Uncle Mike folded into their overly-glittered Christmas card every year. At the bottom was their address and a phone number that Lydia wouldn't use unless forced. Her mother may have been Uncle Mike's younger sister, but they had nothing more than DNA in common, and Lydia followed her mother's example.

Unfortunately, she didn't have time to waste. She punched in the numbers before she could talk herself out of it, and the phone was answered almost immediately.

"Franzelli." The gruff voice boomed across the phone line. Lydia pulled the receiver from her ear and adjusted the volume.

"Uncle Mike? It's Lydia. Lydia Meyer." When he didn't answer right away, she added, "From Short Hills." And she cringed at how stupid and awkward she sounded.

"Hello, Lydia. What can I do for you?" His voice was cool. She remembered instantly why she didn't like him.

If he wanted to treat this conversation as a business exchange, she could do the same.

"I'm calling to see if we have any relatives named Jensen."

"*You're* calling *me* to see if you have a relative? Wouldn't you know?"

He could simply have answered the question, but he was making it purposely difficult. He thought he was better than she was, and that was just one of the reasons she didn't like him.

"Yes, Uncle Mike. I am. Elizabeth and Lloyd Jensen. Do you know them?" She kept her voice level and calm.

"Weren't they invited to your wedding? Big shin-dig like that, they coulda been there and you'da never known."

Six years ago. Their wedding was six years ago and Uncle Mike still held a grudge about not getting an invitation. It was an upscale wedding; important people from her work were there, Greg's clients, friends they needed to impress, so inviting her crass uncle from Bayonne was never going to happen. She was wasting her time; she'd find out about the Jensens another way.

"Okay. Well, thank you for your help." As she moved the phone away from her ear to hang it up, she heard him call out.

"Wait! Now that you mention it, I do remember Lloyd and Elizabeth. She was your grandmother's sister, on your father's side. No relation to me, but she was nice."

"You met her?"

"Yeah. She was nice." He added as an afterthought, "They both were."

She hoped he could tell her something to trigger a memory, but really, how much did she need? Getting even the most basic information from Uncle Mike was an ordeal. The attorney was vetted and Uncle Mike vouched for the Jensens. If a relative she didn't remember wanted to leave her a share of their beach house, why would she refuse?

She hung up quickly after with barely a thank you. He didn't really deserve one.

The next hurdle was deciding if the value of the property were worth her time. Switching on her laptop, she researched the property and Inlet Beach using the address the attorney supplied in his letter. Arial views showed the property was large with the widest part set on a bluff overlooking the ocean. A quick search for similar sized homes in the area showed they sold for close to a million dollars.

Her heart began to thump in her chest.

Two structures occupied the property: a large Victorian set back from the bluff and a smaller outbuilding set a bit apart, but the structures became fuzzy when she zoomed in. The view and the size of the property would be the things to sell the property – the lot looked big enough to subdivide so the condition of the house didn't really matter.

Finally she was getting the break she deserved.

Money from the sale of this property would replace what she had given up to marry Greg, and replace what Tyra had stolen from her. She spent another minute browsing pages about the quaint little beach town nestled between two enormous state parks, the main shopping street spanning the length of four blocks, the hardware store with a microbrew in the back. The marketing copy practically wrote itself, and the money would come from multiple offers.

This was her chance.

The Inheritance

She glanced at the digital clock in the center of the stainless oven. Still early in New Jersey but allowing for the time difference would put the attorney for the estate in his office working. Before she changed her mind, she picked up the letter and dialed the number for Steven Arshay on the letterhead. It rang six times before switching to a tinny answering machine, and she held her breath listening to the hollow message, pushing away a thought that she might be throwing away everything she had on a scam.

When the machine beeped, she took a deep breath. "Hello, this is Lydia Meyer. You sent me a letter last week saying I had inherited property in Inlet Beach. I am calling to tell you that I *will* be at the meeting tomorrow morning. Please call me immediately to discuss the details." After leaving her cell phone number, Lydia hung up, already picturing her new life. One without debt, without anxiety, and without Greg.

Today was Wednesday, and the meeting was in Oregon tomorrow morning, so of course she would have to fly. Calling in sick allowed her to be out of the office without question until Monday. Greg's off-site was in Connecticut, and he would be there through Sunday night. In fact, he didn't expect to see her at all until the awards banquet at seven p.m. on Sunday. Everything lined up so perfectly that it was almost meant to be.

The only thing holding her back, of course, was money. Last minute airfare from Newark to Portland was sixteen hundred dollars. Add that to a rental car and an acceptable hotel room for at least three nights, and she was well over three thousand dollars, an amount she couldn't come close to.

Her bank cards were maxed.

Her department store cards were in collections.

Her personal bank account was overdrawn.

She would have to get money from Greg. Rubbing her forehead with her fingertips, she imagined all the places Greg might stash a bit of money. A quick look online at Greg's checking account, the one she had access to, showed it was also overdrawn with a half-dozen fees posted or pending. No help there.

He must have cards somewhere, or better: cash. Even he couldn't have spent his twelve thousand dollar January bonus in two months.

So where would he hide it?

Tapping her manicured fingers against her lips, she scanned the kitchen. The only place left to look was behind a door locked to her ever since Greg had caught her reading his clients' statements.

Grabbing a knife from the kitchen drawer, she strode to Greg's office, pushed the knife through the door jamb and jerked it up to open the lock. First, she scanned the shelves looking for potential hiding places. The top shelves were lined with half a dozen high school football trophies, but scooping her hand inside the trophy cups yielded nothing. The books lining the shelves were strictly for show – the bindings were embossed and the leather spines had never been opened. She skipped those.

On her way out, she happened to glace at a pile of mail on the corner of his desk. One of the letters in the stack was addressed to Greg, congratulating him on his standing in the world and extending to him an invitation to open a line of credit. Withdrawing the letter carefully from the stack, she took it with her as she left the office and went to the phone to accept.

After an hour on her laptop, she had a flight, a car, and a hotel room. The plane ticket was for the last flight out tonight from Newark to Portland, and the return gave her just enough time to catch the train from Millburn station to New Haven. There wasn't much room for error on the return flight, but if things went well in Inlet Beach, she wouldn't be returning to New Jersey. Reserving the rental car was remarkably easy, so she upgraded the car. It was only when she was asked to leave a credit card on file with the hotel as a deposit for the room that she felt the first twinges of apprehension. The available credit was so low that if the hotel blocked even a small amount against the total bill, there would be nothing left for gas or food. She gave it to them anyway and hoped for the best.

Finally: cash, but Lydia couldn't think of a single place to get it. An advance from any credit card was impossible, a payday loan was beneath her, and there wasn't enough time for anything complicated.

With tension creeping from her shoulders and settling behind her temples, she scrambled for ideas and rejected each as unrealistic. Reluctantly she rose from her chair to wash her teacup. As she rinsed she thought of all the wedding presents boxed in the garage, only coming out for parties – when the idea came to her fully formed. It was almost too daring and if there had been an alternative she would have used it. But she didn't have one.

After drying her hands on the towel, she rushed upstairs to change her clothes and then to the garage to load her car.

Four hours later, she'd pawned most of her wedding gifts. In a strip mall near the parkway she found a shop to take the most valuable pieces, offering far less than the value but refusing everything else. She placed what they hadn't wanted with a consignment shop closer to town, knowing the area clientele would appreciate the pieces more. She was several hundred dollars richer, and could buy everything back if she wanted to with her inheritance money. If she came back.

Congratulating herself on a very nice morning's work, she ran upstairs to change her clothes and pack for the trip. If the parkway was clear, she would just make her flight. Scooping the cashmere throw from the window seat drawer and the teacup and saucer from the kitchen counter, she left for the airport with barely a backward glance.

Because really, a fresh start would be good for both of them.

***

The main shopping street of Inlet Beach looked much like it had in the aerial views on Lydia's computer. About four blocks long, lined with quaint bricked alleys and small shops with painted window boxes. A beach house in a town like this would practically sell itself. With even a bit of luck, she could give notice at work in a month and have her share of the inheritance in two, and she could leave Greg and start another life.

Pulling to a stop directly in front of the signpost for The Arshay Law Group, she slid the rental into park and turned it off. The wiper blades, slapping across the windshield constantly since leaving the airport lot in Portland, froze upright, making the ugly red car look vaguely surprised.

The drizzle and the dim light made the drive slow and exhausting. Resting her head against the window, she looked at the sky hoping to see a promise of sun, but dull gray clouds stretched low across the sky, refusing to yield. She glanced at her suede boots; such a good idea the dry cold of New Jersey, seemed like a mistake in the drizzly Oregon morning and she was afraid the raindrops would mark them.

Following the sign for the lawyer's office, she entered the bricked alley and lost her footing almost immediately. The bricks were filmed with moss, making the path was slippery. She grit her teeth as she made her way to his office, almost at the very end. Only a gray house with lavender trim was further down, and Lydia wondered how anyone could attract business in a place like this.

She pushed open a glass-paned door to an empty lobby, dark except for the light from a single floor lamp standing guard near the window. She swallowed, her hand frozen on the knob. Did she just sell everything she owned for a lie?

The oscillating fan in the corner turned toward her then, blowing the faint smell of mildew across her face. She was exactly on time for her eleven-thirty appointment, and at this time of day, she expected some level of activity in what should be a business office. She pushed back the suspicion that the inheritance letter was a scam or a timeshare and was remembering that no one from this office had actually returned her call before she left for the airport when she heard the heavy footsteps of someone walking across the thin carpet.

Disheveled and pudgy, the young man who approached Lydia did not inspire confidence. His smile was too eager, his suit shiny and ill-fitting; he looked fresh out of law school as he clumped down the hallway, his hand outstretched in greeting a moment before appropriate.

"Welcome. I'm Steven Arshay. You must be Lydia."

He grasped Lydia's hand limply in the fingertip grip she hated and pumped exactly twice before releasing. "I wasn't expecting you for a few minutes yet, or I would have coffee ready."

Twisting her gold watch around her wrist, she glanced at the time. "Didn't your letter say the meeting was at eleven thirty?"

His wide smile faltered a bit as he broke eye contact. "Yes, but Marilyn hasn't come in yet, and she makes the coffee."

"Marilyn?"

He swallowed. "My receptionist. She's kayaking."

Goosebumps rose on Lydia's arms. Without proper research, she had gotten on a plane and flown to Oregon, assuming there would be a fat check waiting for her, or at least the possibility of one in the immediate future. What if this estate, this inheritance was simply a timeshare? It could be. She left without doing even a cursory search of public records. Or the property could be real but stacked with so many mortgages and liens as to be worthless?

As a full understanding of what she'd done came to her, she stared at the young kid fresh out of law school, who didn't look like he had been practicing long enough to master the most basic skill of masking emotion.

She narrowed her eyes and shot him with what she hoped was a withering stare as the regret of what she'd done turned to anger. "Steven, you didn't return my call yesterday, but I came to your meeting anyway on the assumption the inheritance you represent is real and your practice is aboveboard. Is that correct? Because if I let you conduct your meeting, and find what you represent is a time share or an investment presentation, I will make such trouble for you that you will be disbarred at the very least but more likely will be put in prison, are we clear?"

Of course she had no basis for putting this boy in prison.

Even pulling himself to his full height he didn't quite reach Lydia's shoulder. He deepened his voice and answered her question. "Everything I stated in the letter I sent you last week is true. I am the attorney of record for the Jensen estate. The house is real and you and your sisters own an equal share of that estate, free and clear."

The careful wording of his statement concerned her, but she accepted his explanation because she wanted it to be true. Later when she looked back she would ask herself how she could dismiss obvious red flags so carelessly. And she would answer herself: it had been the money.

She followed Steven across the creaky lobby floor and down a stuffy hallway into an office smaller than Greg's dressing room. Spanning the width of two entire walls were metal racks of ugly green reference books, the bindings cracked, the edges torn; they looked to have been in the legal profession longer than their current owner. Mounted precariously near the books, a plastic wall clock snapped the passing seconds and the sound echoed in the empty room.

While she waited for him to settle behind his desk, retrieving his folders and arranging his pens, she wondered if her sisters would come. Probably not. Maureen was indifferent to anything but her own family, and Tyra was flakey. As long as they got their share of the inheritance, they wouldn't care how the estate was liquidated.

So the first order of business after Steven turned over the keys would be to sell everything – everything – from both buildings. She would research liquidators when she checked into her hotel. Then offer the listing for the buildings and the land to builders and agents and let them fight over it. After deducting expenses, including her plane ticket, her hotel and meals, and the rental car, of course she would divide the remainder three ways and send her sisters their money. If things went well, she would have a check for the furnishings in a month and the remainder of the estate at closing – three months at the most.

Relaxing into her chair she exhaled slowly, feeling her shoulders drop.

When his pens were all lined up and his yellow pad perfectly centered, Steven put both palms on his desk and smiled at Lydia. "The coffee is about ready, would you like some?" Atop the rickety old table was a black plastic coffeemaker sputtering through the end of the brew cycle, great clouds of steam rising in the air in a last dying breath. She would no more drink from that than she would drink from a garden hose. She declined and he fussed with making a cup for himself.

The tinny bell mounted over the lobby door rang.

"I'll be right back." Steven set the mug beside the coffeemaker and made his way to the lobby.

After a moment he returned, escorting a short woman Lydia didn't recognize into the room. She was shaped like a teapot and had the halting step of someone who carried too much weight on bad knees. Her brown hair was windblown, and she dressed like someone who had given up, wearing dark knit pants that bagged at the knee and old-lady walking shoes.

Just as she wondered if this was the elusive Marilyn, they locked eyes, and Lydia recognized her.

Maureen.

Lydia's heart lifted as memories of her sister swirled around her: perched on the bathroom sink on her thirteenth birthday as Maureen showed her how to properly line her lips before filling in with lipstick, eavesdropping in the hallway while Maureen talked to a boy on the phone so Lydia would know what to say when a boy called her, and later, watching as Maureen demonstrated the only proper way to make a grilled cheese sandwich.

A smile pulled at her lips as she began to rise from her seat to run to her favorite sister until newer memories pushed their way in, poisoning the old ones.

Maureen leaving for college and never coming home.

Maureen sneering at Lydia's sample wedding invitations.

Maureen not bothering to reply to her invitation and skipping the wedding altogether.

Thinking about the last erased the smile and anger bubbled to the surface like acid. So she sat clenching her hands together in her lap, at a loss for what to do.

Her sister paused at the coffee machine giving Lydia a chance to compose herself, and by the time Maureen made her way to the conference table, Lydia had made her decision. The money from the sale of this property was essential to her, but Maureen was not. As far as Lydia was concerned, Maureen had disappeared from her life when she left for college after promising to return for Thanksgiving, then Christmas, then summer, but not once keeping her promise. She deserved nothing, especially now.

"Hello, Lydia." Maureen's smile was warm, but Lydia didn't return it. Nodding once, she picked up her phone and flipped through the screens, projecting an image of importance.

Silence filled the room. The hand on the clock ticked off the seconds and the coffee machine sizzled as a drop hit the hot plate, but no one spoke.

His eyes darted first to Maureen, then to Lydia. Maureen placidly sipped her coffee as if Lydia meant nothing to her. And Lydia's heart shattered all over again.

Finally Steven cleared his throat. "Ladies, thank you for coming this morning." He pulled two pages from his folder and slid one to each of them.

"Steven, shouldn't we wait for Tyra?" Maureen set her cup on the paper napkin and looked up.

"Well, I was able to contact you and your sister fairly easily, but I had a bit of trouble reaching your sister, Tyra." He ran his finger down the length of a page stapled to the inside of the folder. "The last contact address I have is New..." he stopped and bit his lip. "Old. The last address I have is very old."

The tips of Steven's ears reddened as he read from the page. Lydia's skin prickled in warning; no one stumbles over contact information. She craned her neck to see what was on the page, but Steven closed the folder before she could see.

"Do either of you have contact information for your sister?"

Maureen drew a deep breath. "The last contact I have for

her is a group home in Ohio. She served some of her time there."

"She served her time at a group home?" The injustice of Tyra exchanging a jail sentence for some sort of sorority group home was too much. Everything had been handed to Tyra already and after what she did, Tyra should have been confined to prison. Only prison; nowhere else.

"Yes." Maureen answered the question.

Lydia shifted in her chair and crossed her legs under the table, smoothing the fabric of her tweed skirt as she did. She reminded herself that with the money from her share of this inheritance, she could have a closet full of skirts like this. And she would be happy. Where Tyra spent her incarceration didn't matter.

But Maureen kept pushing, allowing her sister more privileges than she deserved. "Should we wait for Tyra? Isn't she a part of this?"

"No." Lydia placed her palms on the conference table. If Tyra was late, they would start without her. She had managed to be on time and it took a night flight to do it. "I don't have time to wait."

"We can proceed without her for now." Steven opened his folder and recited, his finger moving down the page as he read. "Your grandmother had a sister, Elizabeth Rose Haskins. She married Lloyd David Jenkins in 1944 and eventually had seven children. As a wedding present, he bought her a parcel of land on a bluff overlooking the beach and almost immediately began to build her a summer home."

Steven stuck his finger on the page to mark his place and looked up. "Actually, he bought her an acre of land in the center of town at first, thinking she would like to be around people, but when she saw the view of the ocean from the bluff, he bought her that parcel of land as well."

"Have you known them long?" As Maureen posed the question, Lydia's gaze swept the reference book titles lining the industrial metal shelves. They were standard titles, but some of the versions were outdated and the creased bindings made them look well-used. Too used for a small town attorney. Lydia wondered how Steven acquired them.

Steven blinked, shifting his weight in his chair. "Um, no. Not at all."

"Steven. What is your connection with the Jensens? You had to have known them if you are the attorney for their estate." When Maureen spoke, Lydia heard the slightest hint of their mother's voice, the tone she used when she realized one of her daughters wasn't telling the truth. Maureen, too, must have sensed something was off.

When Steven didn't answer, Maureen continued and Lydia listened carefully. "I have trouble understanding why relatives I don't remember would leave us a bequest as big as this property. I live only a few hours from here, in the same area for the last twenty years, and I don't know anything about them. How is that possible?"

Steven's eyes widened, and Lydia saw the entire inheritance dissolve because Maureen looked too closely at the details. She would not let Maureen, who had everything already, ruin this for her.

She leaned forward in her chair, catching Maureen's eye. "Steven can't be expected to know why we don't know the

Jensens. Our parents kept plenty of things from us as I recall, and maybe this was something else they didn't tell us."

Maureen's fingers tightened around her coffee mug. "There must be other descendants with a better claim. They might deserve the house more than we do."

Lydia's patience with her sister crumbled, like a sandcastle under an ocean wave, but she held her temper, keeping her voice even. "We wouldn't be here if there was someone else with a better claim. We must have been specifically named in the will, isn't that right, Steven?"

Both sisters turned toward Steven. He adjusted his eyeglasses and looked at the papers in his folder. "I can assure you both surviving children have signed away their claim to the estate. The relevant documents are filed with the court, and I can give you a copy if you like." He opened a desk drawer and rifled through the file folders.

Maureen held up her hand to stop him. "It's fine, you don't need to show me."

Nodding, Steven continued to read from the file, but there was something odd about his presentation, as if reading from a script.

"Only two of the Jensen children are still living, both are elderly and neither have an interest in this property. The estate is mostly land, two acres of beachfront just outside the town of Inlet Beach. On the property is a main house, and a small outbuilding that first served as storage, and was later converted to an art studio. It's rather large – about a thousand square feet – and it's wired for electricity and has running water, so you can use it as a guest house if you'd like."

He pulled several pictures from his folder and slid them across the table. "Unfortunately, the main house is in need of extensive repairs as you can see."

Lydia waved the pictures away. "It doesn't matter what condition the house is in. We'll sell the property, of course, and the new owner can do whatever they like to it."

"This property was left to all of us, and we should wait for Tyra to see what she wants to do."

Lydia whirled on Maureen, her control cracking. "When was the last time you saw Tyra? Fifteen, twenty years ago? I don't plan to wait another twenty years – until she decides to show up – to ask her what her preference is."

She glared at Steven. "You should have told me before I came that you need to track down our errant sister."

Pressing his finger on the page to hold his place, he looked up and shook his head. "Technically we don't need to wait. I've tried my best to notify her, and if she doesn't show up by tomorrow's contractor meeting, then she won't share in the inheritance."

"Tomorrow's contractor meeting?"

Steven sighed. "I already mentioned ... at least I think I did." He drew his finger down the length of the page and stopped abruptly. "No, I didn't. Here it is. There is a required contractor meeting tomorrow morning –"

"Why?" Lydia asked.

Steven blinked and looked at his page. "I don't know."

In the corner, a space heater clicked on and the fan whirred in the quiet of the office.

"Is there anything *else* we don't know?" Maureen's voice,

usually placid, held an edge.

Running his finger down the rest of the page, Steven slowly shook his head. "Oh, wait!" Steven looked up with a wide smile. "There is a bit of money included in the estate, dedicated for repairs."

That news hit Lydia like a jolt. She never imagined there would be cash. Depending on the amount of her share, she might be able to stay in town to wait for the listing to sell. She didn't have to return to New Jersey, didn't have to go to Greg's banquet in three days. In fact, she didn't have to see him ever again.

Her heart pounded in her chest as she waited for Steven to tell them how much was in the account.

He removed an envelope from the folder and withdrew a small black passbook. "Here it is. A separate account to fund the repairs. The rounded balance as of this morning is $128,591."

An unexpected windfall. If she lived very carefully, she might be able to live off of her share of that for almost a year. More time to market the property meant a bigger return. This was turning out better than she expected.

Steven breathed deeply, straightening his shoulders. "So if you agree to the terms, all I need is your signature –"

"There are other terms beside the contractor meeting?"

Steven rubbed the back of his neck. "Yes. Didn't I say?" He leaned back in his chair. "The property has been left equally to you and your sisters with the expectation that any decisions made regarding the property will be made together and in complete agreement."

Lydia folded her hands in her lap and squeezed them

together. "If we want to sell the property, what do we have to do? Wait for Tyra? List it now? What?"

Steven shifted in his chair. "If you both want to sell –" He paused to look at Maureen. After she nodded, he turned his gaze to Lydia, who nodded as well. "Fine. Then you attend the contractor meeting tomorrow and if you still both agree, you can sell it."

"And we get the money in the account?"

Steven nodded. "Assuming you still want to sell after meeting with the contractor, you can break up the property however you choose. But you both have to agree."

Steven opened his desk drawer and removed two keys, each on a seashell keychain. "I don't know if you have a hotel room booked, but if you don't, you are welcome to use the art studio as a guest house. It's in good condition, although it hasn't been used in years and could do with a thorough cleaning." He smiled, too eagerly, as if he wanted them to stay. "It has a wood burning stove for heat and a small working kitchen."

As Lydia and her sister each reached for a key, Steven concluded. "If you decide you don't want the property, just return the keys to me." He shrugged. "Either way, I'll see you after the contractor meeting because I have papers for you to sign if you don't want to the house and papers if you do."

Lydia couldn't imagine a circumstance where she would want to keep the house, the property, any of it. If they accepted the inheritance and sold the house, they could split the cash in the account right away and by this time tomorrow, she would be forty-two thousand dollars richer.

Another thought hit her, making her jerk upright in her

chair. "If Tyra doesn't show up tomorrow, we split the account, don't we? Instead of a third, we get half." Half would allow her to live comfortably until the property sold. Half would be good. She deserved half.

From the corner of her eye, she saw Maureen's disapproving frown, but she ignored it. It was easy for Maureen to disapprove; she didn't have to worry about money.

After a long moment, Steven swallowed and nodded. "Yes, I think so. If Tyra doesn't show up, then you get half. But you have to attend the meeting, as scheduled – the entire meeting. My client wants to be sure you know the scope of the project and the history of the house."

Lydia snapped her gaze toward Steven. "Your client? I thought this was an estate."

Steven kneaded the back of his neck with his fingers. "Yes, I meant me. I would like you to be aware of the project before you agree."

When Maureen spoke, her voice was low. "Steven, who is your client?"

Steven held both hands palms up. They trembled slightly. "The estate, of course. The estate is my client. Whoever owns the estate. Of course."

Maureen's eyes narrowed. "I am sure you will agree that it's very unusual for your client, the estate, to want us to be aware of the scope of the repairs before we accept the property. Something is not right here." She counted off on her fingers. "We don't know the relatives who left us this estate, there is a mandatory contractor meeting tomorrow, and a cash account that none of the heirs wanted." When she was finished, she folded her hands and gave him a pointed look. "I need copies of the will and the deed before I do anything else. I will review them tonight and decide if I want to proceed."

Steven's head bobbled up and down as he pulled the pages from the file. "Of course. I have these ready for you to review." He pushed a set across the desk to each of them. "But I suggest you keep the appointment tomorrow to discuss repairs. That's one of only two restrictions, easily met."

"In my entire life, I have never heard of a mandatory contractor meeting. Why does this sound not quite right?" Maureen locked eyes with Steven.

He sighed deeply, folded his arms on his desk and rested his head on top. When he spoke, his voice was muffled. "Because I'm not good at my job."

"What?"

"I just bought this practice. You're only my second client. This is not what I thought private would be like. I can't believe I took the bar four times for this."

Maureen and Lydia exchanged a look. Maureen's eyes were wide with shock, and Lydia rubbed her mouth with the back of her hand to smother a giggle, something she hadn't done since she was a kid.

Not bothering to lift his head, Steven pulled one hand free and waved them away. "You have the address. Charlie Gimball will meet you at the property at ten thirty a.m. Call me if you want it. Or want to sell." His hand flopped to the desk. "Just call when you're done."

Maureen unhooked her purse from the back of the chair and Lydia followed her through the lobby, out the door, and down the alley to the main shopping street. The misty drizzle continued to fall and an ocean breeze blew into their faces. Overhead the clouds were low, an indifferent gray. Above the shaded buildings across the street, Lydia saw seagulls circling and could hear a faint rumble of the ocean waves in the distance.

On the main street, Maureen zipped her fleece against the damp blowing across the street from the ocean. She spoke as she fumbled with the collar. "We have the rest of the day; would you like to grab something to eat? Have you seen the house yet?"

Lydia shook her head automatically. After the contractor meeting tomorrow, they would agree to sell the property, and she would very likely not see her sister again. Why make an effort now? As she watched Maureen's smile waver, Lydia felt a tiny thrill of revenge. "I have work to do. Email to send."

"I understand. See you tomorrow." As Maureen turned away, Lydia's heart squeezed, and she wondered why she hadn't just said yes.

***

Even after Steven heard the bell ring and the lobby door close he kept both elbows on his desk and his head on top. Sorting through the events of the last hour, he wondered how things could get so far off track. He thought this meeting would be simple. His client had said it would be easy.

Growing up with four sisters, Steven understood from a very young age never to get between fighting sisters. They were like cats. His sisters argued all the time over clothes or makeup and it was no big deal; the fights were flash fires – quick to ignite and quick to dissolve – without lasting damage. The tension between these sisters smoldered, like lava. The crust on top looked stable but was deceptively thin, and the true anger, powerful and dangerous, lay beneath the surface.

He scrubbed his face with both hands before leaning back in his chair. He was supposed to call immediately after the meeting, but he didn't know what to say. After seeing both sisters together, he couldn't imagine them working together in any capacity, much less restoring a house. And they would have to work together because there wasn't nearly enough money in the account to hire a contractor and be done with it.

His law partner wandered into his office and settled into his favorite place by the window with a sigh. "What am I going to do with this one, Walter?"

Walter snorted and went to his bed by the window. After shifting his weight to be closer to a weak patch of sunlight, he put his head down and stared at Steven in reproach.

As the only practicing attorney in a small town, Steven had anticipated unusual cases, but this one was out of his league. Aspects of this case forced him to bend rules that shouldn't be bent; the consequences of his decisions and the effect they would have on his client kept him awake at night.

Because he couldn't think of another option, he decided to simply do what he had been hired to do. He slid open the desk drawer and reached for the folded yellow paper on top. Picking up the phone, he dialed the number printed on the page. It was answered on the first ring.

"Yes."

"They both attended the meeting, arriving separately. It appears they haven't seen each other in quite a while and are not close. They have agreed to meet the contractor tomorrow morning. Other than that one meeting, I don't believe they have any plans together."

"I understand. Thank you." The client hung up.

Steven stared at the receiver; somehow he thought there should be more to the conversation, a briefing of some sort. "That's going to be some meeting tomorrow, buddy."

His partner groaned.

Steven smiled, the first real once since meeting the sisters. He reached down to rub the yellow lab's massive head. "We need a break, buddy. You want to go for a run on the beach?"

As Walter leapt from his place by the window and ran for the door, Steven pulled the leash and treat bag from the bottom desk drawer and followed.

***

Tyra slipped her cell phone into her pocket and waited. Heavy vines woven through the lattice of the arbor overhead protected her from the worst of the rain and more importantly, shielded her from view. After spending a dry winter in the desert, the mist and the coolness of the weather on the coast was a welcome change. Breathing deeply, she closed her eyes to identify the elements mixed into the thick ocean air. The sweetness of the winter honeysuckle vines threading through the trellis came first, followed closely by the heaviness of seaweed churned in a recent storm and deposited on the shore. More faint but still present was the comforting smell of fresh roasting coffee beans drifting on the breeze from Declan's coffee shop nearby, and blanketing it all was the comforting scent of sea air.

The soft echo of approaching footsteps, the sound muffled in the morning fog, drew Tyra's attention. She opened her eyes and focused on the two women emerging from the brick courtyard, watching them carefully. The first was heavy, walking unevenly and stiffly as if it were an effort to move. Hair that used to hang in a single sheet to the middle of her back was cut short and pulled back. Clothing that had always leaned more toward comfort than fashion was now an afterthought, dark and rumpled.

But it was the second woman that Tyra almost didn't recognize. She carried an umbrella as a buffer against the rain and wind blowing across the street from the ocean. The blue cashmere coat and suede stiletto boots were clearly out of place in the relaxed atmosphere of this beach town, and Tyra wondered why she would wear either of them in this weather. Winter rain and salty ocean air almost guaranteed damage to both. The woman used to be a runner, Tyra remembered, and her body looked the same, her movements graceful, but the pain etched on her face was new, as if the world had beaten her.

As they approached the red compact parked on the street near the alley, the older woman paused by the curb, but the other barely broke her stride as she walked to the driver's door and opened it, her face a mask of indifference. As the older woman continued down the street alone, the other woman's facade cracked just enough for Tyra to glimpse what looked like longing and sadness buried underneath. And that was enough to work with.

When the compact pulled away and the older woman was no longer visible down the street, Tyra rose from her place on the bench. Her green tea had grown cold while she waited for the meeting to end, but she needed to know their reaction, and she didn't mind waiting. Tipping the cup to her lips, she drank the last bit and tossed the cup into the recycle bin as she decided how to proceed. Throwing her backpack over her shoulder, she stepped away from the protection of the arbor and tilted her face toward the sky. She breathed in the cool air, smelling the ocean and pine trees. In the distance was wood smoke; someone had started a fire to keep out the chill of the not-quite-spring day. After being forced inside for so long, she would never tire of the outdoors, but she had things to do before tomorrow; so with a sign of resignation, she tucked her scarf into her collar and zipped up her coat.

As her fingers skimmed the front of her jacket, she felt the familiar crinkle of the wrapped note she kept with her always. The note gave her permission to move forward, offering forgiveness and reminding her not to waste any of the time she had left because it could be gone in a blink. And it gave her courage because what lay ahead of her would not be easy.

The main street was still deserted as she walked toward her hotel; the shops lining it catered mostly to tourists. At the edge of town was the public library, squatty and shingled with cedar; Tyra noticed a small orchard of flowering trees in the space behind it and a raised garden beyond.

The small hotel she had chosen sat right on the beach, but at the far end of town, a good distance from the town's largest hotel. She wanted solitude and she booked a corner room, her bed pulled close to the sliding door. She looked forward to drifting off to sleep listening to the waves tumble to the shore and watching the boxy white lighthouse balancing on the rocks, guarding the coast.

As she approached the last shop before crossing the side street to her hotel, she saw an older couple sharing a table inside. They smiled at her as she walked toward the shop, and she lifted her hand in a hesitant wave. This was a nice town, and Tyra wondered how long she would stay this time.

Chapter Five

The newspaper crumpled, she laid the pen on top, crossword puzzle completed. She'd been doing them for years, starting as something to fill the pockets of empty time at the restaurant, a habit kept because it occupied her mind with something besides staffing, ordering, and running the restaurant.

With a satisfied sigh, she lifted her arms in the air and pushed her palms toward the ceiling, working the kinks from her shoulders. Snapping off the bedside light and ready to officially begin the day, she padded across the hotel room to slide open the glass patio door. A breeze from the ocean just outside her hotel room pushed its way in, rustling the curtains that framed the door. Outside the sky had lightened to a watery gray, but the drizzle from yesterday continued to fall. On the beach below heavy fog drifted low across the shoreline obscuring the rocks in the surf and muffling the seagulls' cries and the breaking waves.

A glance at the clock urged her to get ready for the contractor meeting, and the unlit message light on the phone told her she would be driving alone. She and her sister were staying in the same hotel, for goodness sake, but Lydia was clearly trying to prove a point by not returning messages, so Maureen let it be.

Unzipping her suitcase and digging through it to find

something to wear, Maureen considered Lydia's point. Maybe she was right; maybe the easiest thing to do was sell the property and go their separate ways. After all, Lydia lived too far away to get any use out of the house, and no one had seen Tyra in years. Joe would be thrilled to have more money to fund the restaurant's second location, or they could divide it among the kids' college accounts. Finding a place to spend the money was not a problem, but her share alone wouldn't buy what she realized she really wanted: a beach house where her family could come together.

An hour later, showered, dressed, and looking forward to seeing the house again, Maureen stopped by the hotel's breakfast service on her way out. Four tables, loaded with food and draped with crisp white cloths, were arranged in the center of the room; small table seating along the perimeter took advantage of the ocean view. Shelves of books lined the inner wall of the alcove, and a framed sign encouraged guests to borrow and read anything that seemed interesting.

The moment she saw the buffet, Maureen promised herself another night in the hotel with enough time for a leisurely breakfast in the morning because right now she didn't have it. Selecting a puffy cheese Danish from the tray, Maureen folded it into a napkin for the ride and grabbed another to eat on the way to the car.

The drive through town and up the hill was easy. Traffic was light and the scenery was beautiful. Avoiding the potholes and mud puddles that lined the driveway, Maureen pulled in behind the studio, near the plum tree garden. She was purposely early for the meeting because she wanted a minute alone to wander the property, but a glance across the driveway showed Charlie was early as well, his brown pickup already parked by the house.

The crunch of tires on the gravel driveway caught her attention, and she turned in time to see Lydia's car, carelessly pulling behind Charlie's truck, blocking him in. From her place across the driveway Maureen could see her sister seated in the car, cell phone to her ear, her face a mask of fury. Whomever she was talking to was getting an earful, and Maureen sighed as she remembered the reasons she avoided her sister. She came to the beach hoping to at least reestablish contact with her sisters, but her patience with Lydia was wearing thin.

Maureen got out of her car and stared across the driveway at Elizabeth's house and all the work that lay ahead of them if they chose to accept the inheritance and restore the house. She knew Lydia wanted to sell it, and from experience Maureen knew any type of construction was not for the faint of heart: it really did take twice as long and cost twice as much as projected. Years ago, she and Joe changed the layout of the dining room and updated the kitchen appliances in the restaurant. The gap between their projections and the actual work involved was staggering. Since then, they had learned to hire both an architect and a good contractor for all the work they did, but even guided by professionals, the process was difficult. The amount of money in the repair account might seem like a lot, but just one problem with electrical, plumbing, or structure would wipe them out and leave them with an abandoned house they couldn't sell.

So Lydia was probably right wanting to sell. But the history of Elizabeth's house beckoned to her.

Lydia's door opened and as she emerged from the car, Maureen was again startled by how much she'd changed. Her sister's thick auburn hair, constantly pulled into a ponytail for one sport or another, was now a slick helmet of blonde that Maureen couldn't get used to. And the clothes she wore now seemed out of character for a sister who had spent years in track pants and team jerseys. Her blue overcoat was absolutely beautiful and certainly expensive but out of place around a construction site. But more than that, Lydia carried an anger with her that didn't seem to have a source or a solution. Maureen wondered what could have happened in her sister's life to make her change so completely; the woman walking toward her was not the sister she had known.

As Maureen started across the driveway toward the house, a yellow convertible bug entered the property, parking casually next to Charlie's truck. The woman emerging from the car was young, maybe late twenties, dark hair bobbed at her shoulder and edged with a swipe of bright purple. After stacking a cardboard tray of hot drinks on top of a flat pastry box, she tossed a worn leather backpack over her shoulder and walked toward them, her long navy coat swaying with each confident stride.

Maureen felt a smile creep across her face as her brain confirmed what a sister's heart already knew: this was Tyra.

Even if she had wanted to she would have been powerless to stop what happened next. In an instant the years fell away from the confident young woman walking across the driveway, revealing the bubbly girl Maureen remembered, so like Dilly. Maureen moved toward her sister, walking slowly at first, then picking up speed and breaking into a run. She felt her arms open wide and embrace this woman with the fierceness of an older sister, despite what Tyra had done, the lives she'd ended, and the ones she had ruined. Maureen hugged her because they were sisters and because Maureen loved her.

It was only when Tyra wriggled in her grasp that Maureen realized with a start that her sister might not *want* to be hugged. And to her shame she understood that Tyra had been out of their lives longer than she'd been in them. That sliver of knowledge made its way to Maureen's heart and embedded there. She released her sister immediately.

"What are *you* doing here?" Lydia's voice came from behind them and was edged with hostility.

Maureen closed her eyes and exhaled softly. Lydia's anger was exhausting. Tyra showing up today meant the estate was divided three ways instead of two, and that was obviously what Lydia was focused on: the money. Years ago, when Tyra had been pulled from public school, Lydia demanded an amount equal to Tyra's tuition deposited into her own college savings account.

Moved by an older sister's need to protect a younger, Maureen opened her mouth to defend Tyra, but the transformation of Tyra's face showed that Maureen wasn't needed. Before her was a woman with confidence and strength, head tilted slightly, the hint of a smile. A sudden breeze teased a strand of hair across her face; Tyra tucked it behind her ear before addressing Lydia. "It seems as if I've inherited a share of a beach house." She lifted the boxes slightly. "And I've brought breakfast. Both are equally important, I'd say."

Charlie Gimball crunched across the driveway from the main house, looking extraordinarily pleased with himself. Smiling as he approached the group, he reached past Tyra and offered his hand to Lydia. "You must be Lydia. I'm Charlie Gimball."

Giving Tyra a quick nod of thanks, he scooped the shortest cup from the cardboard tray. "Thank you, this is just what I need."

She waited to see if Charlie would introduce himself to Tyra, and it was odd that he didn't, so Maureen did it for him.

"Charlie, this is my youngest sister, Tyra."

Charlie jerked the cup away from his mouth and stumbled on his words. "Yes. Yes, of course. It's a pleasure to meet you, for the first it – nice to finally meet you. I've heard so much about you."

Tyra quickly extended her hand to Charlie and cut him off. "I'm Tyra. It's nice to meet you."

Lydia pulled the plastic flap from the lid and sipped without a word of thanks, and at that moment Maureen's desire for a relationship with her sister evaporated.

"How many square feet would you say the house is? Just the main house, not the outbuilding." Lydia balanced her coffee cup on a notebook and clicked her pen, waiting.

"Well, I don't know for sure." Charlie pulled at the brim of his baseball hat, readjusting it over his round head.

"You might look at the house's rental history." Tyra sipped her drink quietly. "Or the tax records from the county."

Lydia's eyes narrowed slightly but she said nothing.

"Well." Charlie set his empty cup on the edge of his truck bed and pulled a clipboard from the open cab. "Let's get started."

Maureen followed as he led them across the yard to a wide courtyard directly behind the house. Using the toe of his boot, Charlie pushed aside a clump of weeds to reveal a gray slate flecked with mica. "Underneath this mess is the garden Lloyd built for Elizabeth because he wanted her to have her own space closer to the house."

Stubs of dead rosemary branches dotted the borders of the raised beds, poking up from underneath a blanket of yellow pine needles, weeds, and decaying leaves. Only a few of the branches were still green, and those were sprinkled with delicate blue flower buds, making Maureen wonder what the garden had looked like when the Jensens lived here.

As they approached the front steps, Maureen noticed the metal fence blocking the stoop yesterday had been rolled neatly to the side and the steps were recently swept.

His blue eyes twinkled as Charlie pushed the door open, letting the sisters enter first. As soon as Maureen entered she understood why the transformation from yesterday was astonishing. Gone was the plywood sheeting that covered every first floor window and the jagged glass had been removed from every pane, bathing the first floor with a flood of natural daylight. Gaping holes still marked the walls, but the chunks of plaster and the rotting carpet had been cleared from the floor, along with the splintered furniture and garbage. Most important, the smell that had forced them both to wear respirator masks yesterday was gone, making the project of restoring the house seem almost reasonable.

Following Charlie and her sisters into the kitchen, she noticed all of the battered appliances had been removed, making it easier to imagine a finished kitchen.

In the winter storm porch, someone fastened thick plastic sheeting between the exposed studs and Maureen saw the reason the Jensens put the kitchen in the back of the house. The view stretched to the wide back yard, past the bluff to the ocean below and onto the horizon and Maureen understood why Elizabeth liked her parties in the back yard: the sunsets from this house had to be breathtaking.

Maureen gaped at Charlie and he grinned back. As they locked eyes she saw a satisfied smile tug at the corner of his mouth, as if he were relieved that she might recognize the magic of the house. She returned his smile with a nod because she was beginning to.

As Lydia roamed the house, scribbling furtive notes and snapping pictures, Tyra stood apart, hip against the countertop, watching.

Maureen decided to approach her sister again, this time gently. "This is a great house, isn't it?"

Tyra smiled slightly. "Do you think so? The kitchen seems big enough for everyone and the storm porch has a good view of the ocean."

"How do you know so much about this house?"

Tyra replied easily. "It's all online. When I got Steven's letter, I researched the house."

As Charlie led them through the kitchen to the dining room, he explained that the subflooring and the structure of the house was sound and that most of the work would be hauling out the demolition from Kenny's shoddy construction.

"What about mold?" Lydia set her empty cup on the counter for someone else to collect before joining the group.

If Maureen hadn't been watching Tyra closely, she would have missed the shadow of doubt that drifted across her face. But it disappeared as quickly as it surfaced, like a smoke trail from an extinguished candle, impossible to track.

Two hours later, they left the house and walked to their cars; Tyra apart from the rest, Charlie and Maureen together, and Lydia trailing, scratching notes on her paper as she walked.

Charlie started to speak. "I know you ladies have a big decision to make, so I've drawn up a rough budget and construction schedule." He pulled stapled pages from the back of his clipboard and handed a set to each of them. "There are some things you should keep in mind as you review the proposal." He tucked his clipboard under his arm and counted off on his fingers. "One, know that the structure of the house is sound and set well away from the bluff, with a thick tree barrier in between so there is almost no chance of erosion or mudslide." He ticked off another finger. "Two, the main problems are caused by substandard materials and shoddy workmanship used when they converted the original home into a seasonal rental." He pointed to the back of the house. "For example, the outdoor shower was built by pulling pipes from the downstairs bathroom through the wall to the outside of the house. Those outside pipes were never insulated and the hole was never caulked and water seeped in from outside." He continued almost reluctantly.

"There is also water damage from a badly installed skylight on the third floor–"

Lydia stopped writing and looked at Charlie. "You said there wasn't any mold inside."

Charlie shook his head. "There isn't any visible mold. I've patched the hole and I've been spraying, but the leaking roof needs to be addressed immediately."

Charlie flipped the pages and put down his clipboard. "This house used to be beautiful. There were six-panel hardwood doors in every room, each with a glass knob that sparkled projecting rainbows onto the wall when the sun hit it just right. Every window had white lace curtains that fluttered in the breeze and smelled like the ocean. When the Jensens were home and the house was open for the summer, the wood smelled like lemon oil, and there was always something baking in the oven or cooling on the windowsill. And everyone was welcome.

"Of course, each door and knob is safely in storage. I took down most of the original molding, too, before the house was converted to a rental."

"We can sell them for salvage."

Maureen opened her mouth to speak, but Tyra got there first. Her voice was sharp. "We should let Charlie finish before we make any final decisions."

Lydia continued as if Tyra hadn't spoken. Flipping to the last page of the report, she said, "The schedule says construction will take four months. Can we speed that up?"

Charlie rubbed the back of his neck. "The most time consuming work is demolition and haul out. I can hire extra crews to do that work up front, but that will put you over budget."

Lydia arched her eyebrows. "We might have the extra budget if we sold the knobs, doors, molding. People love reclaimed salvage."

"It's not salvage." Charlie took a breath. "If you want it to be ready faster, there is work you can do yourselves, either working alongside the crew or at nights and on weekends."

"But that means you won't be finished until late summer."

Maureen pursed her lips into a thin line. She knew where Lydia's logic was headed so she bit back words she might regret later. A beach house, sold during the summer would sell for much more than the same house sold in the winter. Lydia's vote would be to sell.

"Thank you, Charlie. We'll look at this estimate and get back to you."

Cringing at the way Lydia dismissed him, Maureen offered her hand to Charlie. "Thank you so much for your time, Charlie. This is a beautiful house, and it certainly holds wonderful memories for you. Thank you for showing it to us."

"Glad to do it. This house is special, and I just want you to know that." After shaking Maureen's hand and nodding to Tyra and Lydia, he headed back to the main house to lock up.

Maureen turned to face her sisters. "We should look at this report together before we decide what to do." She shook her head. "There is one restaurant downtown that was open yesterday when I drove in. It overlooks the ocean and probably serves Northwest chowder and sourdough bread."

Tyra nodded, smiling. "We can follow you down the hill."

Lydia, still flipping pages of the estimate, spoke without looking up. "Fine. I'll meet you down there."

"Do you know where it is?" Maureen pressed and immediately wished she hadn't.

Lydia gaped at her. "There are maybe three open restaurants, all within two blocks of each other. And the main street is probably still deserted, so all I really need to do is find your car."

"Lydia, really?" Maureen blew her frustration out in a huff.

But Lydia had already unlocked her car door and was getting inside. She waved them away. "Go. I have to make some calls. I'll be there in a few minutes." She closed the car door and reached for her cell phone before they could answer.

Maureen looked at her sister. Tyra shrugged. "She's calling realtors."

"How do you know that?"

"Lydia hasn't changed."

Before pulling out of the driveway, Maureen paused to look at the house one last time through her rearview mirror. At the lawyer's office yesterday, Lydia had made it very clear she wanted nothing more than to sell the house and collect her share, and at the time Maureen had agreed. But seeing the house again, hearing Charlie's stories and imagining it as it used to be, almost made her reconsider.

Almost.

The restoration would be difficult, even with Charlie as a contractor and money to pay him, because construction always was. But when would she ever get a chance like this again? The gift of a house and money to restore it, a contractor familiar with the original? The only hard part was sharing with her sisters.

She drove down the hill toward the restaurant wondering what to do.

***

For the first time in his life, Charlie Gimball walked away from a conversation without expressing wishes for a good day, and he wasn't proud of himself. Elizabeth and Lloyd Jensen taught him better manners than that.

The middle sister reminded him of Kenny, always aware of what things cost and overlooking their value. He knew she wanted to sell the house, and that might be for the best because he couldn't imagine working with her, even if it was for the good of Elizabeth's house.

The oldest was more like Elizabeth, kind and quiet, and he tried to interest her in Elizabeth's story, like he had been told, but he wasn't sure he had gotten through to her.

The youngest was strong but not nearly as strong as she wanted people to believe. Bruised people can recognize one of their own, and Charlie recognized Tyra.

As he approached the picket fence surrounding the front of the house, he pulled his work gloves from his back pocket, slipped one on and pushed one of the points with his palm. Dank water oozed from the wood, and he knew at once this wasn't the original fence. Lloyd's fence was designed and cut so the end cap shed water, protecting the grain from rot, as a good fence should. This one was mass-produced, probably from pressed wood or scrap, and absorbed moisture like a sponge. Charlie's shoulders sagged at the thought of Kenny scavenging something undetected. Lloyd's fence would have been worth something at salvage, but it would have been worth more to Charlie here.

He sat down on the middle of the three porch steps, tired and sore after last night's work and dismayed that he needed to rest. In his younger days, that inspection would have been just part of a regular work day, but recently he found it took him longer to recover from even the smallest things. He wasn't ready to get old, at least not until Elizabeth's house was in good hands.

He needed to call the one person who had known him the longest, knew him even before the Jensens rescued him. Who recognized what Elizabeth's house meant to him and what it did to him when Kenny had taken it.

Fishing his cell phone from his front breast pocket, he snapped open the lid with his thumb and speed-dialed the first number. After three rings without an answer, he felt his chest tighten and realized he was holding his breath.

He let it out the moment she answered the phone.

"Inlet Beach Animal Clinic." Her voice was warm, and Charlie relaxed into over sixty years of friendship.

"They just left."

"Did you call that girl yet – the nice one with the happy car?"

"No, I wanted to call you first. I wanted to make sure you're okay."

He was afraid he'd let Tyra down, and he needed Colleen to tell him it was okay, like she'd been doing their whole lives. She was a reassuring presence in his life for almost as long as he could remember. They met on the first day of first grade, and by the end of the week, somehow she had noticed that he didn't often bring a lunch so she packed enough to share. By fifth grade, he spent at least two nights a week in the shed behind her house because even that was better than being at his own house. And she was the one who brought him to Elizabeth Jensen, the woman who had turned his life around.

"I may be getting older, but I can still wield a broom for goodness sakes."

"Well, I'm not so sure. At the meeting this morning, I noticed a couple of spots you missed." One final poke.

She snorted before she spoke as he had known she would, and as he imagined her exasperation, it made him smile.

"I missed nothing, Charles Gimball, and you well know it." She drew an excited breath, what she always did when she remembered something. "You won't believe this, Charlie." She dropped her voice to a whisper. "When Declan and June found out what we all did at the Jensens, how we fixed it up, they sent a basket of coffee and scones to the clinic."

Charlie was speechless. Declan never delivered.

Anything.

Ever.

Several years ago a tech-guy had come down from Seattle flush with start-up money, and leased the biggest house on the beach for the entire summer. The parties were endless and every restaurant in town suddenly catered multi-course meals for a hundred, hoping to make a year's profit in an eight-week tourist season. Except Declan. If the tech-family or their guests wanted his coffee, they drove to town and got it, same as everybody else.

"But enough about that. How did the walk-through go?" Underneath her effort to sound cheerful, he heard the weariness that laced her voice, so he gave her an abbreviated version of what he thought of the sisters and how he hoped the house would be in good hands now. He thanked her again for her work yesterday, knowing she would brush it off as nothing, but he knew the hours of scrubbing, sweeping, and hauling would leave its mark on her, just as it had on him.

After hanging up, he slipped the phone back into his pocket and buttoned it shut, pushing himself up from the step. It had been a mistake not to sweep the house and remove the garbage before letting Maureen see it yesterday, but he hadn't realized that until he saw the look of horror on her face as she entered the front door. His memories of time spent in the house allowed him to see past the destruction, but without those memories all she could see was a project too massive to undertake.

Pushing open the door, he headed for the kitchen to replace the plastic sheeting across the sun porch. Scooping up the extra roll of tape that Steven left on the countertop, Charlie peeled off a section and went to work. It was a simple job and he finished quickly. As he stood in the kitchen reviewing a mental checklist of things he still needed to do to close the house, he noticed the smell of a roasting Thanksgiving turkey, and he smiled.

"Good morning, Mrs. J. Welcome back."

Elizabeth Jensen had saved his life and Thanksgiving had been one of the many ways she had done it. As an only child born to parents who actively hated each other, he absorbed the brunt of their displeasure at the injustice of their lives, and holidays had always been the worst. All day long his mother complained about a lost day's pay, and his father's anger simmered below the surface like lava, spewing to the top as he worked his way through a bottle of gin. Thanksgiving at the Jensen house showed him how families were supposed to treat each other, and Charlie had drunk it in.

Sometimes he felt foolish talking to the air, but he did it anyway because often it felt to him as if Elizabeth were still there, watching over the house she loved. The way he saw it, Elizabeth and Lloyd Jensen had changed the course of his life, and it was a small thing for him to take care of her house and to talk to her while he did it. "I'm finished here – everything is buttoned up. I'll just check your studio before I leave."

As he left the house, he passed the plywood boards leaning against the walls in the living room and knew he didn't have the strength to remount them. The moment Maureen drove away yesterday, he called for help and within an hour had commitments from a crew of volunteers to set the house in order. Within two hours, the grounds were a hive of activity. Rebecca closed her veterinary clinic and brought her father, Colleen, and a few other locals from Declan's to help. All night they scrubbed, swept, and hauled using car headlights and lanterns to finish the job. They didn't leave until well after midnight and the result was the cleanest construction site Charlie had ever seen. With luck, it might sway the decision.

Crossing the courtyard of Elizabeth's garden, he happened to glance at the corner where Elizabeth kept her chickens and where Charlie had slept in the summer waiting for the Jensens to arrive. It wasn't long before Elizabeth figured out that he was sleeping outside and put him in a spare bed made up with fresh sheets that smelled like sunshine and ocean air. She spoke to his parents. He didn't know what she said, or even if they had cared, but after that he lived with the Jensens in the summer, moving in when they arrived and staying until September.

When Elizabeth got sick and Lloyd her home to care for her, Charlie had promised he'd watch after her house. And even when that little snake Kenny practically ripped the house out from under them, Charlie still checked on it, repairing and rebuilding whatever the renters destroyed. At first there wasn't much to fix, but as the class of renters deteriorated, the repair work increased. And only recently had it gotten to be too much, especially in cold rainy weather when his old bones preferred the warmth of a blanket and his recliner.

He walked across the driveway, removed the padlock, and unlocked the Dutch doors to Elizabeth's art studio. Strictly off limits to the renters, the inside was exactly as Elizabeth had left it six years ago, a few canvases stacked against a far wall hastily covered with a grubby drop cloth, and a scattering of paints and brushes across tabletops. Colleen had been after him for years to clear out Elizabeth's studio, but Charlie resisted. Sometimes he went in there still, closed his eyes and concentrated, and under the musty smell of neglect he could detect the faintest hint of turpentine and imagine Elizabeth was coming back. But this time it pained him to see a thick coating of dust on the art table and all of best paintbrushes warping in glass jars, so he closed the door as the sight of what he couldn't do reproached him.

***

Gathering the pages of information compiled on the airplane–comparable properties, names of real estate agents, and builders working in the area – Lydia pushed open the door of her rental car and prepared to meet her sisters in the restaurant. She was able to email pictures and basic information to two agents before her data connection was dropped, but she planned to finish the process when she got back to her hotel. Flattering pictures of the house were difficult to capture, so Lydia focused on the acreage and the view knowing they would interest both agents and builders.

Because Maureen had already agreed to sell the house, all Lydia needed was Tyra's consent before returning to Steven's office to sign papers and take possession. One third of the cash in the account, over forty thousand dollars, could be hers by the afternoon if she could convince Tyra to sell, but her sister was hard to read and that made Lydia uneasy.

The door of the restaurant was dark wood and heavy as Lydia pulled it open, the metal handle cold and sticky. Lydia would have preferred to go directly to Steven's office to claim their inheritance, but if Maureen wanted them to have lunch together, pretending to be a family before they sold the house, she would. If only to keep the peace until she got her cash.

The inside of the restaurant was dimly lit and smelled like cooking spray, metallic and fake. Lydia followed a well-worn path on the ugly carpet through the empty dining room to the her sisters' table. Both of them sat on the same side of the table, Maureen spilling over the narrow seat, her ratty fleece jacket slung over the back and tangled on the floor behind. Tyra sat in the chair by the wall, a steaming pot of tea in front of her, reading the menu as if she had a right to be there, as if she had never stolen Lydia's money.

Or destroyed their family.

Or killed someone.

Grasping the back of the rickety chair nearest the wall, she scraped it across the floor and set her purse on the splintered wicker seat before settling into her own chair. "Sorry I'm late. I brought a list of comparable that we should look at before we decide on a selling price."

Before her sisters could answer the waitress arrived, brandishing a stained coffee pot, an inch of black sludge festering at the bottom. She swished the contents and held it up. "Too late for coffee?"

Knowing she wouldn't drink anything from that pot, Lydia dismissed the waitress with a flick of her fingers.

Maureen frowned.

The waitress eyed the pot dubiously before nodding in agreement. "I'll make fresh. Won't take a minute."

Maureen leaned in. "Lydia, we might want to –"

The tone for a new message beeped from deep inside Lydia's purse, and she scooped her cell phone from the inside pocket and flipped through the screens to her email. The message was from a realtor who said she might have an interested buyer and would call later when she got reception.

"We may already have someone interested." Lydia flashed a real smile this time. Things were working out.

Maureen leaned back, shifting uneasily in her chair as Tyra set her teacup on the saucer with a soft clink. "Good. We should explore all the options before we make a final decision."

Goosebumps rose on Lydia's arms, but she ignored the warning. They already *had* a final decision; she and Maureen had agreed to sell.

The waitress returned to their table holding a stubby pencil and a spiral notepad, ready to take their order. Lydia spoke first, ordering her usual. "I'll have an egg-white omelet with fresh spinach and minced red pepper – minced, not chopped or sliced. No onion. No cheese. No butter."

The server's pencil never moved; it floated above the pad as if waiting for something it could hold onto, something from the menu it recognized. After a moment, the woman licked her lips, and her brow furrowed as if she were choosing her words carefully. "We don't have red peppers and you don't want the spinach. John won't separate eggs no matter how slow it is back there, so I never ask." She dipped her chin and fixed Lydia with a pointed look. "You want to try that again? Maybe use the menu this time?"

Lydia grit her teeth, not wanting to make a scene and upset her sisters. If she handled this meeting correctly, she would leave this town in a few hours with a pile of money, never to return. "One slice of whole wheat toast."

The waitress smirked as she scribbled on the pad. "Whole wheat, you say? I'll see if the bread is still good."

As her sisters ordered, Lydia checked the messages on her phone. One from Greg, forwarding a list of things he needed her to bring to him on Sunday, three days from now. That she deleted without reading because if things worked out here, she wouldn't be going to that banquet. Another automated message from her work reminding her that she was expected at her desk on Monday morning. She deleted that, too. With forty thousand dollars in her pocket, she didn't plan to return to work.

"Lydia." Maureen's voice was gentle, the voice used to deliver bad news.

Lydia's heart thumped in her chest as her sister continued.

"Now that Tyra's here, I think we should talk about the house – review our options before we decide to keep it or sell it."

Lydia gaped at Maureen. "We already agreed. We're selling."

Tyra leaned forward in her chair, resting her elbows on the table, hands folded, voice clear. "Before we vote, maybe we should discuss the options, just so we don't miss anything."

Lydia's head buzzed. She hadn't been told anything about a vote.

As if she were watching a movie, Lydia saw Maureen's face soften as Tyra addressed them both. "Can you imagine the history in that house? Lloyd buying it as a wedding present for his wife after seeing it just one time, then building a house big enough for a family of nine? The structure was beautiful, wasn't it? So many beach parties in the summer. That bluff must be perfect for a big summer party."

Smiling, Tyra brought the tea cup to her lips and looked at Maureen over the rim, her gray eyes unwavering.

Tyra couldn't know the history of the house – even Steven didn't know the history of the house.

After taking a slow sip of tea, Tyra replaced the cup on the saucer and turned her attention to Lydia. "Of course, you can't overlook the value of two acres on the shoreline. Every plot of land within two blocks of the beach has been subdivided at least once and all the houses in town are practically built on top of each other. The Jensen house sitting on two acres by itself, restored and presented correctly, could sell for close to a million."

Tyra rested her elbow on the table and cupped her chin with her fingertips. "The house as it stands is worth something, of course, but not as much as it would be if we restored it."

She pointed to the report Charlie had given them, lying in the middle of the table. "We're here for lunch anyway; we can at least look at the report while we eat."

Logically what Tyra said made sense, but Lydia felt the tug of everything she wanted slipping from her grasp, as if being pulled away by the tide.

As Tyra flipped through the contractor report; Maureen leaned in to look even though she had a report of her own "The repairs are certainly extensive, but I understand Charlie is very competent and familiar with the original house. Did you notice here –" Tyra flipped the page and pointed, her finger resting on the page. "Charlie's offered to use volunteer crews for unskilled labor, and he's donating all of his own time."

"Why would he do that?" The words rushed out before Lydia could stop them. "Did you promise him something on the side? Maybe a cut of the profits once the house is sold?"

Maureen pulled her attention from Charlie's report and looked at Lydia for a long minute, as if trying to process what to say. Finally, with her brow furrowed, she answered. "Charlie is very attached to the house, and both of the Jensens. He used to live with them during the summer when he was a boy, and I think he knows this house better than anyone."

Lydia saw Tyra's lips curling into the barest of smiles before she brought her cup to her lips.

Lydia glared at Tyra, sitting like a Cheshire cat, her eyes squinting through the steam of her tea, and her temper flared. "Did you promise him something, Tyra? Maybe this contract is rigged?"

Maureen looked up with a jerk. "Lydia, this contract is very straightforward. The only thing out of the ordinary is the way Charlie pulls labor from the community, and I think that's remarkable how the people in this town help each other. Charlie told me that almost everyone in Inlet Beach is indebted to the Jensens in some way, and they want to restore the house as a way to honor them and their contributions."

Folding her hands in front of her, Maureen shifted uncomfortably in her seat. Her eyes lost their dreamy expression, and she seemed to consider her words before she spoke. "However, even in the best of circumstances, construction is hard, and we don't have the best of circumstances."

The waitress came, delivering their lunch orders. The puff of green parsley next to Lydia's dry wheat toast seemed like a slap in the face, and Lydia pushed the plate away.

Maureen reached for the salt, generously shaking it over her fries, following with a squirt of ketchup. Picking up her fork she continued. "And while I don't begin to understand how an account filled with money happened to be included with this estate, it does give us room to work."

Tyra paused to refill her cup with watery green tea, and it occurred to Lydia that Maureen looked to Tyra for information now, as if she were the one in charge. Tyra put down the pot. "Of course we have obstacles to overcome if we decide to take this on, but do we agree at least that a repaired house will bring the most return?"

Maureen answered immediately, "Of course."

A restored house might bring a bigger return, but Lydia needed her money now so she threw some tacks into the path of their discussion. "Is this something we can hand to Charlie and come back when it's completed or will he need one of us to be a contact?" She held up her hand because Tyra opened her mouth to interrupt. "Because I don't live close, and I don't plan to move here. I can't see how anyone can manage a project this big without daily contact." Arranging her features as if an idea had just occurred to her, she drew a breath and continued, proposing something that would benefit her even more. "So I have a proposal of my own. You can buy my share and do whatever you like with the house."

Maureen wiped her mouth with her napkin and shook her head. "Joe and I don't have that kind of money."

Lydia shrugged as if she didn't care while her heartbeat picked up speed. "You can give me the repair account, and I'll take the rest when the house is sold."

Maureen reached for her water glass. "Without the money in that account, we'd have to fund the repairs ourselves, and we can't afford that either."

Neither sister seemed willing to give her even a small fraction of what the house was worth, so she turned to Tyra and said the first thing she thought of. "You owe me money anyway."

How different her life would have been if Tyra hadn't stolen her college fund. Already accepted to a prestigious four-year college, she would have majored in something lucrative and maybe joined the track team. She wouldn't be married to Greg because she would have met a better husband at college. Her life would have been perfect, and Tyra had stolen that from her.

Lifting the teacup from the saucer, Tyra cradled it in her palm as she sat back in her chair. She looked almost pleased though Lydia couldn't imagine the reason.

"How much?"

When she didn't get an answer, Tyra repeated the question. "How much? It seems to me that if you are this upset about something you should know the details. How much was in the account?"

Lydia raised her chin and pulled a reasonable number out of the air. "Six thousand dollars."

Maureen's fork dropped to her plate. "You did not have six thousand dollars saved for college."

"I had a job."

"A summer job. For one summer, working regular hours for minimum wage. "

"I worked during school, too."

Maureen snorted. "You babysat for the Endicotts down the street. Every other Saturday."

Lydia opened her mouth to speak, but Tyra stopped her with a raise of her hand. "How much did you make every Saturday?"

"Fifty dollars." Heart thumping in her chest, she continued the lie. Lydia had no idea how much she earned every week, certainly not that much, but it was the idea of what Tyra had stolen, not how much.

"Okay then." Tyra reached into her backpack and pulled out a checkbook. "I am going to make it right."

Lydia was stunned. Did Tyra have money? She looked at Tyra as if for the first time. After withdrawing her checkbook, Tyra flicked the front pocket of her backpack closed, the brass fittings clinking, metal on metal. The sound was solid, the pack substantial. Dark brown leather with deep pockets in the front and side, worn to a honey brown finish as if it were used instead of displayed. Tyra rummaged inside her pack for a pen. As Lydia watch her sister hook a strand of hair behind her ear, she noticed the purple streak edging the bottom of her sister's dark hair was expensive and recently done.

But Maureen continued to poke a hole in Lydia's claim. She slowly put her coffee cup down. "Lydia. They were gone for three hours. You made less than thirty dollars for the whole night."

"They tipped well."

Tyra didn't answer. She was busy writing a check and after ripping it out she looked at Lydia. "I wrote it for cash because I don't know your last name." Stuffing her checkbook back into her pack, she cinched it closed.

Holding the check with the tips of her fingers, she offered it to Lydia. "I made it for nine to include interest on the money you lost." As Lydia reached for it, Tyra's eyes flickered. "In return I will never hear another word about money stolen from your college account."

Lydia felt herself blush but accepted the check anyway. As she folded and slid the paper into the inner pocket of her purse,

Tyra added, "You should realize that I was eleven years old at the time and couldn't possibly have stolen anything."

But Tyra did steal it – or close to it. If it hadn't been for Tyra's crime, their parents wouldn't have taken Lydia's college money to pay for her defense. Lydia was the victim here, but her sisters refused to recognize that.

As she looked away, she noticed Maureen frowning at her and Lydia's breath caught. Shoving the check into the furthest corner of the pocket, she vowed never to cash it. Cashing it would mean Tyra was forgiven and it wasn't allowed to be this easy. Lydia's face burned with anger, furious that Maureen thought her small for accepting money Tyra had stolen in the first place.

Reaching for her water glass, Lydia drank the contents to steady her nerves. As she finished, she saw Maureen rest her elbows on the table and lace her fingers together.

"There's something else, Lydia." Maureen's smile was thin and it didn't reach her eyes. "I know I agreed to sell the property and split the money in the account, but Tyra's idea has merit and we should at least consider it."

Lydia's breath caught and blood pulsed in her ears; only snippets of what Maureen said next registered.

"Charlie's finish date . . . only three months . . . volunteer crews ... weekends to supervise."

When Maureen's lips stopped moving, she unfolded her hands as if to reach for Lydia's then abruptly changed her mind and stilled them. "I'm sorry but I think it's a better idea."

Lydia moved her hands to her lap and pushed them together into a fist. She glanced at Tyra, calmly spearing pancakes with her fork as if she had nothing to do with Maureen's reversal. Lydia could not lose this money. "I live in New Jersey, Maureen. Am I supposed to go home and wait for you to tell me when the construction is completed?"

It was the first idea that came to her and not the problem at all. Lydia was happy to hand over control of the house to her sisters. She didn't care at all what the finished house looked like. She did care, however, about keeping a windfall this big from Greg and with a three- to four-month construction schedule, she knew she couldn't.

When Maureen didn't answer, Lydia's vision blurred as she turned on both of her sisters. "So I guess I'm outvoted then?"

She glared at Maureen. "When did you two become such best friends?"

Grabbing her coat and purse from the chair next to her and rising to leave, she turned on Tyra. "Congratulations, Tyra. You stole something else from me."

As she strode across the dining room, she scrubbed the tears from her eyes before they had a chance to fall. She would show them.

***

From his desk chair, Steven had a perfect angle to bounce the damp tennis ball against the metal shelf of reference books, and that's what he had been doing since unlocking his office door at ten that morning. So when the phone rang it startled him, not having rung since Thursday despite his new business card being tacked prominently on the corkboard at the grocery. He answered on the second ring.

"Hello?"

"Steven, this is Tyra." Tyra scared him a little so he sat up straighter in his chair, ignoring his law partner nosing at the ball. "Lydia is going to call agents and developers to sell the property. I need you to make that not happen."

"Okay." He had not the slightest idea what to do, and he hoped she would provide some direction.

"If she calls you for information, you can give her the name of the builder from Astoria. But then you need to remind him the property is on septic not city, and the system won't support more than one house."

"Is that true?" Steven opened his desk drawer and rooted around for a pen.

The hesitation in her voice made Steven uneasy.

"Yes."

And she didn't elaborate.

"Okay...." Popping the pen cap off with his thumb, he began to scribble a note on a legal pad – but the pen didn't write, and Walter ran away with the cap, so he would have to remember.

"This part is important: if she's already working with an agent, find out who it is. If she's not, then suggest one but remind them that the house has historical significance and can't be torn down.

"You think Lydia wants to tear it down?" Steven's voice was a whisper even though the office was empty.

"Please do it as soon as you can and call me the minute it's done so I'll know."

"Of course." Steven hung up, eager for something to do and looking forward to billing a client.

***

Seated at the small desk in her hotel room, Lydia scribbled both numbers on the hotel's notepad. "Thank you, Steven. I'll call them right now."

After hanging up, she closed her eyes and exhaled. Finally, something easy: a builder who had already expressed interest in the house and an agent who specialized in beach property.

As soon as she had a solid interest in the house, she would present that as proof the property could be sold easily, and Maureen would see the logic in selling outright. Tyra would lose.

Moving to the bed for more room, she positioned herself in the center and fanned everything she had about the house in a circle around her: a copy of the will from Steven, her notes from the property tour with Charlie, and her phone in case the builder or the agent wanted pictures. Once again without enough signal to use her cell, she pulled the phone from the nightstand onto the center of the bed and dialed the first number.

She counted six rings before a man picked up.

"Blue Sky Construction, this is Benjamin." The sound of heavy machinery thundering in the background made it difficult for Lydia to hear.

"Benjamin Cranford?" Lydia pressed the phone close to her ear and plugged the other ear with her finger.

"Yeah."

"This is Lydia Meyer calling. I am an owner of the property on Pacific Drive, and I understand you were interested in buying it just after Christmas."

"We were looking into it, yeah. Until someone else—" The beeping of a truck backing up cut off the end of his sentence.

Lydia rushed forward, anxious to keep his attention. "I'm

calling to see if you're still interested in it because I have a business proposal for you."

"Hmm." His voice muffled as he switched the phone to his other ear. "I'm kind of busy right now, and we expressed interest in the property months ago...." The sounds of heavy machinery in the distance, and the weak connection made his words waver. "... have on that property and get back to you."

Lydia raised her voice to compensate for the connection. "You can call this number but I will be available only until Saturday morning –. that's tomorrow. But I should tell you that there are other interested buyers."

"There always are." He cupped the phone and shouted to someone in the distance. His voice was muffled when he returned. "I'll call you later today after I get back to the office."

After replacing the receiver, she reached to rub a knot twisting behind her shoulders. She couldn't sell the house without her sisters' consent, but if she could show solid interest, Maureen would realize how easy it would be to sell the house in its present condition.

Flipping through screens on her cell phone, she found the number for the agent she sent the email to, with pictures and notes on comparables, just after Charlie's construction tour. It rang once and rolled directly to voice mail. Suppressing a groan, she left a message, reminding the agent other parties were interested, and the property was available to see only through Saturday.

Even if forced, Lydia doubted Charlie or Steven would show the property the way she would so she needed to make sure she did it, not them.

Flopping back against the pillows, she scrubbed her face with her hands. Anxiety balled and churned deep in her belly, flashing images of what awaited her if she couldn't pull this deal together. The least of which was the overnight flight tomorrow and attending Greg's banquet as if nothing were out of place; the worst was that all of their wedding presents were cast out in a fifty mile radius from their house, either sold or on consignment to be sold. With her eyes still closed, she groped atop the pile for the bottle of ibuprofen she always kept with her and swallowed four round tablets, dry.

She calmed herself by promising the next call would work out. It had to. She couldn't return to the mess she had created before she left New Jersey.

After 20 minutes, the medicine began to work, and the edges of herself felt fuzzy and her body lighter. She pulled herself up from the bed and dialed the last number.

"Bunny McGivvers, how can I help?" Her voice was chipper and urgent. Lydia could almost picture frosted nail polish and poufy hair.

Lydia drew a breath. "Hello, Ms. McGivvers, this is Lydia Meyer. I am one of the owners of an estate on Pacific Drive at Inlet Beach —"

She was cut off almost immediately.

"Yes. The Jensen house. I'm very familiar with the area. Are you interested in having me list the property?"

Lydia wasn't, but fortunately Bunny didn't need a reply.

"I can meet you as soon as this weekend." Pages flipped in the background as Bunny paused briefly. "I have Sunday morning free. I can come to take measurements and pictures and we can go over the listing agreement."

She was moving too fast. Measurements and a listing agreement weren't what Lydia wanted, interested buyers were. "We have other options to consider, Bunny, and we're not quite ready to formally list the property. At this point I'm gauging interest. I called to ask if you knew of any interested buyers."

Bunny drew a deep breath and let it out in an excited gush that rolled over her words. "Oh, of course. Inlet Beach is a hot market and you have quite a property. I keep an updated list of clients who are waiting for something similar. In fact, I have a family in mind who would love it. Of course, there would have to be a signed listing agreement before I show it to them."

Lydia heard the sound of rustling papers, and when Bunny spoke next her voice was muffled, as if the receiver were pressed to her shoulder. "Now, I assume you are selling the house as-is, which let me tell you might be a bit tricky because very few buyers are willing to take on a construction project of this magnitude for a summer house. So I was pleased to get your note that renovation plans specifically for the house comes to the buyer at closing. At least that's something. Did you have any trouble with the historical society when you submitted your renovation plans to them?"

Did they submit the plans? Lydia had no idea. But she recognized the game Bunny played, so she answered without hesitation. "Oh no, no problem at all. Charlie Gimball's working on the project, and he is one of the original builders."

"Charlie Gimball, you said? I know his reputation. That's good." Lydia heard the sound of a pen scribbling.

"Is the house on the city line or is it septic?"

"Septic right now, but it's easily hooked to city." Charlie told them the nearest city line was two miles away.

"That's just fine." More scribbling. "Now one last question: I know the house has been vacant for some years; has it been thoroughly checked for black mold?"

"Mold?" The question brought her up short. "What mold?"

Bunny exhaled softly. "The climate here is very conducive to black mold, especially in homes that aren't occupied. I need to assure my buyers that precautions have been taken to protect the house and that it's been inspected recently, or I won't even present the house. Something as serious as black mold could get a house condemned. It spreads quickly and exposure is toxic."

Lydia cleared her throat. She was in too deep to start telling the truth now. "The contractor assures us there is absolutely no mold present, but I don't have a report for that yet."

"If Charlie Gimball says there's no mold, that's good enough for me. I will contact my buyer and get back to you. Of course, you know we have to come to terms with a listing agreement before I show the property."

"Yes, of course."

Black mold was something she hadn't considered and didn't remember seeing. Reaching for her cell phone, she flipped through the pictures of the house and realized most of them were of the view and the grounds so they weren't helpful. Lifting the lid of her laptop she starting researching.

Thirty minutes into looking at pictures of mold damage, her cell phone chirped signaling an incoming text. Flipping the screen, she read the message from the first agent, the one who had seen the pictures.

My buyers aren't interested in a house with that much work to do, sorry. I've attached my listing agreement, please contact me if you'd like me to market your property.

The room stilled as Lydia read the text again. Exhaling slowly, she pushed her hair back from her face and reminded herself the builder wanted the property three months ago and Bunny already had a family in mind, so the rejection from this agent wasn't devastating. She saw only pictures, after all. But it was so abrupt that Lydia suspected that something had happened. What could it be?

The shrill ring of the hotel's telephone startled her. She opened her eyes and stared at it, not bothering to answer. Only her sisters knew she was here; anyone else would call her cell, and she was not ready to face either of them.

By the time the red message light flickered on the phone, Lydia was dressed and ready for the treadmill in the fitness center. Grabbing a towel from the bathroom on the way out, she congratulated herself on finding a way to fill the time until the builder or Bunny called back. A quick run would clear her head, and with luck she could present an interested buyer as a reason to sell the property immediately.

Things might work out after all.

***

The only way to the fitness center was through the lobby, and Lydia had been forced to avoid the lobby, entering and leaving the hotel by the beach entrance or the side door since check-in. She knew the hotel would run her credit card for a five-day stay, blocking at least fifteen hundred dollars, and the card she had given them didn't have that much credit.

Treading softly on the carpeted hallway, she paused at the end and glanced at the lobby. A few restaurant workers were busy setting up an hors d'oeuvres table in the alcove facing the beach. Bottles of wine cooled in ice buckets and the smell of savory pastries floated in the air. Her stomach grumbled in protest, but she covered it with her palm and pressed, silencing it. Dinner for her would be alone in her room, not here.

Seeing no one at the front desk, she skirted the corner and pushed open the door to the fitness center. A blast of warm air from an overhead vent hit her full on, rustling her bangs and pushing her hair from her face. She scraped it together into a short ponytail as she considered her choice of treadmills. Late model and battered, they were certainly not what she expected for the guests of an upscale hotel.

Choosing the one that faced the picture window overlooking the ocean, she straddled the belt and punched in more buttons than seemed necessary to program a simple hill climb. As the belt accelerated, she adjusted her stride to match the pace, her body remembering the movements. She felt the muscles in her shoulder relax and the dull throb in her head slow. She used to love running; she had run track in high school, medaling in distance events, and the college she had chosen had an exceptional track program with renowned coaches.

An image unexpectedly flashed before her and she didn't have the strength to push it away this time. She stumbled on the belt, catching and righting herself with the side rails as she relived the moment again. The night before she was to leave for college – with the family car loaded and her room empty – her parents matter-of-factly had sat her down and told her that she wouldn't be leaving for college in the morning after all. All the money in her college fund, even the money Lydia earned herself was gone. Most of it was spent on lawyers for Tyra, the rest for expert witnesses to sway the jury. Lydia, who had done nothing, was left with nothing. And in the end, they hadn't needed the lawyers after all; Tyra had admitted her crime and was sent to detention anyway.

Turning the dial on the machine to speed the belt, she easily lengthened her stride to keep up with the new pace. Her heels pounded the belt and pinpricks of sweat gathered on her face and neck. It had taken seven years and two community colleges to do what she could have done in three short years if she had been able to go to university full-time, and she still wasn't finished.

When her phone signaled an incoming text, Lydia snatched the phone from the plastic tray and flipped through to her messages.

But it was from Greg.

Bring my new dk blue BB suit when you come on Sun.

She tossed the phone back on the tray, not caring if it broke. As more time slipped by without a decision to sell right away, it seemed likely that she would have to return to New Jersey. At least for a while. The last possible flight to get her to Greg's banquet in time to pretend everything was normal was an overnight flight leaving Saturday, forcing her to leave tomorrow at least by early afternoon.

The mess she had left in New Jersey and how she had hidden it was too much to think about. Twisting the dial on the machine even higher, she pushed herself to match the pace.

When she had seen the aerial view of the property she and her sisters had inherited, she thought it would sell immediately. She left New Jersey without planning to return, and it made sense to sell wedding presents for enough money to live on until she got proceeds from the sale. After all, half the gifts belonged to her anyway. But the stress of balancing so many lies at once was wearing on her. Greg thought she was still at work, still in New Jersey, even though she was three thousand miles away. What kind of husband didn't know his wife was across the country? What kind of wife would hide that?

Pulling her towel from the hook on the machine, she wiped the sweat from her eyes. The money from pawning the wedding gifts wouldn't last as long. She had a return plane ticket but just enough gas in the rental to get her back to the airport, not enough to refill the tank. Her only option was to leave the car in the rental lot, hoping they wouldn't run the charge through her card until she was safely on the plane.

She ran faster, pounding the belt with her heels, waiting for a reprieve that would come with a call from the builder or the agent.

***

Maureen heard the pounding on the treadmill even before she opened the door to the fitness center and couldn't imagine why anyone would want to run that fast or that hard.

Opening the door slowly, she intended to slip through to the steam room to relax a few minutes before dinner in the lobby but something about the way the woman was running made Maureen hesitate. She ran frantically as if she were being hunted. Rivers of sweat streamed from her shoulders, pasting her shirt to her back, and her breathing was uneven as if she weren't used to the speed.

Closing the door softly behind her so she wouldn't startle the woman, Maureen watched for a moment to see if she needed help. The runner was alone and the dial on the machine dangerously high; if she tripped or had a heart attack, there would be no one to help. Maureen moved closer, unsure of what to do. At that moment, the woman turned her face to wipe it with a towel, and Maureen recognized her sister.

Without hesitation, Maureen reached for the door and walked through it, leaving the fitness center and her sister.

Chapter Six

An incoming text pulled Lydia from a restless sleep. Groping for the phone on the hotel nightstand, she squinted as she entered her password and opened the text.

We're going to pass on the Jensen property. While the land is prime for developing, the house is too difficult to work around. It might have been a good opportunity if the land was vacant.

It was from the builder, Benjamin Cranford, who Steven had said was interested in buying the property a few months ago. Maybe so, but he wasn't interested now.

Tossing her phone back on the nightstand, she flopped onto the pillows as the acid in her stomach churned. Yesterday with three solid leads to broker the sale of the property she had practically felt the proceeds check in her hand. Yesterday she had thought her life was finally turning for the better: she wouldn't have to return to New Jersey, wouldn't have to attend Greg's banquet – wouldn't ever have to see Greg again, in fact. Now the only one still expressing an interest was Bunny McGivvers, but Lydia suspected all she wanted was a listing to add to her portfolio and that she didn't have a client ready.

Rolling onto her stomach, she looked through the sheer

curtains to the ocean. The sky was still dark, but she should get up and plan the rest of her day. Greg's banquet wasn't until tomorrow night, but there was a two-hour drive to the airport in Portland, time to check in and wait because her return ticket was stand-by, the drive from the airport in New Jersey, and the train ride up to New Haven. With a quick count on her fingers, Lydia estimated that she had an eighteen-hour day ahead of her and with the three-hour time difference, she should probably start packing now.

Sliding from under the warm duvet, she reached for the remote and clicked on the news. Even the weather man looked annoyed to be up this early. Scowling as if he knew no one would be listening, he reported snow storms over the Rocky Mountains and a travel advisory over the Great Plains.

Lydia flicked the channel. The weather in the middle of the country didn't affect her in the slightest and his urgency was giving her a headache.

A few more clicks of the remote and she found a home-decorating channel and let it drone in the background while she turned her thoughts to the inheritance and her sisters.

It wasn't fair that she had no way to get her share from this property, that her share was controlled by her sisters.

Maureen had been ready to list the property, and if Tyra hadn't shown up to cause trouble, this weekend would have been spent interviewing brokers and arranging an open house, not packing to return to New Jersey.

Tyra had ruined everything, and she couldn't be allowed to get away with it this time. Yanking open the dresser drawer, Lydia snatched a handful of clothes and threw it into her suitcase. Tyra always got whatever she wanted, and Maureen never cared enough to oppose her.

Well not this time.

Lydia flopped onto the bed and pressed her fingertips to her eyebrows, willing an idea to come to her. The pounding in her head eased as she exhaled, and after a moment she reached for her cell phone and dialed a number. If anyone would know if it were possible to stop Tyra, it would be Janice.

"Aaron Harper's office."

"Jan, it's me, Lydia."

"Lydia! How did you get out of the support staff meeting? And why aren't you here today? It's Mandatory Saturday, you know. Where are you?"

Lydia heard the creak of Janice's chair in the background. Apparently, she had settled in for a story and Lydia suppressed a groan. Janice was a senior secretary and very well-connected. She'd been at the law firm from its inception and knew, or could find out, anything about anyone. But she wasn't free. To get information, you had to give some and Lydia couldn't let Janice find out where she was, not when everyone thought she home in bed.

"Out sick." Lydia faked a cough and hoped it was enough.

"Hmm. I see how it is. I'm feeling something coming on myself, and if I don't get the bonus Fisheye promised me for working every Saturday since Groundhog Day, I'll be out sick, too."

"Janice, you have time for a quick question?"

"Oh, sure." Lydia heard the chair creak as Janice adjusted her considerable weight. "He's locked in the conference room, conquering the world with the other partners. What'cha got?"

"Well..." Lydia paused, considering her words. "Hypothetically, is there a way to force a property sale on a jointly owned inheritance?"

Janice laughed, low and directly into the phone. "Girl, what have you gotten yourself into?"

"It's just something I'm working on, something at home. So can it be done?" Lydia prodded.

"Oh, sure. Happens all the time – Fisheye's whole practice is built on greedy relatives and in-fighting." Her voice muffled as she switched the phone to her other ear and her voice flattened, as if reciting from memory. "If the beneficiaries inherit a set percentage of the property, they can usually sell their share outright. But if they inherit jointly –"

"That's the one – jointly." Lydia pressed her lips together, her heart pounded as she waited for Janice's reply.

"Okay then, you – or whoever it is – has to file a lawsuit to force a partition. The judge usually sides with the plaintiff and orders the property sold."

"How long does that take, do you think?"

"Oh, honey, the attorneys will tell you what they always say: it depends on the caseload of the courts, but really it depends on the size of the estate and the hours they can get away with billing."

Lydia said nothing, calculating how long the process might take and if she had to file before she left this state or if she could manage the lawsuit from New Jersey.

Janice laughed into the phone, thick and gravelly from too many cigarettes and too many secrets. "Something's going on –

you're going to have to fill me in on all the juicy details the very second you get back."

"Oh, I will." Lydia cleared her throat. She had no intention of telling Janice anything, but she knew she had to offer something so she stalled for time. "I'm back on Monday. I'll fill you in then."

"But be careful though. I've seen families ripped apart by a partition lawsuit. It can get bloody and there's no way to fix the damage." The phone muffled as Janice's chair scraped. When she spoke again, her voice was a harsh whisper. "Oh – here they come, the lot of them, walking out of the conference room as if they own the world. Gotta go, Lyd. Call me. I'll be here all weekend."

And with that, she was gone.

Lydia's stomach growled reminding her she hadn't eaten in quite some time. She ignored it and considered what to do. While she was the first to admit they had never been one big happy family, she wasn't sure if she wanted to destroy all hope of reconciliation with something as serious as a partition lawsuit. The property would be sold eventually, all her sisters wanted to do was restore it first. The big question was could Lydia wait another three months? Could she hide it from Greg?

Pulling herself upright, she crossed the room and pulled open the sliding glass door to her oceanfront porch. The sky had lightened, the rain had finally stopped, and people were venturing out to the beach to walk. A patch of blue sky peeked from behind light gray clouds as if apologizing for its absence, and the air smelled scrubbed and clean with a hint of pine, reminding her of Christmas trees and how Tyra had always insisted on a real one.

She leaned against the door, pulling her bathrobe tight around her, imagining where she would finally settle when they sold the house and she had her money. One third of almost a million dollars would take her anywhere. All she had to do was wait.

A sharp knock on the door startled her and she crossed the room to answer it. Because she wasn't expecting anyone, her first thought was that Maureen had found her room number. She'd been avoiding both her sisters since they voted against her and didn't have plans to say goodbye before she left today.

Behind the door stood the front desk manager, the same college kid who had checked Lydia in. Lydia's breath caught. There was only one reason a front desk manager would bother to knock on a guest's room this early in the morning. A quick assessment of the young woman – mousy brown hair pulled into a thin pony tail, plastic name tag pinned to the collar of her cheap navy suit, black tights and sneakers – showed she wasn't a threat and could be easily intimidated.

"Good afternoon, Mrs. Meyer. I hope you're enjoying your stay?" Her words were rushed and ran together, but it didn't matter. Lydia knew what she had come to say.

"Yes, thank you." Lydia gestured to the stack of papers on the bed. "But as you can see, I have quite a bit of work to do, so if you'll excuse me." Lydia smiled dismissively and stepped back to close the door.

Eyes widening for the briefest of seconds, the woman licked her lips and continued. "Actually, I came because the credit card you left on deposit has been declined." She offered an apologetic smile and waited to be given a new one. Lydia almost felt sorry for her.

The same lie Lydia had used for years slid effortlessly from her lips, and she paired it with a tilt of her head as if she were thinking, and then an accommodating smile as if she'd arrived at a solution. It never failed. "Hmm. The card I gave you is newly issued – there must be a problem with activation. It was just to hold the room anyway; I planned to use a different to check out." Lydia clasped her hands together as if a solution had just presented itself. "Tell you what: let me just finish up here," Lydia gestured to the stack of papers on the bed, carefully blocking the manager's view of her suitcase. "And I'll come down to the lobby and straighten it all out."

The girl's brow furrowed. She hadn't expected to leave without a card.

Lydia added what she knew would clinch the deal, a local name-drop. "It's okay, really. I just came from Steven's office, my sisters and I plan to stay –" She let her voice trail off.

The woman's face cleared with sudden understanding, and she nodded. "You're the one who inherited the Jensen property? I thought your name sounded familiar." She handed Lydia the declined credit card, the one she had opened in Greg's name. "I'm not supposed to, but I guess I can wait a little while. Please hurry because I have to update your account before I leave and I don't want to get into trouble."

"Of course. Just let me finish up here, and I'll come right down."

Lydia closed the door without giving the woman another thought. Her sisters' decision not to sell the property immediately practically had forced Lydia to leave the hotel through the side entrance. If she had been allowed to take her share of the money this weekend, she wouldn't be on her way back to New Jersey today.

Gathering the last of her things from the bed, she noticed her email inbox registered one unread message from Bunny McGivvers. Lydia clicked on it

As soon as we complete the listing agreement, I can start showing your property to my clients! So many of them have expressed interest already, but we can't proceed without a listing! Also, I would need assurance the home is mold free–it's so toxic! The county health department has the forms you need.

Lydia never trusted anyone who spoke in exclamation points. There wasn't really any point in replying to Bunny, so she tagged the message and prepared to delete it until the comment about toxic mold drew her attention. Pulling her laptop closer, she clicked on the link for the county health department and read all about toxic mold.

Thirty minutes after that, she reached for her cell phone and dialed, a little parting gift for her sisters.

"Ocean County Health Department."

"Hello. I was just hiking on the city property that borders Pacific Crest, and I think you should know about the abandoned house along the trail."

"If the house is private property we don't get involved; that's another department." The clerk sounded bored so Lydia checked her notes.

"I understand. I just thought someone should tell you that

there is mold on the house – and rats on the property." She faked a shudder and hoped the clerk could hear it. "I can't imagine the disease they carry."

"There is a form to fill out and submit on the website, and if you have pictures it would be helpful to include them."

Lydia drew a deep breath and tried one last time. "I don't have access to a computer –" she scrambled for some sort of reasonable explanation. "– I'm on vacation – hiking. I'm on vacation hiking. I just called to warn you about the dangers on the property up there. I'd hate for someone to get hurt on a city trail." She paused for exactly one beat. "A lawsuit would be such a shame."

The clerk started typing. "Do you have the address?"

She gave him the address and added: "I think someone should get up there and check it."

Savoring the thrill of getting even, Lydia gathered the last of her things, packed her bags, and softly closed the hotel room door behind her.

She slipped through the side door and didn't look back.

✷

The candy bag crinkled on the bed next to her as Maureen reached in for another toffee. Outside, rain pounded against the wooden balcony and the wind pushed through the doorway, rustling the curtains and filling the room with the smell of a churning sea. Inside, Maureen lay against a mound of pillows, cocooned in a down blanket, watching the flames dance in the fireplace, and waiting for room service to bring an early dinner before she started the movie.

Beside the bed, her cell phone rang with Joe's custom tone

141

and she smiled as she reached for it.

"I thought you weren't supposed to be home until tomorrow afternoon. Did the park rangers throw you out? "

Joe's chuckle rumbled low over the phone line. "Nope, not this time." His voice muffled as he called to Dilly. "Go on and get in the shower – pizza'll be here by the time you're done. And wash with soap...."

"Real soap," Maureen added.

Joe called up the stairs, "Real soap, not pretend." He sighed into the phone. "I thought she was done with pretend soap."

Maureen smiled. "The fairies made it and she didn't want to hurt their feelings, so she uses it sometimes." She plumped the pillows behind her, settling in for a good conversation. "So how was it?"

She heard footsteps and the pull of a zipper as Joe unpacked. "It was fun until a storm hit and blew away one of the tents. When it started to hail, we packed up and came home."

Maureen looked out the window. The sky had darkened; fat raindrops blew sideways across the beach. "You know, there's a storm porch in the house. It was glassed in and it has a wood burning stove. Charlie said the whole family used to gather to watch the ocean."

"I asked around about Charlie Gimball to find out more. He's a good man; they say he knows what he's doing. Apparently, he's a master stonemason, and I'm surprised he's doing general contracting." A drawer banged shut as Joe put something away. "Did you see your sisters? Did Tyra show up?"

Maureen swallowed, closing her eyes. Tyra had changed so much since Maureen last saw her as to be almost unrecognizable, but she didn't know how to explain it to Joe.

"– Maureen – I've got to go, hon. I think the pizza's here and Dilly's still in the shower, and I haven't taken one myself yet."

"Go ahead. You guys have fun. I'll be home in the morning."

After she hung up, Maureen leaned back against the pillows and drew the comforter up, pulling the pocket of warmth around her. Tyra's crime had been unimaginably stupid – selling drugs to impress the cool kids in her new school. Of course Tyra had been unaware they were tainted, but her actions still killed two children, and Tyra had to answer for that. And the shame of how Maureen responded, leaving her little sister to fend for herself, was almost too much for her to bear.

She needed to talk to her sister, but she couldn't find the words.

★★

A late spring snowstorm blanketed the runway at Denver airport, forcing Lydia's plane to remain on the tarmac while the snowplows cleared a path. Her heart pounded as the minutes ticked by. She could not miss this final connection.

From her middle seat, she reached for the window shade and pushed it up. Outside in the waning light of late afternoon, fat snowflakes continued to fall. As she watched the whirling orange lights atop the plows she leaned back against her seat, knowing there was nothing she could do.

***

Late Sunday, Lydia finally arrived home. The taxi pulled to a stop at the top of the driveway, and she made sure to have everything out of the car before she paid the driver because he wasn't getting a tip. When he realized she had given him exact change, he scowled and drove away in a huff, coating her with a fog of blue exhaust smoke.

Except for the taxi speeding away, the neighborhood was quiet and dark. The dim streetlights cast weak pools of light only on the patches of sidewalk directly underneath, and the only light in any house was the one in her living room, activated by a timer. Greg's party had ended hours ago, and she had missed all of it, but maybe he was still there. She deserved a bit of luck, so maybe he had gotten the promotion and stayed overnight and all she had to do was explain her absence instead of her suitcase.

After more than thirty-six hours of travel – including a twelve-hour weather delay and a cancelled flight, all she could think of was sleep. She quietly opened the storm door and fit her key into the back door lock.

As soon as she flicked on the switch, her breath caught and her stomach dropped to her knees.

They had been robbed.

All of the cabinets in the kitchen were open, dishes missing from the shelves; appliances had been taken from the counter. In the den, the flat screen and sound system were pulled from the wall, wires left dangling. Greg's office was almost empty, his computers, his screens, and the football trophies on the shelves were gone.

In a daze she walked through the hallway to the den and into the dining room, wondering who would take football trophies and smash the framed pictures beside them.

"Lydia." Greg's voice came from the dining room. He sat at

the table, his laptop casting an eerie blue light across his face.

His red tie was loose around his neck, the top button of his pressed gray shirt unfastened, his suit jacket folded neatly on the tabletop beside him. And he stared at her with a hatred that cut the air in the room.

With her hand resting on the base of her throat, she tried to make sense of what she was seeing. "Greg. What happened here? Were we robbed?"

Greg's laugh was sharp and the sound of it sent chills ricocheting along her spine. "No, Lydia. We weren't robbed."

In front of him was an avalanche of paper. Lydia squinted in the dim light and gasped when she recognized the pile. "Where did you get those?"

"From under the couch, Lydia. Where you left them." He scrubbed his stubbly face with his hands, the sound echoing in the quiet house. He glared at her with a loathing she hadn't realized he felt. More than she deserved for missing his party.

"Where have you been?" The moment he spat the question from his lips, Greg held up his hand to stop the answer. "Actually, I've been knee-deep in lies since you left, so I really don't want to hear it."

As he cocked his head, his mouth twisted. "Harrison got the promotion by the way. I probably would have, but you didn't show up, and they don't promote men who don't have supportive wives. So I came home, and it's a good thing I did or I would have missed all this."

"This one is my favorite." Snatching a bright orange page from the stack, he flicked it across the table. Across the top in bold capital letters were the words, "Final Notice of Eviction."

As Lydia slumped into the chair, Greg continued. "This was posted two days ago. Apparently, no one was home. They will take possession of the house tomorrow –" He glanced at his watch. "– today, actually. It's already Monday. So, today at six p.m."

As Lydia held the paper she tried to read the words, but they ran together as the page shook.

It had to be a mistake. "How did this happen?"

He closed the lid of his laptop and pointed his finger at her. "This is your fault, Lydia. All of it. Your one job was to manage the money I brought home, and you couldn't even do that. We had four credit cards when we got married, Lydia. Four. We have nineteen now. I know because I spent the last seven hours adding everything up, and there is no possible way to avoid foreclosure. We have no money to hold them off."

Without another word, he pulled the computer cord from the wall and coiled it on top of his computer. When he reached for his suit jacket, she reached across the table to stop him. "Wait. What do we do now?"

Greg stood. "We have sixteen hours to leave – actually, you do. I've already left." He pulled a business card from his front shirt pocket and dropped it in front of her.

"What is this?"

"My divorce attorney."

Chapter Seven

With Dilly safely tucked into bed, Maureen made her way down the stairs to help Joe with the dishes. Crossing the hallway to the kitchen, she heard the hum of the dishwasher and saw her husband facing the sink and pulling on a pair of rubber gloves.

"Where did everyone go?" Maureen grabbed a dishtowel from the hook.

"Scattered." Joe aimed a squirt of detergent into the sink, mixing it with the stream of hot water from the faucet. "I saved your wine; it's on the table." Joe nodded his head toward the kitchen table.

"Don't you want any help?"

When the mound of suds had reached almost to the faucet, Joe turned off the tap, stretched off his gloves and laid them near the sink. "Changed my mind. Let's just let them soak for a minute first."

Maureen followed him to the table. On the way, Joe grabbed an orange from the bowl.

"So what happened at the beach? Did you make a decision about the property?" He settled himself into his chair and looked at her, brows furrowed. "Did you find out who left it to you?" He nodded knowingly. "That's textbook haunted house, right there: relatives you don't know leave you a house...."

His voice trailed off and Maureen laughed. "Joe! You aren't allowed to suggest it's haunted until after we sell it."

"So you've decided to sell then?"

"Maybe. I don't know." She reached for her glass, flustered that the conversation she had planned wasn't the one that was happening. After a moment, she changed the subject. "Joe, why don't we go to the beach more often? It's not that far – only about two hours without traffic." She stared at the wine in her glass. "Do you remember the last trip we took, before Dilly was born?"

Joe snorted as he dug his finger into the orange. "What I remember most was chucking everything into the car and driving over without a plan because if we spent another weekend spackling or scraping the new dining room, we'd go nuts."

Maureen laughed. As Joe bent back the peel, the sweet citrus smell wafted out. Joe continued talking as he peeled. "It was sunny then, I remember, but cold, just before Valentine's Day. The only restaurant we found open served breakfast and closed at three – big pancakes and good bacon."

Maureen twirled the stem of her wine glass. "We had to get take-out orders for dinner before they closed. We spent the whole weekend eating nothing but pancakes, drinking hot chocolate, and walking the beach."

Joe popped a section of orange into his mouth. "And watching movies. It was dark at four and we spent both nights watching every G-rated movie we could find."

"That place had a great fireplace." Maureen paused, remembering Joey and Juliette bundled up in blankets in front of the fire. The room had been cold, but the fireplace worked and the firelight in the dark room had seemed magical. "It was the best vacation I've ever had."

Joe stopped, mid-chew. "Really?"

She nodded, a little surprised he didn't realize that. "Joe, all of us were together in one place with nothing to do but relax. That never happened before and hasn't happened since. The kids have their own friends now, and in two years Joey will be at college. Before long we'll be alone."

Joe laughed. "That might not be a bad thing. I won't have to see you and Juliette glaring at each other with your claws out. But Dilly's only seven, you know. She has eleven years before we kick her out."

Instead of laughing with him, Maureen took a deep breath and considered the man she married, usually perfectly reasonable but sometimes not too bright. Something happened to her at Inlet Beach, the moment she saw Elizabeth's house, and she was trying to explain it to Joe, but he didn't understand. How could he, though, when she didn't understand it herself?

As soon as she had seen the property, she had fallen completely in love with everything – the tiny guest house, the plum fairy garden, the huge Victorian house, Elizabeth's garden– and she wanted more time there, but all Lydia wanted to do was sell. So Maureen agreed, because it was easier than fighting with her sister.

Then Tyra arrived and showed them it was possible to restore the house before they sold. And now she wanted to, but didn't know how to tell Joe. The whole thing was a tangle of confusion to her – she was drawn to the house even though they would have to sell eventually.

She tried the direct approach. "Joe, I want to restore the house."

"What about your sisters?" Joe looked at his orange, concentrating on separating another section.

"The house is huge, so even if they're –"

Joe interrupted. "No, honey, I mean what about working with your sisters? Have you forgotten how stressful construction was on the restaurant? We *like* each other, and we almost killed each other."

Maureen rested her chin on her palm. "I know. But this time we have a contractor –"

"Charlie Gimball." Joe nodded. "You told me. He's good, and I'm still surprised he's willing to take on such a big project. He's got to be early seventies."

Maureen blew out a breath she didn't know she'd been holding. "He is. But he's got a crew of people willing to volunteer on the weekends just to learn from him and work on Lloyd Jensen's house."

"And you've worked out your budget? As much as I wish we could, we don't have any money to contribute."

Maureen immediately thought of the money Joe had set aside for the second restaurant and bristled, but now wasn't the time to dig up that old argument.

She finished the last of her wine and answered his question. "If we use the money in the cash account that came with the house to pay for things we can't do ourselves then we should be okay. Each of us will contribute twenty hours a week doing whatever Charlie thinks we're able to do." Placing the glass on the table, she leaned back in her chair. "So we can work whenever we have time. I can be here during the week for you and the kids, then drive down on Friday after school or early Saturday morning."

"Doesn't Lydia live somewhere on the East Coast? How is she able to contribute twenty hours a week labor?"

Maureen shifted uneasily in her chair. It bothered her a little that she and Tyra made these major decisions without Lydia's input, but they had tried to find her. "We would have liked Lydia's input, but we didn't know where she was and she didn't answer her phone."

Joe looked at her suspiciously, the last section of orange halfway to his mouth. "How hard did you try to find her?"

Maureen sniffed and waved away his words with her hand. "You know how she is, Joe. We don't need her."

Joe's expression grew softer. "Maybe she needs you." He held his hand up when Maureen opened her mouth to object. "I know how difficult she is, but you are all equal partners, and she deserves to be treated like one."

Maureen looked away, pulling one of the orange peels from the pile and twirled it absently in front of her. Of course Joe was right, but he didn't understand that no one could irritate her faster or more completely than Lydia. When she was with Lydia, Maureen never felt quite good enough, always too fat or too frumpy.

Giving the peel one last twirl, she snorted. "Fine – if we can find her, we will." Her voice sounded childish, but she didn't care.

"Where'd she go?"

"Probably out shopping." The words snapped out before she could stop them.

Joe's eyebrows drew together as he shook his head. "That's not like you. You don't know what her life is like."

Maureen bit her lip and nodded. "You're right. I shouldn't have said that." She took a deep breath. "Sunday morning, just before I left, Charlie called. Seems someone filed a black mold report with the health department and want the property inspected for mold and vermin. I think Lydia did it. She didn't want to repair the house; she wanted to sell it right away."

Shaking his head, Joe gathered the peels from the orange into his palm. "Sounds like her. First step before condemning a property is the inspection. I don't like her any more than you do, and just because I think she should be treated like an equal partner doesn't mean you have to trust her." He snorted and shook his head again. "In fact, it's better if you don't."

Maureen looked away but felt Joe reach across the table for her hand. "Do you know for sure it was Lydia who filed the report?"

Maureen bit her lip again. "No, I don't know for sure. Tyra and Charlie are going to handle it this week. There's not much I can do from here, but they're going to let me know."

Joe walked to the sink with her wine glass. "I read the proposal you brought home. Charlie's donating most of his time. And he's got a good reputation for honest work so if he projects a finish date of June or July, depending on start date, and doesn't require any personal investment other than your time, you'd be crazy not to do it."

Maureen followed her husband to the sink. "I'll be gone almost every weekend for at least three months, probably closer to four. That's the part I wasn't sure about."

Joe widened his eyes in mock horror. "You're going to leave me with my own children? Surely you have room to take at least one of them with you sometimes?"

Maureen laughed and kissed his cheek. "Probably."

He waved his hand in dismissal. "And who knows, maybe I'll come with you sometime. The restaurant practically runs itself since we hired Josh, and I'd like a chance to meet the famous Charlie Gimball."

"That would be wonderful, but you might have to reserve a hotel room until the house is livable. Tyra's planning to move into the guest house during the worst of the renovation, and I'm going to join her on weekends." She shrugged. "I guess we'll tell Lydia this when she decides to call. I don't even know if she's back in New Jersey."

Joe swirled a scrubber around the rim of a pot. "You'll see her when the money comes in."

***

Lydia let herself sleep for exactly three hours; otherwise, she wouldn't be able face what had to be done. With a little over twelve hours to gather what she wanted, pack what she needed, and leave the house before the neighbors witnessed her eviction, she didn't have time to waste.

As the coffee brewed, she combed through the wreckage for anything Greg may have overlooked. Because they entertained mostly in the den, that was where Greg displayed the showy electronics. She moved through the room like a vulture over a battlefield, but everything valuable – three flat screens, game consoles, and the fancy remote control – was gone, leaving gaping holes and dangling wires in the walls.

Beyond the den in the dining room was a sideboard along the far wall, custom made and worth something but too heavy to move without help. Deep divots in the carpet where the sideboard had been moved were proof that Greg had realized its value, too. Running her fingers along the dark wood, she lifted the corner of the lace runner to touch the burn mark she had made placing a chafing dish on bare wood. For two years she hid it from Greg, draping the surface with linens and decorating for the season, but it didn't matter now; the piece was financed and the store was going to take it back.

Moving to his office, she opened the door to destruction so complete she didn't want to imagine the fury behind it. Papers dripped from his overturned desk and spilled onto the floor. His collection of leather bound classics was gone, yanked from the shelves leaving only faint lines of dust, and the wedding picture he had displayed to demonstrate his happy marriage was smashed, lying on the floor in a puddle of glass. She closed the door. There wasn't anything she wanted in his office.

Upstairs her jewelry case was gone leaving a gaping hole on the dressing room shelf. She had taken her favorite things with her the first time and wouldn't miss what had been left. Greg's suits had been torn from the hangers, the hangers scattered on the floor like bones, and Lydia vaguely wondered what he would hang his suits on once he got to wherever it was he was going.

The suitcases were missing from the storage closet behind the dressing room: Greg had taken the matching set of luggage, leaving only the single battered case Lydia had planned to take to college years ago. Whatever she wanted to take would have to go into garbage bags. Lydia pushed down a bubble of despair rising in her throat. She could collapse later, when she had time. Right now she had decisions to make.

The coffee machine downstairs beeped to signal the end of the cycle. Lydia padded back down the stairs in her bare feet, feeling the deep pile of the carpet, wondering if they would take that, too, As she sat drinking her coffee at the kitchen table, she saw two paths laid before her. One was easy, the other wasn't.

She still had a job as far as she knew, even though she didn't like it. Though it felt like years, she'd really only been away from work for three days. If she wanted to, she could get another sick day and use the rest of the day to gather things from the house and furnish a very small apartment. Tyra's check would cover deposits and fees, and within a week the only thing changed about her would be her address.

Or.

Or she could try something different. *Become* something different.

Technically she was allowed to live in the little house with her sisters because she owned a third of it, although she was positive they wouldn't welcome her back. If this was her decision, then whatever she put in her car needed to be considered carefully because she wasn't coming back.

Another sip of her coffee and a quick glance at the clock pressed her decision. Nine hours until they came to padlock her front door and repossess everything inside. According to the letter Greg had thrown at her, the store that financed their furniture wanted all of it back, and two of the credit card companies were coming to take almost everything else. She had time to find and rent a storage locker and fill it with her favorite things to hide them from the creditors. But to keep any of it, she would have to fight the creditors and the very thought of more hiding and fighting, just exhausted her.

Folding her arms on the table, she rested her head. Her decision rested on a single, glaring fact. The life she had made here was not the life she wanted.

So she would take a long hot shower and a short nap in a bed she loved. She would load her car taking only things that were paid for and things she would use. And after a final meal in this house, she would drive to Inlet Beach to begin something new. Packing her own food and sleeping in her car at rest stops along the way would conserve what little cash she had. It would be hard, and her sisters would not welcome her, but she would fix that, too. She had four days alone in her car to figure out how to do it.

Decision made, she felt a shiver of adrenaline throughout her body and for the first time in years, she felt hopeful.

After rinsing the Spode teacup and saucer, she wrapped it in a linen tea towel and set it on the counter to take with her. She added the yellow cashmere throw to the pile and went upstairs to take a hot shower.

In the end she pawned the kitchen appliances Greg had overlooked – the espresso machine, pasta machine, and juicer – for a few hundred dollars. Gas money to get her across the country because she didn't want to use Tyra's check. She packed food in a cooler, threw clothes in garbage bags, and stuffed everything into her car.

Pulling out of the driveway at five forty-five p.m., she passed a procession of three big SUVs that didn't belong in her neighborhood. Her heart lurched at the thought of what they were going to do to her house and her things, but it didn't crush her like she thought it would.

A nap, a hot shower, and a new path might be all she needed.

***

Joe closed the tailgate of Maureen's truck softly so as not to wake the neighbors. The neighborhood was dark this early in the morning; the only sounds were an occasional thud of a newspaper and the rattle of the car delivering it. The sun would be fully up in less than an hour, and he knew Maureen hoped to be on the highway by then, excited for her first weekend of restoring the beach house.

The truck was packed and ready to go. Oil changed, tires balanced, air pressure checked, current insurance card in the glove box, and the emergency road kit under the seat. Some of the boxes Maureen and the kids loaded had to be rearranged to evenly distribute the weight, and he tucked a few extra tools and a sturdy extension cord into the pocket behind the seat. He was locking the truck bed cover when Dilly came back with another duffle.

Dilly offered it to her father. "Mom says this is the last thing she needs packed."

Joe took the bag with a short nod, at a loss for where to put it. "This is the final – *final* – thing?"

Dilly called over her shoulder as she skipped back to the house. "Yes, Daddy."

Joe squeezed the bag into a space on the floor of the passenger side and hoped this really was the last bag. Nothing else would fit.

He would have liked to come with her, but she needed time to work things out with her sisters. Maureen missed them, he knew, especially around holidays. From a family of boys, Joe didn't pretend to understand the dynamics of sisters, but he did know that not a week went by without knowing where his brothers were or what they were up to. Maureen hadn't spoken to her sisters in more than ten years and it was past time to fix that.

Joe heard the back door creak open and Maureen and Dilly tumbled out, Maureen holding Dilly in a tight hug and Dilly attempting to break free. Joe watched as Maureen tilted Dilly's face to hers and gave her a raspberry kiss on the cheek. As they walked toward the truck, Maureen's arm was firmly around Dilly's shoulders, and Joe was surprised to see that the top of Dilly's head almost reached Maureen's waist. When had Dilly gotten so tall?

Joey followed, ear buds firmly plugged into his ears but carrying a plastic cooler stuffed with food for his mother's trip. Joe stifled a laugh as his son raised his chin in a dude nod as he passed, and then settled the cooler in the front seat where Maureen could easily reach it. His son was a good kid and he was a lucky man.

"You got everything you need?" Joe heard his own voice, clipped and short without intending to be.

The front door creaked again as Juliette emerged, bleary eyed and wrapped in an oversized fleece bathrobe hastily tied, its edge dragging across the wet grass. Joe glanced at his wife. Maureen stood still, stiffly, as if the wrong move would frighten Juliette back up to her room, behind a slammed door. Juliette carried Maureen's coffee mug, the coffee inside sloshing over the rim as she stumbled toward the truck. His oldest daughter was not a morning person. Never in her life had she voluntarily gone to bed before midnight so she probably had no idea that Maureen had finished her coffee hours ago and what she was carrying was cold dregs. At least it was an effort.

He watched his wife offer a tentative smile and reach for the mug. "Thank you, Juliette, I almost forgot this."

Dilly's brow creased with confusion. "But Mom, that's –"

Maureen placed a hand gently on Dilly's shoulder. "It's just a bit cold, Dilly."

If he had blinked or looked away, he would have missed it. Juliette's eyes snapped with anger, and she looked at Maureen with contempt before turning to walk back to the house.

Joe was stunned at the pain in his wife's eyes. When had Juliette become so mean? How could he have missed a change that big?

As he watched his wife drive away, he put his arm around Dilly's shoulders and walked back to the house to have a conversation with Juliette.

***

It was well after midnight when Lydia finally turned into the driveway of the Jensen house. The trip across the country had not gone well. The cooler of food she packed in New Jersey and meant to last the entire trip, had not lasted beyond Chicago. Everything she packed was wrong somehow – yogurt

159

without spoons, dry protein bars without bottled water, and sandwiches wrapped in tin foil that looked dodgy by the time she unwrapped them. Three full days of nothing but fast food and soda had given her a dull greasy headache, and only the hope of a hot shower and a clean bed had pushed her past Utah.

She pulled her car to a stop near the studio but was so exhausted that she had to sit for a moment fighting waves of nausea; it felt like the car was still moving. Her head throbbed, her shoulders ached, and her legs cramped from almost three thousand miles of almost continuous driving. Getting here was one of the hardest things she'd ever done. The first night she had slept in her car had been so cold she hadn't slept at all, and even the second night, wrapped in a sleeping bag hastily bought from a discount store the very next day, she had slept fitfully, dreaming of fugitives breaking into her car, stealing the few things she had left.

She had kept the key to the studio that Steven had given her and hoped no one had changed the locks.

Overhead a night breeze pushed aside the clouds to reveal a bright spring moon turning everything silver in its light. The crushed oyster shells in the driveway sparkled like pirate's treasure and the house, light against the night sky, was full of possibility. It really was a beautiful house, especially in the moonlight. And what a project that would be, to restore it, to breathe life back into it.

Lydia snorted, a short puff of disbelief. She must be more tired than she though, delirious almost, to think that she and her sisters could work on anything together.

With no other thought than she would finally be lying flat

to sleep, Lydia scooped the key from the zippered pocket of her purse and opened the door. Pulling the cot and the sleeping bag from the back of her car, she dragged both toward the guest house and went inside.

Vaguely she noticed that someone had cleaned inside. Charlie had said it needed to be cleaned, and it had been. So someone must be living here, probably her sisters.

At this point, Lydia didn't care if they threw her out the next morning as long as she was allowed to sleep now. Following a short hallway, she opened a door at random and found a narrow twin bed already made up.

She fell upon it fully clothed and was instantly asleep.

Chapter Eight

The stool by the corner of the kitchen counter afforded a view of the entire studio, so that was where Tyra sat, laptop open, pretending to work. Maureen was pretending as well, engrossed in the thin community newspaper, cradling a coffee mug in her hand. However, the coffee had long grown cold and she hadn't turned a page in quite a while.

Work was scheduled to begin early the next morning. Charlie had a volunteer crew lined up for the first official weekend of work and there were a million things to do before then. In fact, they should have been started and finished long ago, but neither sister moved. As the afternoon light waned and the hour hand inched closer to three o'clock, they waited for Lydia to wake up.

When the door to the small back room finally creaked open, both sisters froze, tension crackling in the air. Lydia emerged from the short hallway dressed in dark leggings and a thick knit sweater. The edge of her blonde ponytail brushed the back of her collar as she padded across the concrete floor.

Without a word of greeting or acknowledgement, she lifted the carafe from the coffeemaker and held it in her hand as she searched the small countertop. "Are there mugs?"

Maureen's eyes narrowed, but she didn't turn. If she had

maybe she would have seen the tremble that ran through Lydia's fingers and sloshed the last bit of coffee in the pot or the tight smile that didn't quite reach her eyes.

That was not the coffee Lydia wanted, anyway. Tyra had made the mistake of trying it once as a change from her usual green tea, and spat it out as soon as the taste registered. It was heavy and bitter, very close to the only time she ever smoked a cigarette. Maureen had laughed then, because it was just the two of them, called it Baker's Coffee and said it was an acquired taste.

When it was clear that Maureen wouldn't answer, Tyra pointed to the small cabinet over the sink. "I think there's an extra in there."

That cabinet was where Elizabeth had kept her jars of brushes and tubes of paint and where a family of mice had lived until Tyra chased them out four days ago before she moved in. Since then she kept everything she needed in plain sight and wouldn't have reached back there for a winning lottery ticket.

Lydia poured the last of the coffee into the mug without comment and Tyra wondered again why she had come back. Lydia flounced off last weekend when the vote hadn't gone her way, and it didn't make sense that she would return suddenly and without explanation. Her SUV sat in the driveway stuffed with lumpy garbage bags and covered with road grime, evidence of a long and hurried trip.

Public records were easy to search, and a complete report on anyone could be accessed in moments. Lydia should know the illusion she projects is easily pierced and it would be better if she dropped the pretense altogether. Tyra's plan wouldn't work as long as Lydia pretended.

With no other place to sit, Lydia made her way to the tiny kitchen table and slid into the chair next to Maureen. In her wake she pulled the scent of her perfume, spicy and expensive, mixed with the exaggerated powdery smell of deodorant, not quite masking the fact she hadn't showered recently.

So Lydia left in a hurry and had driven straight through.

Interesting.

It was to Maureen's credit that she didn't watch Lydia drink the Baker's Coffee, and it was to Lydia's credit that she finished it. Both of her sisters were strong-willed, and Tyra was running out of time.

Lydia didn't stay at the table long, and it was only when she left, to put her mug in the little sink that Maureen finally addressed her. "Lydia, before you left did you file a black mold complaint against the house?"

Tyra watched Lydia's reaction carefully. Of course Lydia was the one who had filed the report. The coincidence of a hiker just happening to file a complaint against an abandoned house that could barely be seen from an overgrown trail was too much to accept. She waited for Lydia to admit the obvious truth.

Instead Lydia slowly rinsed her mug under the faucet and overturned it on the rack to dry. "I don't know what you're talking about."

"Why did you come back?" Maureen turned in her chair, her gaze locked with Lydia's.

Lydia lifted her chin and arched a perfectly shaped brow. "I still own a third of this property. I came to restore it."

Maureen's mouth tightened as she considered Lydia's reply.

"Work starts tomorrow morning."

Lydia smirked. "And that is why you see me today."

They were like two cats in a bag, clawing and hissing, neither giving an inch. Lydia clearly not going to tell either of them the real reason she came back, and Maureen refusing to accept anything but the truth.

Maureen turned to fold her newspaper with short, deliberate strokes as if Lydia's very presence annoyed her. When she finished she rose from her chair and leaned stiffly against the table. "Since you say you don't know, I'll tell you: someone called the health department and filed a formal complaint for black mold against the owners of the property – us. An inspector came out and went through every inch of both buildings. It took Charlie and Tyra two days to escort the inspector and in the end they found nothing, but they charged us nine thousand dollars for the inspection anyway. They said we can expect at least one more inspection when demolition is finished." Her eyes flashed with fury. "You might not care about the extra expense, but I do. We can't afford it."

Lydia broke eye contact and turned toward the sink. If Maureen had been paying attention she would have seen Lydia pressing her lips together and the tremor in her fingers as she turned on the faucet.

But she wasn't.

Maureen had paced the length of the studio and stood by the front door, her face flushed with anger. Snatching her jacket from the peg by the door, Maureen pushed her arms through and pulled it on. "Lydia, there was barely enough money in that account to cover basic repairs for the house, much less pay for the mold inspection. So after three days of juggling numbers, Tyra came up with a proposal that we are going to follow –"

"– *Tyra* did? Since when is Tyra in charge?" Lydia glared at Tyra, then back at Maureen. "I told you it wasn't me – I didn't call in that report. I won't be punished for something I didn't do."

"We are all being punished, Lydia. All of us. Because this restoration project just got nine thousand dollars harder." Maureen snapped her collar and slid the zipper. "So this is what is going to happen: each of us is expected to contribute twenty-five hours a week now instead of twenty, doing whatever Charlie needs done. No questions, no exceptions." She dug in her pockets for her gloves and slid them on. "You will pay for one-third of all expenses, including electricity for the house and studio and food for the volunteer workers "

"We're *feeding* workers? Can't they bring their own lunch?"

But Maureen continued, holding up her hand and finishing her sentence as if Lydia's objections had no value. "And finally, the money in the household account is to be spent for repairs only. And because Tyra is the one who drew up the new budget, she is in charge of the money."

Lydia faced Maureen with a desperate fury. "You can't do this – you can't arbitrarily decide this. We're supposed to vote."

Maureen froze and fixed Lydia with a glare so ominous that it would have been noted, even in prison. "You left last weekend like a thief in the night because you didn't like the outcome of our vote, and the next day the county comes to inspect for mold, even though everyone knows Charlie's been spraying and the house is vacant and not remotely a health hazard." Her voice slowed, the last words edgy and sharp. "And don't you think for one minute that I believe you had nothing to do with it. Your whole life is about money and isn't this the perfect payoff."

Lydia's face drained of color as she stood by the sink, motionless, giving Maureen an easy target.

And Maureen wasn't finished. Her face blazed with fury. "And know this: if you do anything to sabotage this project –"

"– we should go." Tyra stood and moved to join Maureen at the door. "We have errands to do before work starts tomorrow, and Lydia still needs to get settled."

Maureen blinked.

Lydia glanced at Tyra as if she hadn't realized she was in the room.

Tyra pulled her coat and backpack from a peg. Purposely turning away from her sisters as she slipped her arms through the sleeves, she hoped Maureen would see that Lydia deserved none of her tirade. She needed Maureen to apologize.

Instead Maureen scooped her purse from the table and reached for the door. "Charlie and his crew will be here at eight. You should be dressed and ready to work by then."

***

It was only when she heard the door close behind them and the crunch of the gravel under her sisters' feet as they walked away, that Lydia let herself take her first full breath. She barely made it to the chair before she collapsed. With her elbows on the table, she buried her face in her hands and let the tears come. Hot tears of frustration she had been holding back for almost a week, telling herself that all she had to do was get to the house and everything would be okay.

Only it wasn't.

***

Lydia woke without opening her eyes. The lace curtains ruffled softly as the breeze drifted through the small open window near her narrow bed. In the distance seagulls called to each other and the ocean waves rolled toward the shore. Her sleeping bag was warm and the air smelled fresh as if the rain had scrubbed it clean. She sat up in bed and unzipped her sleeping bag, letting cold air from the room chase away the warm pocket of air she was sleeping in because she had to.

Demolition began today.

She went to bed shortly after her sisters returned and could easily have slept longer. Tyra brought her dinner and she accepted it reluctantly, not wanting to be indebted to her sister. The tender, roasted chicken, basmati rice, and garlic asparagus were delicious and almost put her body into shock after the greasy food eaten over a steering wheel. The sisters ate in silence. After pulling out money to repay Tyra for dinner and contribute to expenses for the week, Lydia returned to bed.

Gathering soaps and lotions into a bag, she grabbed her towel and rushed across the short cold hallway to the makeshift bathroom. Someone had constructed a shower curtain using a blue tarp clipped to a wire strung across the ceiling, almost preventing the naked pipe from spraying cold water onto the floor.

Almost.

Dressed and ready in record time, she blotted the final coat of red lipstick and opened the back bedroom door. As she followed the sound of muted conversation and the smell of baking bread into the kitchen, her stomach grumbled in delight. She couldn't remember the last time she had eaten a muffin. Ever since Greg had accused her of letting herself go, she eliminated bread altogether. Entering the kitchen she hoped for a small tin of freshly baked muffins, instead stood a buffet for forty.

A sturdy wooden door was set atop saw horses and pushed against the overhang outside the studio. The surface was spread with a blue cotton blanket, and on one end was a pile of mismatched ceramic plates scattered around squatty jelly jars filled with a collection of forks and dull knives. Toward the front was a bundle of thick paper napkins loosely tied with raffia and tucked with a sprig of rosemary. Spread along the length of the table was food she hadn't seen in a long time, completely unlike the fussy appetizers she arranged for Greg's parties. Two trays of fat cinnamon rolls sat in the center of the table next to a basket of blueberry muffins covered with a crisp yellow napkin. Next to that, containers of yogurt chilled in a shallow bowl of ice, and along the back were bottles of juice, water, and milk. Finally, chafing dishes filled with eggs and potatoes were tucked near the plates.

It was an exceptional display. The food looked delicious, and Lydia really did want to tell her sisters how beautiful it all was, until she remembered the three hundred dollars she had given Maureen last night for food. Lydia assumed it would cover food for a month, but it looked like everything had been spent on this one meal.

Tyra stood by the sink, a bright red dishtowel draped over her shoulder while washing dishes. Lydia walked past her looking for Maureen and found her lifting coffee mugs from a plastic rack propped on a stack of cardboard boxes.

"What is all this?" Lydia's voice sounded unexpectedly harsh, even to her.

Maureen hesitated, her fingers tightening around the handle of a mug. She set the mug on a wooden tray, and her voice was clipped as she answered. "For Charlie's crew."

"The workers?"

Maureen nodded and turned to pull a blue speckled tin pitcher from a shelf above the sink.

Before she and Greg had been able to move into their home in New Jersey, they hired a construction crew to repair damage done by the previous owners. It had taken almost six weeks to repair and during that time, she never once fed anyone anything. During the hotter part of the summer, she allowed the landscapers to drink from the garden hose, but she hadn't encouraged it because it took focus from their work and they were paid by the hour.

"Why are we feeding construction workers? Where did you get all this – did you buy it all?"

Maureen's lips compressed into a thin line as she turned from the tray, and she drew a breath before answering. "Charlie brought the door and the sawhorses, Tyra contributed the blanket –"

"– and the flowers." Tyra entered the room with a large box of bread and two bunches of bright yellow daffodils picked from the side garden. She set the box on the edge of the kitchen table, pushed the hood of her raincoat from her head, and hung the jacket on a peg by the door. She brought the smell of rain and salty air into the room with her, and Lydia found herself relaxing into it.

"– and the flowers," Maureen repeated, with a smile for Tyra that pierced Lydia's heart like a shard of glass. When had those two become such good friends? Tyra didn't deserve Maureen; Maureen was hers.

Maureen reached into the box and pulled out a great loaf of crispy bread. "The plates, cups, silverware are old. I brought them from the restaurant when I drove down yesterday...." Her voice trailed off as she rummaged in another box of serving dishes.

"Maureen." Lydia's voice was sharper than she had intended, and Maureen jerked away from the box. Lydia clasped her hands together and continued now that she had Maureen's attention. "Why are we feeding construction workers a full breakfast? In fact, why are we feeding them at all?"

"Because, Lydia, the workers who come on the weekends are volunteers – electricians, carpenters, plumbers. They don't bill us for their time because they want the opportunity to work with Charlie Gimball. And we feed them to thank them for their time."

Maureen's reply was condescending, as if speaking to an errant child. Lydia felt the anger rise to her face. She crossed her arms and addressed her sister. "As someone who contributes equally to the expenses, Maureen, I would have appreciated knowing what you planned to spend and why, before you do it. Expecting me to contribute and not giving me a choice is not acceptable."

Maureen's brow furrowed, and she looked at Tyra. "She's right."

When Tyra nodded, Maureen put the bread back into the box and gave Lydia her full attention. "We planned this last week. You weren't here, but we should have at least let you know before we took your money." She managed a tight smile. "I'm sorry. I didn't expect things to be this chaotic." She nodded toward the box of bread in front of her. "Brenda and Maeve from the bakery donated the bread and all the pastry in this box." She pointed to the table. "The place settings and silverware came from the restaurant. The table – the door and the sawhorses – are borrowed. The rest of the food I bought at the warehouse store and left in the bakery's walk-in cooler." She hesitated before dipping her head in a slight nod. "We should have told you."

Completely unprepared for an apology, Lydia blinked in confusion. Not knowing what else to do, she uncrossed her arms and mumbled, "Okay."

Just as she was about to offer to help, Tyra interrupted them. "You plan to work in that?"

She was looking at Lydia's outfit.

Lydia's outfit had been carefully orchestrated to show that she was the property's owner, not a worker. Her jeans were dark wash and custom tailored, her red cashmere hoody peeked out stylishly from beneath her khaki riding jacket, and the twinkle of silver on the toe of her black flats tied it all together. She'd worn the outfit before during the neighborhood association garage sale, and it felt exactly right.

Tyra left the room, returning almost immediately with a

dark green sweatshirt, which she tossed to Lydia. The cuffs were frayed and across the front it said *"Pog Mo Thoin"* in white script. "Got it in Ireland." She pointed toward the front door. "I have an extra pair of work boots out front. You're going to want to put them on."

Lydia glanced at her flats. Black leather with a small medallion at the toe, they matched perfectly. Then she looked at what her sisters were wearing: Tyra in baggy faded jeans rolled to mid-calf, a plaid flannel shirt buttoned sloppily over a thermal Henley. Maureen's outfit was worse: baggy knit pants that sagged at the knee and a flowered sweatshirt under a dark fleece vest.

Lydia shuddered.

She was beginning to understand that she might be expected to do more than survey the job site, encourage the workers and keep them fed. Turning on her heel she walked to the storage closet where she slept and changed into the clothes Tyra provided.

An hour later, Lydia had her work assignment and was at her station, fully outfitted in a respirator and foggy safety glasses.

Her job was to pull rotted drywall from the studs with a claw hammer and deposit the soggy lumps into a five-gallon construction bucket. The worst job on site. A college kid, volunteering for the weekend and overjoyed at a chance to work with Charlie Gimball, came by to shovel the whole mess into another bucket and carry it away. She was grateful for his help, but she wasn't able to thank him because the respirator made it hard to breathe and impossible to talk, so she spent an entire morning in silence.

When the whistle blew for lunch, she had no idea how many buckets she'd filled. Her arms felt like rubber, her head ached from the safety glasses, her chest hurt from breathing through the respirator, and her neck was knotted from being so close to the wall. She put her hammer on the floor next to her and just sat, feeling her muscles throb.

"That was the whistle for lunch. You coming?"

The sound of the kid's voice startled her after a morning of working in silence. Lydia turned toward where he stood in the doorway, and shook her head.

"Charlie's lunch breaks are mandatory."

Suppressing a groan, Lydia stood slowly, allowing time for the blood to reach her head and her muscles to adjust to their new position. She pulled off her respirator and took a deep gulp of fresh air.

"Don't let Charlie see you do that. Someone called the health department to report black mold." He scoffed, "They should know Charlie would never let that happen. Apparently once a complaint is filed they have to take it seriously, so the respirator and goggles only come off outside until the site's clear." He shrugged. "After the second inspection."

Lydia nodded, regretting the day she ever filed the complaint and hoping it would never be traced back. Avoiding the worst of the muck on the floor and the construction buckets outside the door, she made her way outside.

When she cleared the house she walked to a grassy spot in the back of the house near the beach trail and pulled the glasses and respirator off. The sunlight stung her eyes and her head pounded from working in the stuffy room. Not caring if the grass was muddy or wet, she laid on the ground, to stretch her shoulders.

Closing her eyes, she breathed deeply and listened to the sound of the ocean beyond the bluff. She could smell the sea kelp and wondered if the tide was out and if there were tide pools at the base of the rocks offshore. When she opened her eyes she saw the clouds overhead, leaden and low across the horizon with patches of fog tucked into the crevices of the yard, low enough to walk through.

A chill pushed its way up over the dune and across the yard. Lydia pulled the collar of her borrowed work coat tighter around her neck. Her stomach growled, and she realized that it would be a long afternoon if she didn't eat lunch. Scooping up her safety equipment she walked toward the studio to find something to eat.

The line to the lunch buffet snaked across the driveway, with the workers first washing off at the water pump in the yard. After washing away all traces of drywall in the icy water, using soap and towels someone had left on a table near the spigot, she reached into the galvanized bucket for a bottle of water, unscrewed the cap, and waited in line for the buffet. She counted eight men still in line to get lunch, another twelve scattered on dry tarps around the yard already eating, and she wondered what kind of man Charlie Gimball was to inspire such a following.

Maureen emerged from the doorway wreathed in smiles, holding a serving platter like an offering. She called out to the workers as she placed the food on the table. "I have enough pasta salad here for anyone who wants seconds."

At least two men rose immediately to join the line. The college kid who spent all morning shoveling muck into a bin, and was now just ahead of her in line, turned to comment on the spread. "This is turning out to be a great weekend. I didn't expect food, and I get to work on this amazing house."

"You're shoveling muck into a bucket and emptying it into a dumpster."

The kid nodded, still excited. "I know, but it's just my first weekend and everyone else has more seniority. It'll happen."

Lydia left the line. Baseless enthusiasm had always annoyed her. She walked through the back yard toward the sound of the ocean and stopped at the edge of the bluff. Choosing a relatively dry patch of ground under a pine tree, she crossed her legs and settled in to watch the seagulls circling the rocks offshore and the waves rolling toward the shore.

"You need to get a job." Startled, Lydia turned to see Tyra standing beside her, a plate piled with food and a fork rolled into a napkin. Her stomach growled, threatening not to work if it wasn't fed.

"I mean it." Tyra bent to offer Lydia the plate. "This project will take longer than you think, and you're going to need your own money."

Lydia accepted the food and unrolled the fork. "This is a very small town, and there isn't a lot of demand for what I do."

Tyra shrugged. "So do something else."

Lydia looked at her sister, at how easy Tyra's life was compared to her own. The moment she tested as gifted when she was eight years old, she had become the darling of the family, the focus of everything. She had no concept of how hard normal life was, how hard Lydia's life was, and Lydia didn't have the words to explain. Instead she sighed. Her life, it seemed, was a series of deep sighs.

"Stop it."

She froze. Her fork balanced with potato salad halfway to her mouth. "What?"

"Stop feeling sorry for yourself. It's depressing."

"You have no idea what my life is like."

"And you are so cocooned in self-pity that you don't see anything yourself. Have you seen how difficult it is for Maureen to walk? Do you know that Charlie Gimball, at seventy-three years old, came out of retirement to restore this house but is only physically able to work three or four days a week? Everyone has struggles, Lydia. Not everyone waves them like a banner." She swept her hand in a wide arc toward the studio. "There are thirty people out there offering their skills for this house, working in the rain and the cold. Half a dozen more in town have donated material or food without a thought of what they will get back. All for honoring the family that lived here. How amazing that is."

Tyra stood for a minute, but when Lydia didn't offer a response, she turned to leave.

"Why didn't you tell me any of this before?"

"We're not exactly close. We've never had a conversation that didn't start and end with, 'Where's Maureen?'"

***

Despite the overcast sky, Lydia slipped on her sunglasses the instant she left the hardware store to cover the hot tears of frustration she felt prickling behind her eyelids. Looking for work at that store had been a mistake; she could barely tell a screw from a nail, had absolutely no interest in any of it, and they could tell. But her choices were limited. This small town wasn't exactly a haven for commerce, especially in the off-season when all of the tourist shops were closed. Already turned down at the library, the community theatre, and the dingy grocery store at the edge of town, the hardware shop had seemed like the last chance.

A patter of fat raindrops hit the sidewalk as she walked to the end of the street where her car was parked. Her entire job search had taken less than two hours, had encompassed every open business, and still she found nothing. She wasn't looking for a career; all she needed was something to cover expenses until the property sold because her pawn shop money was quickly running out. The only source of money left was the silver tea set and the crystal she had placed on consignment in Short Hills, but they carried a high price tag and would take time to sell.

The rich smell of freshly brewing coffee stopped her in her tracks, and she closed her eyes to take a deep breath, not even caring what she looked like or the marks from the raindrops that would have to be brushed from her coat. It had been entirely too long since she enjoyed a good cup of coffee and the smell of it was intoxicating.

"You can come in, you know. First cup for locals is free."

Lydia opened her eyes to see a woman with a kind face and a warm smile leaning against the doorframe.

"Really?" Lydia brightened. She could afford free.

"Nah." She shook her head as her smile widened. "But you looked so pathetic out there that I knew I had to do something about it." Standing beside the door, she waved Lydia inside. "Come on in out of the wet and welcome to Declan's."

Inside the coffee shop was warm and the air was thick and smelled sweet. Behind a glass counter, iced scones and cookies were piled into wire baskets, pastries were arranged on cake plates, and drinking chocolate and mulled cider were on tap. A stone fireplace in the far corner of the room popped as a log gently collapsed in the grate. An older couple sat in the armchairs near the window sipping drinks from thick ceramic mugs. The only other customer sat on a sturdy wooden chair by the fireplace, reading the newspaper, empty cup and a crumbed plate in front of him.

"We're slow this time of day, and I could use the company. My name's June." She offered her hand and Lydia shook it. June's hands were warm, her grip firm, and Lydia felt herself smile for the first time since arriving at Inlet Beach.

June's green eyes sparkled as she continued. "I'm the other half of this coffee shop, and we only named it Declan's because I lost the coin flip. I do the baking when I feel like it, and hire out when I don't. I'm told that I have a fierce temper, but really I don't tolerate tourists very well. My favorite color is turquoise, and I've always wanted to live on a houseboat." She slid behind a long wooden counter and stood in front of a large silver espresso machine. As she twisted one of the black handles on the machine, she smiled. "Now, what can I make for you?"

"Do you always introduce yourself like that?"

June shook her head. "Nope. It's just that I know so much

about you that it's only fair you know something about me."

"Fair enough." Lydia smiled. "And I'll let you choose what to make. I'm just happy to have good coffee."

June's brow furrowed as she looked at Lydia. Finally she said, "You're different than I thought." She flicked her fingers through the air before turning to steam the milk. "Small town gossip."

Lydia spent a good hour in Declan's talking to June about nothing in particular, and when she left the rain had stopped though the sky was the same dreary lead-gray it always was. She was halfway down the block when she felt the smattering of drops hit the shoulders of her good cashmere coat. One of the few nice things she had brought with her, the coat was only for interviews and she couldn't afford to have it spot, so she ducked under the shelter of a shop awning to get out of the rain.

The shop was a veterinary clinic, and it hadn't been open earlier this morning when she started her search. She felt a flutter of hope as she glanced up and saw a faded red "Help Wanted" sign taped to the upper corner of the picture window. The corner of the sign sagged; the tape holding it up apparently lost its stickiness, fading to a dull yellow with peely edges.

Inside was a refuge from the cold and damp outside, bathed in warm yellow light with soft music playing in the background. Leather-ish club chairs for the owners, and nestled between were thick fleece blankets folded into soft beds for waiting patients. The room smelled unexpectedly of lavender, and Lydia felt as if she'd stepped into someone's living room instead of a medical waiting room. The tendrils of her headache, squeezing since she began her job search early this morning, began to lose their strength, and she felt herself relax.

"Well, good morning. Come on in and get out of that rain." An older woman with a kind round face and thick Southern accent beckoned her from behind a large reception desk.

Lydia slipped off her sunglasses and offered the woman her hand. "My name is –"

But the woman waved it away and smiled instead. "I know who you are, honey. I've been expecting you."

"You have?"

"Of course. This is a very small town and there aren't many places to wander. Come on over here so I can see you." As she motioned Lydia over, the collection of bracelets on her wrist jingled together. "Call me Colleen."

She patted the top of her desk with her fingers, almost every one of them adorned. A chunky gold ring with a carved lion head covered her index finger almost to the first knuckle, a sparkling wedding band set was moved to her right hand, and bands of gold encircled both thumbs.

Intending only to offer a formal handshake, Lydia was a bit taken aback when Colleen reached for both of Lydia's hands. Colleen held them both firmly in her own as she stared deeply into her eyes as if she were looking for something specific.

So Lydia waited. Waited because she wanted a job.

After a long moment Colleen released her hands and nodded. Lydia felt as if she'd been evaluated.

Colleen folded her hands neatly on her desk. "Now what can I do for you?"

Confused, Lydia hesitated until she remembered a job interview, years ago, that she had thought went well but hadn't.

When it was over, the recruiter gleefully told Lydia that she wouldn't be considered because she hadn't asked for the job. Lydia replied that it was pretty obvious that she wanted the job because she was there, but the recruiter said if she didn't ask for it specifically, she didn't want it badly enough. So Lydia took a breath and asked. "I'd like to apply for the job in the window."

Colleen blinked. "The job in the window?"

Lydia pointed to the sign. "That one."

Colleen glanced at the sign and shook her head. "Oh, honey. That sign doesn't mean anything. It's been there for fifteen years. The first Dr. Brinkley taped it way up high so the whole world could see it. After I was hired, we just never got around to taking it down. Pretty much everyone who lives here ignores it, and the summer people don't come looking for work. We just kind of forgot about it." She heaved a great sigh as if that sign had plagued her for all of its long life. "If I wasn't so short, I'd have taken it down myself years ago."

"You have nothing?" Lydia's heart sank. She was so tired. Tired of pulling down rotted drywall, tired of avoiding her sisters because they hated her, tired of ... everything. Tired of trying.

"Now you know, honey, things always get worse before they get better. You'll see. It will all work out."

Startled, Lydia looked at Colleen, who just smiled. "June called me. She said you need a job and she didn't have anything. But things are going to work out for you, you wait and see."

Lydia felt her brow furrow. "How do you know that?"

"I just do." She lifted one shoulder. "It's a gift."

183

A swinging door at the end of a short hallway swung open and a woman in a frayed blue lab coat came through. She slid a sheaf of brown folders into a wire basket on the reception desk and seemed surprised to see anyone in her waiting room. After a moment, she smiled and offered her hand. "Good morning. You must be Lydia. I'm Rebecca Brinkley. Welcome back."

Lydia winced at that last sentence.

Colleen reached to hold Lydia's hand. "Honey, small towns have long memories. The Jensen place especially holds a special place in our hearts. But it will be okay."

Rebecca rolled her eyes. "Did she offer to read your Tarot cards? She does that sometimes when she's bored. But she's right about one thing: Elizabeth Jensen was a remarkable woman. She and her husband held this town together in many ways."

Colleen nodded; her eyes danced with memory. "She was and she did. They were both remarkable people. The house you are restoring was a vacation home that Lloyd built as a wedding gift for Elizabeth. He bought a little over three acres in the middle of town and planned to build her house there until she saw the bluff." Colleen flapped the air with her hand, dismissing the story's details and came to the conclusion. "She kept the land in town; they had it cleared, planted an enormous victory garden, then donated it to the community." She looked at Lydia and smiled. "A lot of families with ration cards had food to eat during the war because of the Jensens. And that's a kindness they don't forget."

Rebecca nodded in agreement. "My father still talks about it sometimes, her generosity. Her community dinners were legendary." "I wish I could have been there, but it was before my time."

Colleen shook her head. "It's a shame someone tried to ruin it with one phone call to the health department." She scoffed. "As if Charlie Gimball would allow anything to happen to that house."

"Why is he so attached to that house?"

Colleen looked surprised. "Oh, honey, Elizabeth and Lloyd Jensen saved that boy's life." She reached to pat Lydia's hand. "But that's his story to tell; he'll get to it if he needs to."

Rebecca reached for the spiral pad of phone messages on the edge of the desk. She flipped the first page. "Colleen did the drug rep return my call yet?"

Colleen snorted, clearly not a fan of the drug rep. "He did. He said to remind you that you have to call him before ten in the morning or he won't make the trip out here. He said this clinic is too small and too far out of his way and all you want are samples anyway."

Rebecca shrugged. "He's right. Free is all we can afford at the moment."

***

Leaving the office so Colleen and Rebecca could get back to work, Lydia walked across the damp street and down the beach stairs and sat near the bottom step to watch the ocean. The misty rain had stopped and a weak spring sun poked from behind the clouds, reluctantly, as if to apologize for its absence. With her elbow on her knee and her chin in her hand, she watched the seagulls circling the rocks offshore.

She didn't really expect to find a job in town, especially

before the tourist season, but it would have been nice. With strict budgeting, the money she arrived with might last another two months and maybe after that, the house would sell quickly. If she had to, she could widen her search to another town.

She heard a noise under the stairs and froze.

It sounded like something whining and all the times she had teased Tyra about monsters living under her bed came back to her in one big wave. As she held her breath, she listened again, hoping it was her imagination and mentally checking off every beach animal she could outrun, even in suede boots. When it whined again, high-pitched and urgent like it was in pain, Lydia leapt from her place and peered between the steps. Slumped against a driftwood stump was a matted, skinny, adolescent dog, its breathing shallow and rapid.

Everything she had ever been told about animals in pain came down to one thing: don't go near. And she didn't until he opened his eyes and looked at her. In his eyes was such a cry for help, a pleading, that she scrambled under the stairs without another thought. Pushing up the sleeves on her coat, she hooked her hands together, splaying her fingers to make a sturdy base and tunneled them into the sand under the dog's body. She stopped when she realized he might need something more stable than her hands to brace him, especially if he had broken bones. Scrambling back on her heels, she ripped off her coat, folded it in half and gently draped it across his thin body. Pulling the sides of the coat together as she lifted, she hoped the compression would support whatever injuries he had.

With strength she didn't recognize, she scrabbled across the damp sand, up the stairs and across the street, while bracing the dog's body carefully against her own.

As soon as she reached the clinic, she opened the lever handle with her knee and nudged the door open. A gust of wind took the door and banged it against the wall.

Colleen's eyes widened in surprise and she flew around the desk to help. Rebecca followed closely behind.

"Oh, honey, not another one." Colleen rushed to the supply cabinet and grabbed a tray as Rebecca began a swift assessment of the dog.

"Where did you find him? Do you know of any injuries?" Rebecca's voice was calm and steady despite the urgency of her questions.

"Under the beach stairs. I just found him there." Hysteria bubbled up in Lydia's throat, but she pushed it down. She held the dog as carefully as if she were shielding a puffball from the breeze. But in the stillness of the room, every snap of the second hand on the clock wall sounded like an explosion, putting her on edge. His breathing, not strong but at least regular, sometimes stopped altogether, and she held her own breath waiting for his to restart. When it did, it was labored and ragged as if he were fading.

She told Rebecca, hoping it would help her to make him better. "He barely moved when I picked him up, and he's not breathing right. It sounds crinkly, like a paper bag."

"More than likely he's got pneumonia." She flicked her glaze toward Lydia. "You did the right thing by wrapping him in a coat, but I need to lift some of it away so I can examine the rest of him. Hold him steady." She glanced at Colleen. "Watch his head and catch it if he turns to bite. It will be a reflex because he's in pain."

As Rebecca gently lifted part of the coat from the patient, the air filled with the stench of infection and the metallic smell of blood. The dog's light fur was matted with blood and sand, and Lydia's heart squeezed for what he had endured in a very short life.

Running her fingers lightly across the knobby outline of his backbone, she stopped at his neck and groaned softly. "I was afraid of this. There is a nylon rope wrapped around his neck and it's been there for quite a while." She and Colleen exchanged a look.

Colleen's voice was soft and calm. "Hold him steady, honey. Just like that."

Rebecca shook her head. "I am going to try to unwind it first. Cutting something this deep and this close to his throat requires sedation, and I don't think he has the strength to live through it."

The group held their breath as they watched Rebecca's fingers disappear into the fur of the starved animal. She murmured to him as if weaving a spell that would keep him calm.

Suddenly the animal cried out in pain and everything in the room changed. Rebecca froze, her fingers still buried in the animal's fur but no longer moving. Lydia drew her arms closer to her body, cradling the dog as he fought to escape the pain.

Quicker than a breath, Colleen tossed aside the coat and pulled a white towel from the shelf. Taking advantage of his struggle, Colleen slid her hands under his body, scooped him into her arms and wrapped him in the towel in one fluid motion. He didn't struggle for long; each movement seemed to sap his energy and whatever reserves he found within him were quickly gone. After a moment, he slumped against Colleen's chest. A few shallow breaths rose and fell from his chest, and then he was quiet.

Colleen's face contorted with anguish. "This never gets easier."

She looked at Lydia. "Dr. Brinkley will make him more comfortable in the back, and then I'll come out to talk to you."

Lydia nodded numbly and fell into a club chair, leaving her coat puddled on the floor beside her. She glanced at it, the blue cashmere that was so important a month ago now caked with sand and spotted with blood. Although she didn't remember doing it, there was a rip in her sleeve from shoulder to elbow, and the edges of the silk lining lay jagged against the cashmere. Glancing at her boots, she saw they hadn't fared much better and probably couldn't be saved.

She leaned her head against the back of her chair and closed her eyes. The trembling started deep in her core, radiating out until she had to clench her teeth to keep them from chattering.

She heard the door to the clinic open and someone walk in, but she didn't have the strength to open her eyes. She wasn't exactly a town favorite, so what was the difference if they thought she was crazy, too.

"Heard you might be here."

Opening her eyes, she saw Charlie Gimball standing in front of her chair, a deep look of concern on his face.

All she could do was nod.

He picked up her coat from the floor and draped it over the arm of a chair. Sand splattered to the floor. He chose the seat next to her and sat on the edge of it, elbows on his knees and hands clasped together. Examining the rip in the sleeve of her coat, he shook his head.

"Usually we find them in the fall after the summer people have gone home." His voice cracked. "Never this late. I don't know how he's survived this long."

"Survived what? How did that poor dog get under those beach stairs?" The room was spinning and Lydia's voice sounded hollow.

Charlie pulled out a big cotton handkerchief and wiped his eyes. "It doesn't happen all the time, but it does happen. And even once is too often." He heaved a great sigh and stuffed the handkerchief back into his front pocket. Then he leaned forward and held her gaze. "Sometimes renters with more money than sense come to Inlet Beach and expect a magical family experience. They find a big house for the summer, bring their children, their children's friends, their own friends, and set to living the life they think is perfect." He looked away to collect his thoughts. "And one of the things they bring with them is a puppy. By the end of the summer when they're ready to leave, they realize how much work a puppy really is, and maybe they don't have time to clean up accidents on their carpets at home, and they don't have time to play anymore, or maybe," his blue eyes welled with tears again, "that little puppy just isn't as cute at the end of the summer as he was in the beginning. So they leave him."

"Leave him where?" Lydia hoped she misunderstood because

what Charlie was telling her was too horrible to take in.

"They let the puppy out and drive away without him. Sometimes they leave a bowl of food nearby, sometimes not. And if we're lucky, we find them before they become emaciated and terrified, living in places they don't belong and can't survive."

Charlie's voice dropped and he looked at his hands. "All those renters wanted was the idea of a puppy not a real one. Anything worthwhile takes work."

The doors to the back swung open and Rebecca walked through, her face grim. "Lydia, the dog you brought in is young, close to a year old. And he is in very bad shape. He's got pneumonia, and his breathing indicates at least two cracked ribs." As she tried to draw a breath of her own, Lydia saw Charlie drop his head into his hands. Her heart squeezed in premonition.

"The rope around his neck has caused an infection, and there is another infection, more advanced, in his leg." Rebecca clasped her hands together in a plea for understanding. "I'm sorry but the process to save him will be long and expensive, and I can barely keep the doors open as it is. The process will be painful for him as well as confusing to keep him in a kennel in the back while he heals."

The injustice of it made her furious. Almost without thinking, she pushed her hand into her purse, unzipped the side pocket, and pulled out the paper. "Use this."

Rebecca's brow furrowed as she took Tyra's check and unfolded it.

"Use that, and if you need more I will get it for you." Heat rose to her cheeks, but she didn't care. "And I will visit him every day so he's not lonely. He needs a chance."

Charlie raised his head from his hands, his eyes red rimmed and puffy. Rebecca looked strained. "I can't promise you that I can save him. His injuries are extensive."

"Just promise me he will have a chance," Lydia repeated.

Rebecca nodded, a tired smile creeping across her haggard face. She touched Lydia's knee before she got up. "I will do my best."

After Rebecca left, Charlie fixed Lydia with an appraising look, and sighed deeply as if reaching a conclusion he hadn't expected. "You know, I may have misjudged you, and for that I am sorry." He rose from his chair and offered Lydia's coat to her. "Come on, let's get some hot soup."

"Soup?"

Charlie nodded. "Hot soup and a warm roll will fix near about anything." He went toward the door, opening it for her. As she walked through, he held out the remnants of her coat. "Can this be repaired?"

Lydia shook her head. "I think it's time for fleece, Charlie."

Chapter Nine

After fifteen years of waking before dawn and making the trip to the restaurant to check on morning deliveries and the baking crew, then returning home to get the kids up for school, sleeping past six a.m. was a distant memory for Maureen. So it wasn't a complete surprise that while her sisters slept, she was the one making coffee with only the hum of the clunky refrigerator to keep her company. It was nice, though, listening to the world wake up this way: spring birds nesting in the plum tree chirping happily with the rumble of ocean waves in the background instead of the chaos of the restaurant.

As she waited for the coffee to brew, she wandered toward the window to check the weather. The heavy gray clouds that blanketed the area with fog and mist all winter were beginning to lift. A bit higher in the sky than they used to be and not as stern, with an occasional puff of white zipping across the horizon.

With a loosely zipped fleece jacket keeping out the morning chill and a steaming cup of coffee in her hand she left the warmth of the guest house to wander the grounds before Charlie and his crew arrived. The oyster shells crunched under her boots as a battered spring sun peeked out from behind a cloud to promise to stay on the job today. Even the breeze felt different, crisp instead of raw, like spring might come after all.

The ocean rumbled in the distance as she walked across the driveway, passing the plum tree garden. Sipping her coffee in the stillness of the morning, she stared at it and imagined it raked, weeded, and planted with spectacular spring flowers. Charlie already had work for all of them today, so the raking and weeding would have to wait.

Across the driveway, the yard was scattered with work buckets, tarp-covered power tools, piles of debris. Charlie told them it would get worse before it started to get better, but after a month of nothing but demolition, Maureen could see glimpses of Elizabeth's house before Kenny's interference. And she liked what she saw.

Behind the house was a courtyard with a series of raised-bed gardens that Elizabeth designed herself. Maureen stood before it and considering the layout. According to Charlie, it was a working garden, and every kid had a job from gathering eggs from the coop in the far corner, to pulling weeds from the vegetables as they grew, to harvesting when it was time.

Having walked completely around Elizabeth's courtyard, Maureen stood again in front of the point of the foremost bed, the one shaped like a diamond. Setting her empty mug aside, she stooped to pull a spiny weed growing too close to the border and pushing away the brick. The weed came up in a clump, dirt clinging to its roots. The earthy smell of the wet leaves and damp grass was a welcome change from the staleness of plaster dust, rotted wood, and old wallpaper inside the house where Charlie still had them all working. She knelt to pull another tuft of weed and it came out easily. In no time, she had a mound of weeds and a clean stretch of dark loamy earth, ready to be seeded. It was strange, but she imagined Elizabeth would be pleased.

She moved toward the point of the diamond, clearing the weeds as she went until a section of weeds lifted in a single sheet, exposing a hard surface underneath. Brushing away the dirt, she tried to read the letters carved on the light gray slate, but they were overgrown with moss.

"It is good to see someone working in the garden again."

Maureen looked up to see Charlie Gimball standing on the edge of the courtyard, wearing his usual smile and carrying the clipboard he used to assign work detail.

"This garden is beautiful." Maureen breathed deeply, enjoying the scent of fresh damp earth.

Charlie nodded. "Elizabeth loved her garden. She had something growing all year long. Always something good to eat in there."

Maureen pointed to the gray slate hidden in the ground. "There's a rock here, wide and flat, that might have some writing on it, but I can't read it. Do you know anything about it?"

Charlie pulled a brush from his tool belt and stepped closer to brush the dirt from the stone. After a minute his smile widened, spreading across the whole of his face. "Well, I'll be."

"What is it?"

Charlie turned to Maureen and pointed to the ground. "Come look."

The Inheritance

For Elizabeth Kathryn Jensen,
May your family be
as strong as thyme
as soothing as lavender, and
as abundant as chamomile.
With rosemary to remember

"It's a beautiful sentiment, but I don't understand."

Slipping the wire brush back into his tool belt, Charlie explained. "When Elizabeth and Lloyd knew they weren't going to live in town – weren't going to use the land – they didn't sell it. Though it was worth quite a bit even back then." He tucked his clipboard under his arm and shifted the weight on his legs. "This town was pretty isolated then. Only one road going or coming and hemmed in by two state parks – beautiful parks but restrictive.

Charlie pointed toward town as if Maureen could see what he saw. "The library sits there now, and Elizabeth's fruit trees still grow in the back. Free to anyone who wants to pick them."

Charlie hooked the back of his neck with his palm and tilted his head back. The man loved telling a story. "When they decided to build here on the bluff, they had another garden built and welcomed everyone to use it. Lloyd crafted the stone path and the neighbors commissioned this plaque to be embedded as a thank you for everything they'd both done." Charlie held up his finger to make a point. "Now, you might think this plaque is nothing special, but you have to remember this was an isolated community not easily reached, so food growing already in Elizabeth's garden was more valuable to them than ration cards and the promise of food."

Maureen smiled. "I wish I could have met her. It's hard to imagine we had relatives that selfless, and we knew nothing about them."

Charlie looked at the plaque, remembering. "They were remarkable, the both of them."

An idea shot through Maureen, and she couldn't believe it hadn't occurred to her before. "Charlie. You knew both of them. Did they ever talk about us? Did they know us as children and we just don't remember? How are we related exactly? Because it bothers me that I don't know."

Charlie's face reddened and he cleared his throat. "Well, like I said, it was an isolated community."

"But that doesn't explain why I don't remember them – there are still roads – ways to get in and out."

Charlie pulled out his clipboard. "I really do need to review this work schedule before I post it up." He turned to go. "We can talk later about it if you still want to."

Maureen watched Charlie hurry away, confused at his sudden departure. He never posted the work schedule.

***

Lydia pulled into the driveway, past the thicket of pine trees that sheltered the entrance from the street, and saw Maureen's car in the driveway, up early on a Friday.

Despite what Charlie told her earlier, it wasn't the chowder and warm roll that calmed Lydia enough so she could drive home; it was the two inches of thick cream cheese frosting on the carrot cake she had ordered for dessert. And it was talking to Charlie for almost an hour.

Now she needed to talk to her sisters.

The Inheritance

It was a shaky drive home, and she almost stopped at the clinic to check on the puppy, but Charlie convinced her that Colleen and Rebecca wouldn't welcome the distraction and promised they'd call her when he was stable.

Sliding the car into park, she sat in her car for a moment to gather her thoughts. This conversation wouldn't be easy, and she wasn't looking forward to it, but it was overdue.

Scooping her blue cashmere coat from the floor of her car, she headed for the studio. One of the stilettos on her boot split and she wobbled to the door on her toes. It was time to buy a pair of work boots of her own.

Inside the small guest house, it smelled wonderful, and Lydia paused to breathe it in. Onions, garlic and butter gently sizzled over a burner on the tiny stove. Maureen's big orange stew pot sat on the only other burner, steam rising from it in delicate tufts. Beside it a pile of chopped carrots, and sweet potatoes waited their turn to be added. The kitchen table was set for three, and Tyra's candle was plunked in the middle casting a warm light and smelling like lilacs.

It was a beautiful thing to come home to, and Lydia felt her eyes fill with tears.

Maureen rummaged in the small cabinet above the sink, her back toward the door. As Lydia closed and latched the studio door, she felt her composure splintering.

"Lydia can you get the –" Maureen's voice seemed far away.

Lydia stood in front of the door, detached. Watching emotions play across her sister's face as if she were watching a movie. A clump of sand fell from her coat, landing on the concrete floor with a soft plop. Her foot throbbed where the heel had broken and a headache bloomed at the base of her neck. Something landed at her feet with a thud, and Lydia, curious, looked down to see the contents of her purse scattered on the floor.

Her sister's voice came from far away, and it seemed louder than it should have been. Lydia wanted to say something, but she felt herself begin to tremble.

Someone took her coat; someone else led her to a chair and pressed something cold into her hand, a glass of water. She stared at it until it was brought to her mouth and tipped against her lips.

She drank.

After a very long time, the trembling in her body faded and the pulsing in her ears dimmed; she took a breath and listened to the sound of her own voice. "I found a dog."

Her statement was met with silence. The candle on the table popped, and the stew bubbled softly.

"Did you fight it?" Tyra's face was full of concern, but her eyes twinkled with laughter.

"That's not funny, Tyra." Maureen admonished. "Charlie called us but he didn't tell us you were this upset – or this banged up. "Drink your water. You'll feel better after you shower and eat."

Lydia drank the rest of her water, this time feeling the coolness of it against her throat, and she did feel better. As she sat back in her chair, Maureen returned to the kitchen with Tyra following.

Before she was strong enough to talk herself out of it, she needed to tell them what else she had done. If she ever wanted a fresh start with her sisters she needed to tell them everything. They would never know for sure who had called the health department because the claim was filed anonymously without a way to trace it to her. But Lydia would know.

"The water heater's fixed. Your shower will be hot." Tyra spoke from the kitchen as she gathered bowls and silverware to set the table.

Impulsively Lydia set the empty glass on the table and addressed her sisters in a voice full of conviction. "First I have something to tell you."

Both her sisters stopped: Maureen near the stove with a handful of carrots over the stew pot, Tyra at the table about to lay a soup spoon at a place setting. Lydia thought she saw the edges of Tyra's mouth twist into a smirk but ignored it. After what Lydia had to say, Tyra would almost be redeemed.

Lydia closed her eyes so she wouldn't see her sisters' reaction to the news – Tyra's glee and Maureen's disappointment – and blurted out the truth. "I did it. I am the one who called the health department and registered the complaint on the house. The black mold. I'm sorry I did, and I'll pay the account back. And I'm sorry I didn't tell you."

At the sound of a splash in the kitchen, Lydia opened her eyes to Maureen scattering the carrots into the liquid. Tyra went back to setting the table.

After Maureen replaced the lid on the pot, she looked pointedly at Lydia. "We know you did, but why – just because we decided not to sell the property right away?"

Lydia nodded. "I needed the money."

Maureen wiped her hands on the towel and pulled it back

through the tie of her apron. "You *have* money, Lydia."

Lydia bit her lip as the trembling returned. How could she explain the mess she'd made of her life? The spending, the bills, the horrible marriage, the job she hated. Where would she start? Lydia shook her head as her sisters came to sit next to her. Her hands shook, and she clasped them together on her lap, a little harder than she needed to. What did it matter now? She wasn't the perfect sister anymore. She would tell them everything.

And she did.

She told them about her marriage, her job, her bitterness about not going to college, her spending, Greg's spending, the foreclosure, and what she'd had to do to get here. She held nothing back, and her sisters listened. It took all night, and they stopped only to eat dinner. When she was finished she was emotionally exhausted. Her sisters knew everything about her – that she wasn't anything like the woman she pretended to be.

And there wasn't a doubt in Lydia's mind that they would tell her to leave.

Lydia finished. "I don't have the money to pay you back now, but I will. Before the repairs are complete, I will have the money."

Maureen sat in the only other chair, a blanket over her shoulders, sipping her coffee. "What about the check Tyra gave you at the restaurant two months ago? You could use that."

Lydia shook her head. "I can't. I used it – for the dog." Her voice sounded croaky so she cleared her throat to explain. She told them how she found him under the beach stairs, how she had carried him to the clinic, and his diagnosis. She felt tears welling in her eyes again and wiped them away, impatient with her weakness. "They were going to put him down, and I just couldn't let that happen. He wouldn't have had a chance."

She looked at her sisters for their reactions, hoping they understood. Maureen, obviously disappointed, stared deep into her coffee mug. Tyra scrubbed her face with both hands, clearly upset that her check was spent for a dog and not tuition.

Lydia's stomach fluttered as she made her decision. She had to leave before they threw her out. After revealing her deepest secrets, her sisters had judged her and found her wanting. She would not stay here and be pitied.

Lifting herself from the chair, she intended to go to her room and pack when the look on Maureen's face stopped her. Her sister's eyes were rimmed with red. "Lydia, that was incredible what you did."

Tyra's chin rested on her palms, and she peered from between her fingers. "How is he now?"

Lydia shook her head. "I don't know. Charlie said someone – Rebecca or Colleen – would call me when they were finished."

Maureen nodded. "Then we wait."

"We wait," Tyra agreed.

***

When the lunch whistle blew, Tyra swept the last of the construction dust into the trash bin before slapping the dust from her jeans. Today was the last day of demolition. On Monday they would start to rebuild Elizabeth's house. She looked at the dining room one last time before she left for lunch, stripped of the cheap plasterboard Kenny had put up. With luck, when this room was finished everyone would gather in it for dinner, and they could be a family again.

Tyra sighed. She was almost there.

Making sure she cleared the plastic sheeting before she removed her respirator, she stepped into the gathering sunlight. As she took a breath without her equipment, the shock of cool air filled her lungs and cleared the cobwebs from her brain.

Jerry, the college kid who came to help on weekends, strode across the driveway. "Charlie wants to see you for a minute before you get lunch."

When she found Charlie, he was next in line for the lunch buffet, eyeing his favorite: Maureen's pasta salad. He barely paid attention to Tyra as he scooped, so she started the conversation. "You needed to see me, Charlie?"

He plunked a final scoop of pasta salad on his plate. "Yes. Would you mind extending your lunch walk just a bit today to go to the hardware store for me? We wouldn't need you back for the rest of the afternoon."

"Sure, I will, Charlie, but can't someone just drive down there for whatever you need?"

Charlie's eyebrows shot up and he hesitated over the desserts – he never hesitated over the desserts, he usually selected at least three. "Um. We're out of screws."

"What screws?"

Maureen came out of the studio to refill the salad, and she and Charlie exchanged a look. Charlie reached into his pocket and pulled out a jumble of washers, finishing nails, twine, and pebbles. From that mess, he extracted a long roofing screw. "This one. We're out."

Tyra narrowed her eyes at him. "Charlie, we haven't started

roofing yet, but you need me to go into town – right now – and buy roofing screws. And none of it can wait for the regular supply order?"

Charlie's neck reddened. He shook his head and started to leave the buffet line without dessert. "Nope, sorry. It can't wait."

"And while you're down there would you mind stopping at the clinic to give Colleen this?" Maureen held out a neatly printed recipe card.

Tyra narrowed her eyes, and Maureen's smile brightened. "Sure, but can't Lydia bring it when she goes to visit the puppy at four?"

Maureen's smile froze, and she shook her head. "Uh, no. Colleen needs to buy the ingredients, um, right now."

Tyra took the screw and the recipe card. "I will do this as long as you both know I don't believe a word of what you're telling me."

"Okay, have fun." With a glaringly artificial smile, Maureen grabbed an empty serving dish and skittered back into the studio, while Charlie busied himself with a selection of grapes at the end of the table and said nothing.

"You two are pathetic," Tyra mumbled, knowing neither of them heard. After gathering a walking lunch into a paper bag, she headed across the yard to the beach switchback When she cleared the thicket of blackberry vines, the air changed, turning colder and bringing with it a spray from the ocean. Down below, the beach was deserted as normally docile waves churned offshore, spitting sea foam, and throwing themselves against the rocks and splashing against the driftwood logs along the shoreline.

The beach was wide, and she wasn't afraid to walk along it toward town; in fact, she looked forward to it. As she looked down to zip her raincoat, a gust of wind tugged at her cap, freeing a strand of hair and pulling it into the wind. Brushing her hand across her face, she caught it and hooked it behind her ear before pulling her knit hat lower against her ears. Smiling as she zipped her coat to her throat, she started down the switchback, looking forward to the drama of an offshore storm. Being outside after so many years of being forced inside was glorious.

She walked along the beach, watching the wave crash offshore and the birds circling the rocks. An angry dark cloud pushed away the weak spring sun and the drizzle that had spit out all morning turned to rain as she approached the clinic. As Tyra pushed open the glass front door, she saw Colleen lying in wait behind the reception desk, pretending to be busy.

"Good morning, Colleen."

Tyra knew Colleen was watching as she approached the clinic, but once she entered, Colleen's hand went to the base of her throat in fake surprise. "Oh my goodness, honey, I didn't hear you come in." As she pretended to recover she reached for Tyra's hand. "Let me take a look at you." She looked deep into Tyra's eyes. "Charlie working you too hard?"

Tyra shook her head. "Today's the last day. Maureen leaves later this afternoon, and Lydia and I are going to finish cleaning the jobsite and start repairs with Charlie on Tuesday."

Colleen paused and smiled, as if trying to remember

something she had forgotten. Tyra decided to see how long it would take her to remember the very urgent recipe card.

"How's Mulligan?"

This time the smile was genuine. "Tyra, do you know your sister comes down here almost every day to see that little baby? Giving us that check was the most generous thing I've ever seen anyone do."

"I think so." Tyra unzipped her jacket in the warm room. She had no idea how long this conversation would take, but it seemed to be leading to something.

Colleen's smile widened, and the corners of her eyes crinkled as she gave a short nod. "You were right about that sister." Her fingertips rested on the base of her throat again. "I admit it was difficult to see at first, especially when she called the health department on Charlie, but when she gave us your check for Mulligan's treatment, well, I need to thank you both."

Tyra smiled in return. Charlie was right: people here really did know everything and weren't afraid to tell you they knew.

Colleen reached for her hand again, and Tyra let her. "We could never afford to absorb the cost for that baby's treatment. Shoot, I don't even get paid myself –"

"You volunteer?"

Colleen nodded. "Of course, honey. You don't think Dr. Brinkley can afford to pay both of us, do you?" She shrugged. "Of course, not being an employee frees me up to do whatever I want. So that's good."

The phone rang and Colleen reached for it, resting her hand on the receiver. "I almost forgot: the mailman brought a package here today by mistake. Would you mind just running it over to

Gordon for me? It's kite supplies and he needs them.

"Gordon?"

She flapped her other hand toward the door and she spoke in fragmented sentences. "Gordon at the kite shop. Above Your Head. Next alley. Box is over there. It's not nearly as heavy as it looks."

"You brought me all the way into town to take a package from your clinic to a shop in the next alley? He couldn't come over to get it himself?"

But by then Colleen's attention was on the caller. Tyra had been dismissed.

As Tyra eyed the box, wondering what was really in it and what was wrong with Gordon that he couldn't get it himself, an understanding dawned on her, and she rolled her eyes.

Of course: they were setting her up.

She would deliver the box because she liked Colleen and admired Charlie and realized they were only trying to be kind. She would be polite to Gordon but that is where is would end; she didn't have the time or the interest for anything else.

Muttering to herself as she scooped the box from the chair, she slipped her hood back over her head and went out into the rain to take the package to the next alley. A package that Colleen said was delivered today.

By mail.

On a Sunday.

It wasn't until she had passed the same bricked alley three times, without finding Above Your Head, that she decided to give up and return the box to Colleen. She was quickly losing patience with this fake errand. It had been raining steadily since she left the clinic – the box was waterlogged and getting heavier.

Ducking her head against the rain, which was pelting sideways by now, she turned abruptly and collided with someone.

"Hey!"

Lifting her head would invite a face full of rain, so Tyra peeked up from underneath her hood. It was Steven, walking the street and eating a sandwich, seemingly oblivious of the rain.

Awkwardly resting the box on her hip, she straightened. "I'm sorry, Steven. It's hard to see around this box."

He took a bite and stuffed it into the side of his mouth. "Why are you carrying a box in the rain?"

It was on the tip of her tongue to ask why he would eat his lunch in the rain, but she bit it back. Instead she let out an exasperated sigh. "Colleen asked me to bring it to Gordon at Above Your Head, but I can't find it."

Steven chewed his sandwich and swallowed it before answering. "Gordon doesn't have a sign. He only wants customers who come to him on purpose. He's not big on tourists who browse."

He used his sandwich to point to the alley where his own office was. "It's the last shop on the far end. Come on, I'm going that way."

As they walked the short distance to the courtyard the pounding of the rain slowed as if it were catching its breath. The alley was so narrow that Tyra had to wait for Steven to unlock his office door before she could move past him.

As he pulled a keychain from his pocket and slipped a key into the lock, she asked, "You're working on a Sunday?"

Steven shrugged. "Actually, I'm going to watch the game on my computer. My office gets better reception anyway, and my business partner is already inside, waiting. I just forgot to bring lunch."

Tyra peered down the bricked alley. "Nothing looks open down here, Steven. It's all dark."

Steven jiggled the key in the lock of his office door, but it wouldn't open. "Oh, Gordon's down there, all right. The kite festival officially opens tourist season and its coming up pretty soon. He'll be down there working. Word is that he hired someone to watch the front of the shop this year. Last year, he got a little bristly with customers who browsed too long and ended up losing some business." He glanced toward Tyra. "Be careful when you talk to Gordon. Use short sentences and don't look him in the eye. He's easily annoyed."

As Steven tried the lock again, Tyra shifted the box to her other hip. The cardboard was still absorbing rain and the box was getting heavier. As she was about to offer to unlock the door for him, he pushed it open with a look of triumph. He turned to her with one final question. "Why are you bringing him a box from the clinic? That's just a block away; couldn't he have gotten it himself?"

Tyra's black look must have scared him because he scurried inside, shutting and locking the door behind him.

The last shop in the alley was shingled in gray and trimmed with a deep lavender. Without a welcome sign or display window, it could have been a private home. Tyra pushed the door open and stepped inside. The showroom was dim and smelled like new sleeping bags and industrial glue. Three small windows along the roofline filtered weak sunlight through the forest of kites hanging from the ceiling, casting splashes of color onto the showroom floor; and a fan sent a faint breeze across the room, catching kite tails and making them flutter. The effect was almost hypnotic.

Tyra followed the twang of country music through the showroom and into a back workroom where a massive wooden table was littered with tangles of string, spools of colored ribbon, and a pile of yellow kite fabric. On a stool at the head of the table was a brick of a man who she assumed was Gordon. His denim work shirt was rolled to the elbow and frayed at the collar, his auburn hair gathered at the base of his neck and secured with an elastic. Hunching over his work, he seemed to be attacking a kite seam with a glue gun, pushing a line of hot glue along the edge of a piece of yellow fabric, and growling at it when it skipped and popped.

If she startled him, he might damage his work, but the box was getting heavy so she cleared her throat to let him know she was there.

"Yeah, I see you. Wait a minute." His voice was gruff and impatient.

Tyra let the box fall and it hit the concrete floor with a wet thud. He looked up slowly and glared at her, but she had faced down far worse than him. She raised an eyebrow and lifted one shoulder. "It got heavy."

Sliding off the metal stool, he went to the box and picked at it. A strip of wet cardboard peeled away from the box into his hand. "Colleen sent you?"

Tyra nodded. "She did. And now you have it, and now I'm

leaving." Tyra turned to leave, heart pounding at the nerve of this stupid man. She called over her shoulder, "You're welcome."

"Kite nylon."

Tyra turned and blinked. "Excuse me?"

"Kite nylon. I ran out and I need the extra fabric in that box to finish a custom order." He brushed something from his cuff and brought his hand to the back of his neck. "I had to work with yellow. I hate yellow." He took a deep breath. "Being this busy makes me crazy. Thank you for bringing it over."

"I thought business owners liked being busy?"

Gordon shook his head. "Not me. I don't work well under pressure. Makes me tense." He raked his fingers across the side of his head.

Something chirped, sounding like a chorus of crickets, and Gordon fished his cell phone from his shirt pocket, looked at it for a moment, and flipped open the lid. "Hi, Colleen."

Tyra turned to leave. It would be a long time before she did another favor for this man.

"She's here right now."

She turned to find Gordon looking at her, phone wedged between his shoulder and his ear. He talked as he put the lid back on the glue pot. "I'm fine. But I know you didn't call me just to chat...." He walked around the work table, picking up scraps of kite material for the trash. He glanced at Tyra. After a minute he furrowed his brow. "Really?" He paused to adjust the phone. After a moment, he shrugged. "Okay then."

Without so much as a goodbye, he flipped the lid closed and slipped the phone back into his pocket, then looked at Tyra. "Which one of the sisters are you?"

"Excuse me?"

"Are you the uptight one? You don't seem like it."

She stared at him, not sure if she should be happy not to be confused with Lydia or angry at his rudeness.

Gordon nodded as if she'd answered his question. "The quiet one. You're not weird or anything, right? Just quiet?"

"Okay. Here's what I need you to do." He filled a wire basket with skeins of nylon fabric, mostly shades of yellow, and put it on the table. Collecting a spiral notebook from a bookshelf and a pair of scissors from a bin, he deposited both on the table. Gordon paused, tapping his lip with his finger. "Glue, a metric ruler, are all kept over here. You can take whatever you need but put them back when you're done so the kid who sharpens them can find them."

Tyra held up her hand. She didn't want anything to do with him. He was rude and she was only there as a favor to Colleen. "I have my own work to do. I'll leave you to yours."

Gordon turned from the rack of tools to look at her. "See that's just it. Charlie and Colleen have decided that you're working too hard up at the house and you need something else to do. Something that doesn't involve dust, rotten drywall, or sweeping."

Tyra frowned, trying to piece together everything he said. "Wait. Colleen is your mother?"

Gordon shook his head. "No. Well, yes. Kind of. Everyone in town calls her Mom, and we mostly do what she says. Runs the whole town like it was her own little kingdom. And watch out if both Colleen and Charlie gang up on you – you don't stand a chance then. Pretty sure that's what happened to you."

He pointed to the pile of supplies at the table. "The notebook has basic patterns that anyone can follow. You need to make at least two without straying from the pattern, then once you get the hang of it, you can vary color and shape. Just know I usually run out of basic kites, so make a lot. They sell well to families with young kids."

Gordon waved his hand over the piles on the table. "You can work here. The festival is in six weeks. Tourists start showing up in four. They like bright colors."

From the showroom, someone called out, "Gordon?"

"Back here."

A teenage boy wearing a dark baseball cap and a soggy jacket, stepped into the work room, staggering under the weight of a large insulated cooler. "Declan sent these over for you."

Gordon rushed to take the cooler, and Tyra reached for the thermos tucked under his arm. Gordon pulled a stool from under the workbench and gestured for the boy to sit down. "Billy, I didn't order anything, and Declan wouldn't deliver even if I was dying."

Billy was all sharp angles and acne. "June sent it over. Declan doesn't know. She wants her cooler back as soon as you're done." He shook his head as he stood to leave. "I don't think she liked lending it out. Said you better remember." After snapping the collar of his jacket, he adjusted his hat and turned to leave. "I have to get back."

"Thanks, Billy."

Billy waved over his shoulder as he crossed the showroom.

Inside the cooler was enough food for the rest of the afternoon and even though Tyra wasn't hungry, what was inside looked good. The bagels were toasted and smeared with raspberry jam, the crumb cake was lumpy and perfect, the fruit was cold and ripe, and the thermos was filled with well-sugared cinnamon tea.

"I've never made a kite before."

"It's not rocket science. Actually, the other ones are." Gordon pointed to the more complicated kites hanging from the beam. "But you won't make those. You just stick to the simple ones people buy for their kids. And the ones the hotels buy for display."

He pulled a battered digital camera from a shelf and slid it toward the rest of the stuff. "Take pictures of them when you're done."

"I'd like to be asked, you know." Tyra raised her eyebrow instead of reaching for the camera.

Gordon blinked, so she continued.

"You don't know me, yet you expect me to build kites because you and Colleen bribe me with food? I'm pretty sure I don't even like you."

To her surprise, Gordon laughed. A deep rumbling belly laugh that made her smile.

"You're right." He pushed the piles of kite supplies aside and pulled the food closer. "We should eat first, and when we're finished, you can decide if you'd like to spend a rainy Sunday afternoon building kites. I'd be happy for your help, but I'm just as happy for your company."

And as the rain pattered against the glass of Gordon's shop, Tyra spent the afternoon making kites.

***

It had taken a week to find the shop, and another two weeks to arrange the rest, but she did it. When the letter for Lydia finally arrived in the mail, Tyra couldn't stand the anticipation. She staged the bundle of mail carefully, as if whole thing had been tossed onto the counter, with only the corner of the envelope exposed.

At the sound of tires crunching the gravel outside, Tyra's breath caught. But when Lydia opened the door, Tyra pretended to be so engrossed in slicing and stirring that she didn't notice her sister's entrance.

"It smells good in here. What are you making?" Lydia unzipped her fleece and hung it on the peg next to the others.

"Another one of Maureen's twelve basic recipes. It's not going well." Tyra's answer was purposely casual, a deliberate mix of distraction and courtesy.

"I got everything on the list. It's in the car." She moved to the upholstered chair by the window and sank deeply into it. "I just need to sit for a minute."

Tyra cracked another egg into the bowl before deciding she couldn't wait anymore. "A letter came for you. It's on the counter." She pointed to the pile with her knife and went back to her work.

Lydia opened her eyes warily. "No one knows I'm here."

Pretending to be engrossed in her work, Tyra simply shrugged. Picking up a wooden spoon, she stirred the mess in front of her, her grip tightening as she watched Lydia rise from her chair and walk toward the mail.

As she reached for the envelope, Tyra turned her back, digging into the cabinet for something she didn't need. It was presumptuous, what Tyra had done, and easily traced back. Grabbing a bottle of some orange spice from the shelf, Tyra made sure the top was closed before shaking it over the pan, her voice deliberately casual. "Anything good?"

In the silence that followed, Tyra watched her sister's reaction from under her lashes. The eggs in the pan smoldered and burned, and Tyra poked at them absently before turning off the burner entirely.

When she looked up, Lydia was leaning against the counter, relief flooding her face. "I can't believe it." Lydia stared at the check, turning it over in her hand, her body relaxing as she exhaled. "I can't believe it."

Lydia disappeared down the hallway and closed the door to her tiny bedroom without another word.

And in that moment, all of the time it had taken to research – and call – every consignment shop within a hundred miles of Lydia's house was absolutely worth the effort. When Lydia told them she'd sold things for gas money and consigned the rest, Tyra went to work. Without telling anyone, she found the store Lydia used. The owner told her Lydia had things there still, and while it had taken some convincing, Tyra had bought it all over the phone, with the condition the store send Lydia's proceeds to this address.

In the envelope was a substantial check from the store for everything Lydia had consigned.

Tyra smiled and went back to her recipe.

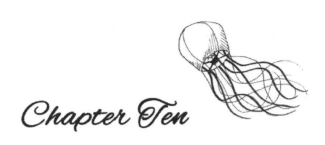

Chapter Ten

The deep rumble of a diesel truck engine entering the driveway and pulling to a stop under her window jerked Lydia awake. Blinking until she focused, then blinking again in disbelief at the time on the clock, she closed her eyes and wondered how the rest of her family could be morning people while she decidedly was not.

Clutching the edge of her sleeping bag, she pushed her head deeper into the pillow and seriously considered faking an illness until she heard a truck door slam and voices of children in the still morning. Today was kitchen day, and Maureen brought her family to help. Two hours of driving from their house in Portland meant they had left well before dawn. If small children could do that without complaint the least she could do was get out of bed to help.

With a deep sigh she slid into yesterday's jeans, pulled Tyra's green sweatshirt over her head, and headed for the door. Yesterday before he packed up the jobsite, Charlie had made sure everything in the kitchen was wired for the appliances Joe was going to install today.

On the way out of her tiny room, she caught her reflection in the crooked mirror and froze, horrified. Even with the flu last winter, when she had slept on the couch and couldn't shower for a week, she hadn't looked anything like this. Licking her finger, she swabbed at the dark mascara circles under her eyes, and dragged a brush through her hair so the dark roots wouldn't show. In New Jersey, she had a standing salon appointment every six weeks with blow-outs in between. Here, well – here, she didn't.

Lydia trudged through the empty studio to the front door, opening it to crisp air and a swarm of activity. The sun had crested the hills, its light not yet reaching the rocks offshore but enough to reveal a sky without clouds. The second sunny day in a row.

A small brown car puttered into the driveway followed by Charlie's truck and another she didn't recognize. Lifting her shoulders and adjusting the sweatshirt's crewneck tight around her chilled neck, Lydia marveled at the way Charlie and Maureen were able to rally help when they needed it. Her sister was already a force in the small town, asking workers about their families and feeding everyone who came to work.

As Steven unfolded himself from a battered green car, his dog Walter pushed past him to run a few victory laps around the yard, and Lydia wondered if Mulligan would ever be able to run with such joy. Colleen said his pneumonia was responding well to the new antibiotics and the wounds around his neck from the nylon rope were beginning to heal, so Lydia was hopeful. She would see him again as soon as she could and bring the boiled chicken he liked.

A lanky boy of maybe fifteen lumbered toward the studio dragging a duffle bag. When he got close, he lifted his chin without a word of greeting or explanation and continued toward the studio. Lydia noticed something vaguely familiar about him, but there were so many college kids working this jobsite, she couldn't be sure.

On her way to find Maureen to ask, she was crossing the driveway and almost ran into a cherub-faced little girl with tousled dark hair and a sleepy face, a puffy pink coat zipped over flannel pj bottoms.

"Can you show me where my mom's room is? She said we could nap there until it's time for pancakes, then we have to help."

Lydia realized with a shock this had to be Maureen's daughter; her little round face looked exactly like a younger version of Maureen's. But Lydia didn't even know this girl's name. She never had met her niece and didn't know what to say.

Another girl came to stand beside the younger one; head tilted to one side, chin slightly raised in defiance, and blond hair swept into a high pony tail. Even with no makeup, her lips pouted into a perfect sneer used by mean girls everywhere, exactly the look Lydia had perfected in high school. A blue fleece blanket was wrapped around her shoulders; loose dark sweat pants were tucked into slouchy sheepskin boots.

"Are you our Aunt Lydia?" The voice was cool and Lydia was met with the smug look of a teenage girl.

Lydia was the queen of the mean girls in high school, and she knew instinctively how to deal with one of her own. She met the girl's stare with one of her own and held it. "I am."

The girl shrugged, conjuring an air of contempt and settling into it. "My mother said we're supposed to be nice to you."

Lydia's gaze didn't waver. "When do you think you're going to start?"

Without breaking eye contact, the girl slipped the strap of a navy gym bag from her shoulder and held it out to Lydia. She raised one perfectly arched eyebrow in expectation.

Lydia jerked her head in the direction of the studio. "Pretty sure you can make it by yourself."

Juliette narrowed her eyes and walked past Lydia without another word, and the little girl scampered after her. When the little girl woke up, Lydia would make a point to introduce herself and get to know her niece.

Staggering behind his family under the weight of a folded camp cot, several oversized canvas totes, and a rolled pink sleeping bag was Maureen's husband, Joe.

Lydia hadn't seen him in years.

"Here, let me take something." Lydia reached to help, pulling the sleeping bag and two totes from the pile.

"The rest is attached." Joe lifted his arms to show that his arm was threaded through the legs of the cot, a tote was hooked to his elbow. He smiled. "How are you, Lydia?"

Lydia smiled, grateful at the second chance. After the way she had treated him at her father's funeral, she wouldn't blame him for not treating her well. Her sister married a good man. "I'm good, Joe. Thanks."

"Some house you got here." Joe started walking toward the studio Lydia followed. When they got to the door, Lydia opened it for him.

After dropping everything into a corner, he turned to her. "I have a favor to ask."

Lydia braced herself. "Sure."

Joe rubbed the dents from his arm. "The kids and I are going to be here for the whole weekend – they don't have school today and Maureen wanted to make a weekend of it."

Lydia nodded.

Joe shrugged. "We have a hotel room, but I'd really like to surprise Maureen by all of us staying here." He held both hands up. "Whatever you decide is fine, but if you don't mind, would you be willing to take the hotel room for the weekend – it's prepaid and comes with breakfast and happy hour, I think."

"Which hotel?"

Joe's brows gathered in confusion and he frowned, but he answered the question. "The Dragonfly, by the inlet."

Lydia released the breath she didn't know she had been holding. She could stay there. "Absolutely. No problem." She took a step toward her supply closet. "Let me just grab a few things and you have it. The bed's sturdy if you don't move around too much, but you don't want the sleeping bag. It needs to be washed."

Joe grinned. "Yeah, you and Tyra have been roughing it over here for quite a while." He put his hand on her shoulder, and she was surprised at the touch. "I'll do my best to hook up the washer and dryer before we go. It'll be a temporary fix and we'll have to move it when the laundry room is finished, but you can at least wash and dry clothes."

The thought of clean laundry whenever she wanted it made Lydia almost giddy. Before she could stop herself, she pulled him into a hug and squeezed, feeling his deep laugh.

***

Thirty minutes later, after a quick breakfast and enough coffee to ensure a reasonable start, Lydia gathered with the rest of her family, and a group of workers in the unheated empty big kitchen, awaiting Charlie's instructions for the day.

"We've got three work groups here, and I've set the schedule pretty aggressively so we can get almost everything done in two days." He tapped his clipboard and broke into a smile. "You should know that Maureen and Joe want to pay you for the day, overtime for the holiday, and they have also offered to pay you for the entire weekend if we get everything done today."

Pulling off his work gloves and stuffing them into his back pocket, he waited until the murmurs circulating the group quieted.

"So we're going to do everything at once. Listen up for your assignment. "After flipping a page, he looked up and pointed to the living room. "Preston, you and your crew hang the cabinets first. They've been repaired, refinished, and are in the living room."

A sturdy looking man in loose coveralls nodded and two other men followed him to get the cabinets.

Charlie turned to the college kid Lydia had worked with on the first morning of demolition. "Billy, everything except cabinets and appliances is in the dining room, stored in bags or packed in boxes. I need you to unpack everything and have it ready. We're going quickly today, and you need to know where everything is." Charlie suppressed a smile. "Take this and lead your own crew."

Billy nodded, his eyes widening at the clipboard Charlie offered.

Charlie turned to Joey, Juliette, and Dilly. "You three will work with Billy today. I need you to do everything he tells you, exactly when he tells you."

Juliette sniffed and pushed her weight onto her hip, but when she saw no one was watching, she followed Billy into the dining room.

The only ones left without an assignment were Lydia, her sisters, and Joe, so Charlie turned to them next. "When Preston's done with the cabinets, he'll move on to the countertops; after that, you can put in the appliances, and you said you can do those yourself."

Joe nodded.

Charlie tucked his clipboard under his arm and clapped his hands together. "Then let's get started."

**

It was full dark when the last goodbyes were said and the last car pulled out of the driveway.

Joe put his arm around Maureen. "We did good work today, and you still have a free weekend."

Maureen leaned against Joe and smiled. "Thank you, Joe."

Joe kissed the top of her head. "Let's round up the kids and put them to bed." He looked at Lydia. "Thanks for giving up your room."

"Are you kidding? This will be the first hot shower I've had in almost three months. You're the one doing me the favor."

Lydia turned to leave, thinking about nothing except a weekend with hot water, good sheets, a real bed, and no construction as she drove out of the driveway.

**

The Inheritance

Lydia woke without opening her eyes, listening to the rain patter gently on the wooden deck outside and breathing the briny smell of low tide through the open patio door. Taking a deep breath, she stretched her arms and legs along the bed as far as they would go, like a starfish. After far too long on a narrow, thin mattress that creaked loudly whenever she moved, this was as close to heaven as she could imagine. Turning over, she buried her head deep into the down pillow, pulled the puffy duvet to her chin, and fell back to sleep.

It was only when she woke the second time to voices of people walking along the beach that she decided to leave her warm bed and get up to start her day. The early morning rain had cleared – the clouds skittered across the sky, looking for someone else to torment.

The second hot shower was as luxurious as the one she had taken when she arrived the night before, and using a second set of fresh clean towels almost made her giddy. A quick glance at the clock confirmed that she'd slept through the breakfast buffet downstairs, but she would make it up to herself with an excessively large lunch, complete with bread basket and extra butter. With a snort she remembered the way Greg had glared at her in warning whenever she reached for any type of carb. Being free of that was life-changing.

The bathroom lighting was good, better than she had been used to. The reflection in the mirror was a bit too accurate, too sharp. Dragging her brush through her wet hair, Lydia decided her first errand was essential. Immediately laying the brush on the marble sink, she walked to the bed and flipped open her laptop and after a cursory search dialed the phone number listed in the review.

"Five-oh-six salon, can I help you?" The woman's voice was cheerful but not weird, a good sign.

"I need to schedule a cut and a color, and I hope you have an opening today." Lydia twirled the phone cord around her fingers as she spoke. A salon with that many good reviews probably wouldn't have an opening for weeks, but she was giving it a try.

The woman laughed. "Well, we just had a cancellation with Kathryn, if you can believe it." Lydia heard the woman flip a page. "And I think Marie can fit you in after that for a cut."

Lydia glanced at the reviews of the shop still on her laptop. "Kathryn's perfect, I'll take that appointment. But is Hannah available for a cut anytime today or tomorrow?"

The woman lowered her voice to a whisper. "Good choice. I'll pencil you in. Four p.m."

Leaving her car parked in the hotel lot, she took advantage of the warmer weather and walked into town to visit Mulligan. With the official opening for tourist season a little over a month away, the center of town was a hive of activity, especially with an unexpected sunny day. Shop awnings were unfurled and scrubbed, window boxes were replanted, and new merchandise graced the display windows.

The door to the veterinary clinic was open, and Lydia walked in. Colleen smiled a welcome from her place at the reception desk.

"You coming to visit Little Bit?"

Lydia nodded. "I am. I have an unexpected day off, and I

want to see how he is."

Colleen waved her back. "He's getting much better. The IV is still in, but this course of antibiotics is almost finished. Go on back."

Past the metal table and the big ceiling light of the surgery was the recovery room and resting in a quiet corner in a kennel lined with clean white towels was Mulligan. If anyone deserved another chance, this little guy did.

Outside his kennel, the IV bag hung from a stand, the clear plastic tubing snaking between the bars and taped to his front leg. The fur was stubbly where they had shaved it, and much of his leg was still wrapped with gauze and taped to protect the IV. His breathing was shallow but strong, and Lydia was glad to see that he'd put on a bit of weight.

As she touched the bars of his kennel, she whispered to him. "Hello, little guy."

The stack of fresh white towels she brought last time to line the bottom of his kennel were still there and didn't look like they should be changed. In the beginning, she brought a load of towels every other day, washing the dirty ones in the laundromat at night. Colleen told her the clinic had a washing machine, and she was happy to wash Mulligan's towels with the regular load, but Lydia wanted to do them herself, using good detergent and fabric softener.

Lydia sat with Mulligan for a while stroking his still-brittle fur, telling him about the house, her sisters, and her thoughts on construction in general. She told him a joke in case he liked that kind of thing and patted him once more before leaving him alone to rest.

"How's our patient?" Colleen looked up from her work with a smile as Lydia entered the lobby.

"It looks like he's getting better."

"You did a wonderful thing, you should know that." Colleen slipped off her green-rimmed reading glasses and folded her hands.

Lydia shrugged.

Colleen looked at her closely, a good sign she had something important to say. Lydia waited.

Colleen reached for Lydia's hand, and Lydia let her have it. "Honey, he's getting much better. We have to think about what will happen to him when he leaves here."

Lydia's stomach twisted. "What do you mean?"

Colleen squeezed her hand. "He's going to need a permanent home, and after what he's been through, it needs to be with people that care for him very much."

Lydia held up her hand. "If you mean me, I can't do it. I don't have a permanent home. We decided to sell when the repairs are finished, but we haven't talked about it since the first vote."

Colleen put her glasses down and reached for Lydia's hand. "Honey, you've already done more than enough. I wasn't suggesting you need to do more. I just wanted to give you the first opportunity to give him a home."

Lydia shook her head. "Thanks for thinking of me, but I can't."

Colleen nodded as if she understood completely. "Okay, well that's settled."

She slipped her coat on and turned to leave when Colleen

called her back. "Wait just a second, honey, we've got some money for you."

"For what?" Lydia stopped, her hand still on her zipper.

"Oh, it's all right here." She pointed to the computer screen. "You gave us a check for nine thousand dollars. Dr. Brinkley donated all of her time, and we tried to cut costs as much as possible. Most of the drugs, Dr. Brinkley bullied from the drug rep, but he didn't have everything, so the total there was eighteen hundred. The surgery was three thousand – and I have an itemized list of everything we used." Colleen touched the screen with her finger to hold her place. "He's finishing the course of antibiotics, and we have him on an IV until he's clear, but he's come through the worst part."

Colleen laid her hand on Lydia's arm. "We are very grateful for what you've done. We've used the money we needed and want to give the rest back to you."

"How much is left?"

"Just about thirty-two hundred dollars."

Lydia drew a deep breath and made some quick calculations. "Okay, you keep five hundred for the medication he's on now and in case anything comes up."

Colleen's smile widened as she squeezed Lydia's arm. "I'll write you a check."

Check in hand, Lydia walked fifty feet to the bank and deposited it into her account. She had one more errand to do before lunch.

Heart pounding, she walked up to the front desk of the only other big hotel in town. "I need to see the manager, please. My name is Lydia Meyer."

"Is she expecting you?" The girl behind the counter couldn't have been more than a senior in high school. Same cheap blue suit, crooked name tag, light brown hair braided behind her ears, Lydia recognized the uniform from the last time she stayed here.

"No, but she'll want to see me." Lydia swallowed and let her breath slowly out.

After hanging up the receiver, the girl pointed to a door around the corner. "Go right in."

Lydia straightened her shoulders and walked the short distance to the manager's office. She offered her hand and her name as soon as she walked in and to her relief, the manager accepted it.

"What can I do for you, Mrs. Meyer?"

"I think we both know why I'm here." Lydia sighed. "I want to apologize for leaving your hotel without paying and I want to pay now."

The manager glanced at her computer screen and gave Lydia a hard look. "You know, we could have called the police and sworn out a warrant for your arrest."

"I know."

"It should have at least gone to collection by now, but I was persuaded to give you a little more time."

"Someone called you?" When the manager gave only a curt nod in reply, Lydia realized she would not be forgiven and pulled out her checkbook. "I have a local check, and you can call the bank to verify funds."

"I will." The manager's voice was frosty. She glanced at her screen again. "The total amount is two thousand, two hundred ninety-five dollars."

The Inheritance

Lydia swallowed. "I am happy to write you a check. I'd like an itemized bill, please."

The manager's eyes narrowed but she complied. She printed the Lydia's account, laid it before her and jabbed at it with her finger. "The standard room rate for your room is four hundred and twenty dollars, off-season. You stayed with us for three nights, but the minimum stay for that room category is four nights. With taxes, resort fees, and three orders of room service, the total comes to two thousand, two hundred ninety-five dollars."

Lydia wrote the check immediately, handed it to her, and waited while she called the bank. When she was finished, the manager nodded curtly. "Before you leave, you should realize this is a family owned hotel. You were stealing from a family who has owned this hotel for three generations."

Something about the way she carelessly opened a top drawer and slid the check inside made Lydia take notice.

The manager started to rise from her chair; Lydia was being dismissed. "And you are not welcome in this hotel again."

Lydia remained in her chair. "I'd like a receipt."

"Excuse me?"

"I'd like a receipt for the check I just gave you. An account statement with my name and a zero balance would be best."

***

The hair salon was a luxury she had completely forgotten. After two hours of primping, cutting, and coloring, her hair was shorter, low maintenance, and back to her original color. Lydia was thrilled with the results and even surprised herself by tipping everyone.

She returned to her own hotel, crossing the lobby as the happy hour was in full swing in the far corner. A woman in a sequined dinner dress lounged next to a red-faced man painfully buttoned into a dark suit, both sipping slowly from their wine glasses without speaking. Several people gathered around a white clothed table, filling their tiny plates with dry crackers and wrinkly cheese cubes while balancing drink glasses and forcing witty conversation. It reminded her of every one of Greg's business parties, and Lydia planned to stay far away.

There was only one thing she wanted before she went to her room.

Ducking around two hipsters in slouchy knit hats and skinny jeans, she laced her fingers around the necks of three bottles of microbrew, pulled them from the ice bucket and headed up. The large pizza box she brought with her garnered some curious stares, but she just smiled. She had big plans of her own.

Pushing open the room door with her hip, she slid the pizza box onto the desk, placed the bottles next to it, and went to take a fast hot shower.

Pink-skinned and tingling from the shower and wrapped in the oversized spa bathrobe, she set up what she needed for the night: pizza box on a towel on the bed, beer bottles lined up with bottle opener ready and gas fireplace lit. After nesting the down blanket all around her, she reached for the remote, flipped a few channels and found Miss Gulch pedaling furiously down a farm road in Kansas. And that was how Lydia spent the last night of her hotel stay: eating triple-cheese pizza, drinking beer in bed, and watching the Wizard of Oz.

She was utterly content.

***

There was still touch-up work to do in the kitchen of the main house, but the plumbing worked and although Tyra's little orange stove was dwarfed in the space reserved for the commercial stove they'd ordered, it was hooked to the gas line and worked just fine. The house was far enough along to move dinner preparations to the big kitchen, and her sisters were thrilled with the extra room, but Tyra missed the coziness of the little guest house kitchen.

"Juliette, take your sister and set the table, please." Maureen's voice came from the dining room over the crackle of the tarp she was folding.

"What table?" Juliette dragged a baby carrot through a bowl of ranch dip, one ear bud stuffed into her ear, the other tossed over her shoulder.

Tyra scraped the garlic across the cutting board with her knife and bit back a smile, wondering how long Maureen would let Juliette get away with her attitude.

The crackling from the plastic tarp stopped. "Outside. We are eating outside." Maureen's words were clipped.

"You mean outside in the *tent*?" Juliette popped the carrot in her mouth and crunched. "You know it's still cold outside, right? And raining?"

"Misting. That's why we're under the tent. Get going."

"I'm supposed to make the salad." Juliette said as she pulled another carrot from the pile.

"Don't make me come in there." Tyra recognized the same tone her mother had used when she had run out of patience.

Juliette popped the carrot in her mouth without dressing,

grabbed the clay pot filled with mismatched silverware, and scooped the pile of placemats from the counter.

"Let's go, doofus." Juliette smacked the back of her sister's head with the placemats.

"Hey!" Dilly rubbed the back of her head. "I'm telling Mom!"

Dilly pulled the stack of napkins from the counter and rushed to catch up to her sister. Before running out the door, she turned her head to look at Tyra and fixed her with a serious stare. "Garlic bread, right?"

Tyra gestured to the pile of garlic pulp topping the bowl of softened butter and nodded. "That's the plan."

"Extra garlic?" Dilly's eyes widened.

Tyra smiled. "They won't know what hit them."

Dilly left, wreathed in smiles, slamming the door behind her.

"Stop slamming that door." Maureen came around the corner from the dining room, cheeks flushed with exertion, arms circling the blue tarp. If the weather hadn't cleared, she planned to use the tarp to partition the usable part of the dining room from the section that wasn't quite finished.

"They're gone."

"Oh, good." Maureen sank onto the stool Dilly had vacated and heaved a sign. "Do you remember how many times we used to slam the door? No wonder it drove Mom crazy."

Lydia came in from the living room with another platter and two large bowls. "Mom locked us out once, do you remember? She said she needed one day where no one slammed the door. Locked us out and told us not to come back until the street lights came on."

"Too bad we don't have street lights," Maureen murmured.

Tyra picked up a fork and poked at the bowl of butter and garlic. It didn't look right; something seemed to be missing, but she couldn't remember what. Maureen was no more than three feet from her, on the stool watching, but Tyra refused to look. Confidence was the key here.

Lydia put the platters on the counter before taking the tarp from Maureen. "I can take that."

"Thanks." Maureen shifted her weight uneasily on the stool.

Lydia disappeared back into the living room as Joe and Joey burst through the door carrying boxes filled with groceries, along with a tornado of dead leaves and raindrops. Joey slid the box onto the countertop by the sink, while Joe greeted his wife.

"So can I have a beer tonight since I brought the whole case from the car?" Joey spoke, apparently continuing a conversation they had started earlier at the store.

Joe snorted at his son. "Takes more than hauling a box from the car to get a beer."

"But I'll be old enough to vote –"

The adults in the room erupted in laughter before Joey even finished his sentence. His face flushed with embarrassment, and he looked at them in confusion.

"Son, kids have been using that old argument since there was something to vote for. Your time will come, just not yet. Don't be so eager." He hooked his arm around his son's shoulder and drew him closer. "If you still want to plate the first course, you better start moving. Because it looks like they've started without us."

After Joey ran off to gather his things, Joe peered into

Tyra's bowl. "Whatever you've got in there smells good."

Leaning in to grab a carrot from the stack, he whispered one word to Tyra as he reached for the dressing. "Rosemary."

Tyra smiled as she reached to add it to the bowl.

As Lydia entered the kitchen again, she paused to look at the little orange stove. "It's cute, Tyra, but I still can't believe you bought an orange stove."

Tyra tightened her grip on the fork as she stirred. Things were better between them, but Lydia still couldn't resist an occasional jab and Tyra's patience was wearing thin. "It's going to perfect for the guest house."

" – and we all are grateful Joe could hook it to the gas line. We wouldn't have a working stove if Tyra hadn't let us borrow this one," Maureen finished smoothly.

Tyra tilted her chin in a show of confidence, to show that the stove had been a carefully considered purchase.

Which of course it wasn't.

The instant she had seen the stove, she bought it without looking at the price tag, without negotiating with the salesman. The orange reminded her of Halloween pumpkins and her hope that somehow all of them would own this property well beyond the summer. The house was almost finished, and they hadn't talked about selling yet.

Joey entered the kitchen wrapped from the waist down in a white apron and carrying Joe's knife roll. "I'm ready."

"Okay." Joe clapped his hands and turned to the group. "Joey wants to do the first course alone, so we've been asked to sit at the table outside and wait. Grab your coats and a blanket or two."

"What about my garlic bread?"

Joey glanced at the bowl and lifted his eyebrows. "I might be able to rescue it for you, Aunt Tyra –"

"Rescue? It doesn't need to be rescued. It's almost perfect," Tyra sputtered as she let herself be led away from the kitchen, secretly relieved she didn't have to finish.

Outside, someone had laid a floor of plywood sheeting on the bluff overlooking the ocean. On top, Charlie's thick wooden door rested on a pair of sawhorses draped with a crisp linen tablecloth, with a collection of driftwood, sand dollars, and sea grass circling a trio of fat white candles sheltered in hurricane glass. During their usual morning walk, Tyra and Dilly had scoured the beach for things to make a centerpiece and brought everything home in a plastic bucket.

The display was beautifully done, artistic and thoughtful because there was room in the center for whatever Joey planned to serve. Someone older than seven must have finished it. Tyra glanced around the table and caught Juliette's eye. Juliette smiled shyly, and Tyra nodded in return. There was more to her niece than she realized.

The soft blue shadows of twilight deepened as the sun touched the horizon. The ocean rumbled below, and the seagulls circled the rocks offshore one last time.

"I never get tired of this view," Maureen sighed.

When the back door slammed, and Joey started down the path with his server's tray, Joe stood to light the candles. As wicks ignited, the table was bathed in a warm yellow light, and Tyra breathed a sigh of gratitude.

This was the moment she had waited for and the sole reason

for everything leading up to it. During the worst times in prison she lost herself in the hope for this exact moment, escaping into it when her placement at the group home had been threatened, and drawing it around her at night when the most unspeakable crimes happened.

With sidelong glances at his parents, Joey proudly presented his creation. Reaching around Tyra, Joey placed a wire basket loosely covered with a linen napkin on the table and Tyra closed her eyes for a moment to breathe the scent of bread fresh from the oven. Under the linen cover was a stack of torn baguette, still warm from the oven with tendrils of steam rising from the basket. In the center of the table, Joey laid a platter filled with at least four types of cheese, scattered among them were toasted hazelnuts, spiced pecans, fat purple grapes, and tiny wedges of fig. Several ramekins, each filled with a dollop of rich chutney or preserves anchored the plate as well.

Tyra opened her mouth to congratulate Joey, but closed it as she realized he was waiting for his parents' approval.

Everyone watched as Joe pulled a tear of bread from the basket, spread it with a smear of blue cheese, and topped it with a dab of what looked like ginger. He bit into the bread and chewed exactly twice before closing his eyes in bliss. "Son, I was going to wait for your mother, but this is just too good. The pairings are absolutely perfect." He cut himself off with a groan to finish chewing.

Maureen eyed the plate for a full minute before looking up at her son with a proud smile. "Joey, this is very well done. Where did you get the preserves? The restaurant? I've got to say, the supplier's really stepped up their quality. I wasn't crazy about the strawberry preserves they left just before Easter –"

Joey cut her off with a laugh. "I made them, Mom." And then laughed again at the expression on his mother's face.

The meal was over much too soon. As evening fog settled over the rocks offshore, the breeze changed bringing with it a chill from the ocean. Bonfires that once burned brightly on the beach below now smoldered, and the sturdy candles on the table burned to stubs. As they divided the last of the wine from the bottle, they decided to call it a night, and too soon everyone started to stir. Lydia finished her wine as Juliette raised her head from her nest of fleece blankets and blinked. Joey had nodded off, too, but tried to look as if he hadn't. Wrapped in a blanket on Joe's lap, Dilly shifted in her sleep. He rose from his seat, lifting Dilly and the blanket in one practiced motion, then turned to plant a kiss on his wife's head.

Before leaving the shelter of the tent, he stage-whispered over his shoulder. "Early start tomorrow, ladies. We have painting to do. Work begins at six a.m. sharp."

Lydia groaned. "Joe, I thought we were friends."

Joe chuckled as he walked toward the house, sheltering Dilly's face from the evening mist.

Chapter Eleven

"Well, what have we here?"

Joe followed the sound of Gordon's muffled voice, walking around to the back of the studio by the plum tree.

He found Gordon standing in the middle of the thicket, bare legged and triumphant. Blackberry vines obscured his boots and tangled around his shins.

"How did you get in there?" Joe's plan was more long-term: start from the edges and work his way in, pulling vines and digging roots as he went. However, he couldn't help feeling a bit of admiration for Gordon, who had just barreled in, ignoring the cuts and scrapes on his legs, something Joe might have done himself at Gordon's age.

Gordon pointed. "This is cool, man. Can you help me haul it out?"

Joe waded into the brambles, feeling the thorns tug his jeans and snag his boot laces. He hoped Gordon hadn't found anything dead.

"What is it?" Joe poked a section of vines with a big stick, lifting them so he could see underneath, but all he could see was something dark and rusted.

Gordon peeled away a sheet of thorny blackberry vines with gloved hands and tossed them to the side, revealing what looked like half a steel drum buried in the mud and dusted with rust.

Did Gordon want help hauling this to the trash? With luck, if they broke it apart the drum might fit in the dumpster, but they were running out of room. Paying for haul-out and another dumpster wasn't in the budget right now. Whatever space was left had to be carefully managed.

Joe decided to redirect. "Aren't you supposed to be building a chicken coop with Tyra?"

"That's already finished. Tyra went to get chickens, and Dilly's painting the coop." Gordon's reply was muffled because he was digging around the drum with his hands, trying to pry it loose from the vines and mud.

After a moment he stood up, face red with exertion. He wiped his face on the sleeve of his sweatshirt and pointed his chin toward the drum. "This will make an exceptional fire pit, man."

"It looks pretty rusted from here." Joe pointed to hubcap sized holes on the end of the barrel where rust had eaten through the metal.

"Not a problem. All you need is –"

But Joe didn't hear the rest because what Gordon said a moment before about the chicken coop had just registered. Dilly was painting it, and Tyra was out buying chickens. If Maureen was inside cooking and Lydia was in town, that meant Dilly was alone. Painting alone. He turned to leave, hoping Dilly wasn't strong enough to open the paint lid. He called over his shoulder. "If Joey's not busy, I'll send him out."

He hurried around the corner toward Elizabeth's courtyard, hoping it wasn't too late.

What he saw stopped him in his tracks. Maureen and Dilly and Juliette were gathered around a half-painted, bright pink chicken coop, drippy paintbrushes in hand, all of them laughing. The joy on Maureen's face was something he hadn't seen in years, and it filled his heart to see all of his girls happy. He watched, letting every detail soak in so it would be with him for the rest of his life.

Maureen peered over Dilly's head and smiled at him. "Joe. Come over and help."

"Daddy!" Dilly waved from her station at the corner, flapping the paintbrush and splattering pink on the damp grass.

"Hey, Dad." Juliette's greeting was more subdued, but it didn't matter. As she stood with her blonde hair stuffed into a baseball cap, arms and head poking out of a black trash bag to protect her clothes from paint, Joe immediately remembered the weekend Juliette had helped paint the new dining room when she had been four. And she looked the same to him.

Joe smiled as he walked toward them. Maureen might have been right about this house being just the thing to force a little family time. "Who picked the color?"

"I did!" Dilly bent over the paint can to refill her brush. "Their house needs to be pink because chickens are girls, Daddy! Chickens are girls!"

Maureen laughed, leaving her paintbrush on the holder before walking toward him and wrapping her arms around his neck. She smelled like paint, salty air, and happiness.

"What about Tyra and the chickens?" Joe kept his voice low so the girls wouldn't overhear.

"She's not going to find chickens anywhere this early,"

Maureen whispered back and dissolved into giggles. He hadn't heard his wife giggle in years.

"What's so funny?" Gordon and Joey rounded the corner covered in mud and sweat. Joey's face was red and his bangs were plastered to his head, but both of them looked enormously pleased with themselves.

Maureen slipped her arms from around Joe's neck and shrugged. "We're just talking about chickens."

As if on cue, the crunch of tires on the gravel driveway came from the corner of the house. Joe held his hand up, wanting Maureen to have more time with the girls. "You stay here; I'll go see if Tyra found chickens."

As he walked away, he heard Maureen call to him. "Or it might be Lydia with the pizzas. She'll need help – we ordered a lot of them, salads and garlic bread, too."

Joe raised his hand to show he'd heard and walked around the corner of the house. He and the kids had to leave to drive back home right after lunch. They had school in the morning, and there were a few things he wanted to check at the restaurant. They had planned to leave earlier, but the warm spring day was unexpected and with everyone working in the yard, pizza for lunch seemed like a good idea. Lydia volunteered to get it, which surprised Joe, but maybe this house was working its magic on her, too.

The car was unfamiliar, a black luxury sedan, a battered older model, covered with a sheen of grime and tagged with Nevada dealer plates. Maybe a renter who had lost his way. Joe brushed the dirt from his hands as he walked toward the car. He had a rough idea of the area, but if this renter asked for a specific house, he'd have to get Maureen or Gordon. Between the two of them, they knew everyone.

The man opened the car door wide, and Joe could see inside. There was no luggage, no family with him, nothing to suggest he was a renter. Skinny and grubby, the man stood and stretched as if he'd been in the car a long time. Putting a cigarette to the side of his mouth, he fixed Joe with a deliberate, calculating stare before putting it to his lips and inhaling.

Joe's skin prickled in warning as he took a step forward. "Something I can do for you?"

An oily smile spread across the man's face, and he took the time to pop the collar on his cracked leather jacket before answering. "Well that depends." He nodded toward the house. "I know this is the Jensen property. But I don't know you."

Joe straightened his shoulders. "If you're selling something, we don't want it, so you should get back in your car and drive away."

"Oh, I don't think so." The man closed the car door and walked slowly toward Joe. "You see, I own this house."

Joe thought of Maureen and his girls just around the corner and moved his feet shoulder width apart to block the man's access. "You need to leave here. Now."

"Joe? Everything okay?"

Joe turned to see Gordon a few yards away, with Joey trailing behind. Gordon brushed his hands on his jeans, but Joey's eyes were wide.

Relaxing his stance immediately, Joe offered a smile to his son. "Son, go tell your mother she should stay where she is and keep painting."

Only when Gordon gave Joey a gentle nudge toward the house, did Joe exhale the breath he was holding.

Gordon wandered toward Joe and stood beside him, deliberately casual but sending the message that the man was outnumbered.

The man cocked his head, a smiled slipping across his face like an oil slick. "Doing some work on the house, are you? Good, that's good."

When the man walked to the front of the house where Charlie's crew had installed the new cedar siding, Joe reached for his cell phone.

"Repaired the siding, I see." After taking a long drag from his cigarette, he flicked his chin toward the sunroom, newly glassed the past week, and nodded. "This is all very nice. Saved me the trouble of doing it all myself."

When the man flicked his lit stub toward the house, Joe felt Gordon's restraining hand clamped on his shoulder; he hadn't realized he had taken a step toward the stranger.

Then Gordon took over. "Enough. We need to know your name and what you're doing here."

The man turned unsteadily on his feet, eyes narrowed. "I told you. I own this house."

"That does it. I'm calling the cops." Gordon fished his cell phone from his front pocket and dialed numbers.

At that moment, Tyra's blue beetle turned into the far end of the circular driveway. Lifting a grocery bag and a bunch of flowers from the back seat, Tyra walked toward the group, smiling. But her smile faltered when she noticed the tension in the group. Each man looked poised for a fight, and she stopped in front of Joe for an explanation.

As Joe opened his mouth to explain, the man called to both of them. "She should hear this, too. All of you are trespassing."

Tyra's eyebrows rose. "What's all this?" She sidestepped Joe and walked toward the man. She wasn't afraid of him; she'd seen worse.

She glanced at Gordon, his back to the wind cupping his cell phone with his hand. Even though she didn't understand, she kept walking toward the stranger, arranging her car keys between the fingers of her fist.

Narrowing her eyes, she lifted her chin toward Gordon and addressed the man, not bothering to find out who he was. Gordon and Joe didn't like him, and that was enough for her. "I see you've already been asked to leave. I think you should."

The man sniffed and spat on the driveway. "Name's Kenneth Jonson. I own this house and you all are trespassing." His lips curled into a sneer.

Tyra stopped in her tracks. Her heart thumped so furiously that she began to feel lightheaded.

"I see you've heard of me." He folded his arms over his skinny chest, satisfaction flooding his face. "Imagine my surprise when a friend of mine tells me a family's moved into a house that I own. Fixed it up nice, though."

A police siren wailed in the distance, getting louder as it approached the house.

Blood pulsed in her ears as she saw everything she had worked for disappearing. Tyra hissed at him through clenched teeth. "Get. Out. Now."

With a smirk he slithered back to his car and started the

engine. But before he drove away, he lowered his window and spit. "I'll be in touch." He left with a spray of gravel.

"You okay?" Gordon's face was so full of concern that Tyra nodded, manufacturing a calm smile she didn't feel.

Gordon bent down to gather the things Tyra didn't know she'd dropped. The grocery bag had split, scattering food she didn't remember buying and flower petals that looked vaguely familiar.

Biting the inside of her cheek, she focused on the pain to keep her in the present. When she tasted blood, she reminded herself where she was: outside, Inlet Beach, with her family. She was safe.

As the edges of her vision blurred, she bit the other cheek and told herself that everything was riding on this one moment, and she needed to stay present. Willing herself to remain upright, she reached into her backpack for her cell phone.

Vaguely aware that a patrol car had arrived and parked hastily at the mouth of the driveway, she watched as Joe and Gordon walked toward the officer.

Tyra dialed the number and plugged her ear with her finger as she listened to it ring. She had suspected from the very beginning that Steven's inexperience might be a problem, but she hired him anyway because he was local and would provide a good cover.

After six rings, the phone clicked to voice mail. Drawing a deep breath, she waited until the machine beeped, then left a message. "Steven, this is Tyra. Someone named Kenneth Jensen was just here claiming to own this property. I need copies of everything you have from our first meeting."

Glancing up, she saw the patrol car backing out of the driveway and Joe and Gordon walked toward her, their faces grim. "Call me at this number, my cell phone, immediately."

***

With his hand on the doorknob ready to leave the office, Steven listened to the message and his heart dropped.

***

At Tyra's feet, the paper bag rustled as Gordon righted it, pushing green apples and celery back in before scooping up the whole bundle. Joe was there as well, lifting the tattered flowers from the driveway and watching her from the corner of his eye.

Both Joe and Gordon looked confused at her reaction to Kenny's name, but the difference was that Gordon looked concerned, only Joe looked suspicious, as if she were somehow involved – which of course she was but not in the way he thought.

The cellophane crinkled as Joe offered the remaining bit of flowers, petals missing, stems broken. "They're a little banged up."

She took the flowers but didn't trust herself to meet his eye just yet. She needed a moment to compose herself. "Thanks, Joe."

Holding onto the bouquet a beat longer than necessary, Joe watched Gordon walk away. When Gordon turned the corner of the house, Joe turned his attention back to Tyra. "You seemed to have a pretty strong reaction, dropping the bag and the flowers like that. Do you know that man?"

Composed now, Tyra shook her head and looked at him. "I don't." It was an honest answer but not the one Joe wanted.

After a moment, he nodded slowly and continued. "You know, Maureen has gotten pretty attached to that house. Kids like it, too – so does Lydia, seems like. It's odd to me that your first reaction to a trespasser is to make a phone call. Unless you know who he is."

Tyra wiped all emotion from her face, something she had learned to do in prison. "I called Steven. He's the attorney who handled the inheritance. If something's going wrong, he would know what it was and how to fix it." She leveled a gaze at him and saw him flinch. "You guys were already talking to the police. Seemed reasonable to call Steven."

They walked back to the house in silence. Joe picked up a paintbrush and joined his family by the chicken coop. Gordon recruited Joey and waded back through a tangle of blackberry vines toward the barrel.

Closing her eyes, Tyra soaked it in. Maureen's laughter, Dilly's squeals, Gordon's deep voice as he called to Joey, the rumble of the waves beyond the ridge, the call of the seagulls, and the warm sun on her face, all woven together in the tapestry of family. Imagining this exact moment had protected her and allowed her to hold onto the edges of her sanity on the nights she was sure she would drown. Now that she was about to lose it, she needed to burn a memory of it into her so she would never forget.

When the judge's gavel smashed against the wooden plate, she was led from the hot courtroom and loaded onto a bus with barred windows and the beginning her nightmare.

Her first night the ache for her family had been so deep she ripped her fingernails across the inside of her arm to draw blood, pain. When the other girls scared her, the angry one–who chiseled a paperclip into a weapon, the crazy one who pulled out her own hair in clumps while she keened, the others who stole her books, ripped her clothes, daring her to fight back – Tyra had pretended her own family was whole and waiting for her.

But they weren't.

Lydia arrived with the pizzas at about the same time midday hunger drove everyone inside searching for food. The chicken coop was painted, the rusted drum rescued from the blackberries.

After everyone's washed hands had been inspected, Maureen spread a blanket on the floor of the unfinished dining room and set up a picnic for the kids: a pizza of their own, salad, and Dilly's favorite: garlic bread. By the ease of her sister's movements, Tyra knew she hadn't been told about the trespasser.

Joe filled his plate in silence and settled into one of the folding chairs scattered about the kitchen. Gordon watched from the corner of his eye, unsure of what to do.

Maureen chose a seat next to Joe and speared a tomato with her plastic fork. "Joe, what's the matter? You're very quiet."

Joe lowered the plate to his lap and blew out a puff of air. "Well, funny thing, actually." As he told them about Kenny, Tyra listened to what he knew and how he presented it. He kept his voice artificially light, as if explaining a minor traffic accident to a child. But reassurance melted into suspicion when Joe told the sisters that he had called the police.

"The police?" Maureen froze, her fork poised over her food.

Lydia put her slice back on the paper plate, wiped her mouth with a paper napkin, and gave Joe her full attention. "What did that man – Kenny – what did he want?"

Scrubbing the back of his neck with his fingers, Joe hesitated too long before replying. "He only said that he was the owner of the property. When Albert drove up in the patrol car, he mentioned Kenny was a relation and might just be upset the property was willed to someone else. Kenny left as soon as he heard the sirens, and Albert doesn't think he's dangerous, just a nuisance."

Maureen looked first at Gordon and then at Joe. "Well, what are we going to do? We can't just leave Tyra and Lydia here alone; what if he comes back? What if he's crazy?"

Joe forced a laugh, hollow and fake. "If he's just crazy, that's fine. We've all seen crazy, and we can work with that."

"Excuse me, Joe." Gordon's deep voice came from his place in the corner and every head swiveled to look at him. He held up his hand. "I know this is family business, and I don't have a part in it, but he didn't sound crazy to me. Pissed, yes. Crazy, no."

Joe's sigh deflated him. "You're right. I was going to suggest Lydia and Tyra come home with us at least until next weekend. School's almost over and we can all drive back next weekend."

Tyra shook her head. "No. I'm not leaving."

The room stilled as Joe and Gordon exchanged looks.

"Is it that serious?" Lydia's plastic chair creaked as she crossed her legs.

"Mommy – we're done." Dilly's voice called from the dining room. "And Juliette has her phone out, even though she's on restrict – OW!" Dilly's voice grew indignant. "Mommy, she *hit* me."

Joey shuffled into the kitchen shaking his head at the mystery of sisters, and Maureen sent him back in to clear his place and pick up the room. He went, but he wasn't happy.

When everyone was finished and the pizza boxes contained nothing more than a scattering of crusts, the kids were sent away to clear their work areas and put the tools away while the adults straightened inside. Maureen collected garbage as Lydia stacked folded lawn chairs out of the way of tomorrow's finishing team. As Tyra broke down the pizza boxes for recycle, she waited for Steven to call. He didn't have much longer before she got in her car and went to find him. He would be easy to find; anyone in town would know where he lived.

When the rooms were cleared and ready for the finishers tomorrow, Maureen went to the window and looked out. "I don't know what to do. Should we tell the kids to put their stuff in the truck? They have school tomorrow, and I'm sure they haven't even looked at their homework." She looked at Joe and Gordon and Tyra, each in turn. "You've seen him. Does he look scary to you?

Gordon shook his head. "No, not scary. Determined maybe but also cowardly. He left as soon as he heard the siren." He turned to Tyra. "If you and Lydia are nervous about staying here by yourselves, I can bring a cot into the house while you stay in the studio. I'll be close enough to hear you if you need me."

Lydia stood behind Gordon, and when he made the offer to stay, she stopped folding chairs, letting her hand rest on the back of the last one. She tilted her head and looked at them both; after a moment, she bit back a smile and continued her work.

Tyra's cell phone buzzed and she snatched it from her back pocket. As she walked toward the empty dining room, she answered with a coolness she didn't feel. "Steven."

***

Later that night, with the kids put to bed upstairs in the mostly finished third floor, thrilled at missing school tomorrow, the adults remained in the kitchen to await Steven's return call. When Tyra told him about Kenny's visit, he was silent for so long that Tyra thought they might have been disconnected. Finally, he asked for time to review his files and said he would call back as soon as he could.

"I guess then you're just going to wait for Steven? Gordon shrugged on his denim jacket and straightened the collar. "You sure you don't need my help?"

Joe clamped his hand on Gordon's shoulder. "We're fine, dude. Thanks for all your help today. I'm staying the night and you have kites to finish."

Gordon nodded. "Okay then, it's back to the salt mines for me."

He reached for the door but paused to look at Joe. His voice was soft and Tyra strained to overhear. "Albert said to tell you that patrols will come by every hour tonight." He rolled his eyes. "I think they're looking forward to it, actually." With one last smile, he wished them good night and closed the door behind him.

***

When Steven finally called at eleven p.m. he said he needed

more time to research and insisted on meeting with Kenny privately. Tyra retreated to a far corner with her laptop, spending the night scowling at her screen and scribbling notes on a pad. With nothing else to do, Joe and Maureen went to bed shortly after Steven's phone call, but Lydia couldn't.

Something wasn't right, but she couldn't put her finger on it.

So it was after a restless night, each of them distracted and edgy, that they made their way into town for an early morning meeting with Steven. A meeting to which they were not invited.

Every light in Steven's office was lit, and he met them in the lobby wearing a business suit and a tense smile. "Good morning."

Lydia was the last to enter the office; she saw Tyra's eyes narrow as she brushed past him in the lobby, but it wasn't until Steven dropped his gaze and his smile faltered that Lydia knew for sure that something was wrong. She had seen that look before on her husband's face, at a broker reception where Greg had sworn to his boss that he would *never* poach a client when she knew that was his standard practice.

As he rounded the corner to his desk chair, Steven wiped his hands on his pants, but it wasn't until he was completely settled in his chair that he spoke. "As I mentioned last night on the phone, it's better if I meet with Kenny alone. If you'll just wait—"

"No." Tyra's arms were crossed, her voice hard. "We're staying, Steven."

Maureen's brows furrowed with confusion; her gaze flickered briefly to Tyra before she turned back to address Steven. "Why wouldn't you want us here, Steven?"

Steven looked away. "Kenny might feel more comfortable, more willing to negotiate, if I am the only one here."

Lydia pressed her hands together. "Negotiate what, Steven? You're only supposed to negotiate when you have something to lose. We don't have anything to lose; we've inherited this property, isn't that right? Kenny has no claim. "

Steven smoothed the top page of a blank legal pad and straightened the pen beside it.

"Steven." Tyra's voice was steely.

Steven's head lifted; his eyes widened when he looked at Tyra, who had leaned forward in her chair, hands flat on her knees.

"Kenny should have no claim on this house. You and I both know that." Tyra leaned forward in her chair. "What is Kenny's claim, Steven?"

Steven's shoulders sagged as he exhaled. "Kenny wants the house. He was excluded from Lloyd's will but believes he has a claim to the property regardless. After speaking with him last night, I gather that he doesn't know much about estate law and that's good for us. All he knows, I assume, is his Grandfather died and someone bought the property."

"Someone what?" Lydia's head snapped up. She stared at Steven.

The bell over the outer door in the waiting room jingled and Steven rose from his chair.

Lydia held up her hand for him to wait. "Steven. You said 'bought.' I heard you – 'someone bought the property.' Three months ago you told us we inherited it."

Steven held both hands up. "This is exactly the sort of thing I can't worry about. I'll explain everything later, but right now I need to prepare for this meeting. I've asked you to leave, and since you refuse, I need you to at least let me do my job. Or we'll lose everything. Please."

He paused at the door, looking utterly defeated. "It would be very helpful if you don't say anything during the meeting. Kenny's case is stronger than he realizes, and we can't give him anything to use against us."

The bell from the lobby rang fiercely; it sounded like someone had grabbed hold of the door and was shaking it.

Only after Steven left the room, did Lydia exhale. Tyra's face was a mask of fury, angrier than Lydia had ever thought possible.

Maureen shifted in her seat. "Something's going on here, and I think we need to look into hiring another lawyer to represent us."

Lydia tucked her hair behind her ear and nodded. "I agree. I'll find one."

Tyra said nothing.

As Steven and Kenny approached from the lobby, Lydia reached for a bottle of water to relieve her dry mouth.

Kenny entered the office first, smelling of stale cigarettes and desperation. He wore the same clothes as yesterday, the same fake leather jacket, dark t-shirt, and rancid jeans.

He stopped mid-stride when he saw the sisters seated at the table, but Steven guided him to a chair before Kenny could object. "You can have a seat right here, Kenny."

As Kenny settled in and hooked his arm around the back of

the chair, he crossed his legs with his ankle on his knee, as if he owned the world. "Kenneth."

Steven was about to sit down but paused. "Excuse me?"

"I go by Kenneth. Have for quite some time." He smoothed the side of his hair with his palm and sniffed.

Steven nodded. "Kenneth. What brings you here, Kenneth?"

A thin smile slithered across Kenny's face. "You know why I'm here. The Jensen property. Should be mine." Kenny jerked his thumb toward the sisters. "They know it. And I know it." He patted his jacket, removed a rumpled piece of paper from his pocket, and recited from it. "See what you did was fail to give me notice." He jabbed his finger on the page and looked up with a smirk. "You must have missed that."

Steven leaned forward in his chair. "You weren't named in the will."

Kenny shrugged. "Doesn't matter. I'm a relative."

"Do you have the copies of the identification I asked you to bring?"

Kenny fished a packet of folded pages from the side pocket of his jacket and tossed it onto the desk. He nodded toward it. "All right there. Social Security number, driver's license. Made copies for you."

Steven unfolded the packet with a nod and glanced through the pages.

When he finished, he leaned back. "I'm not saying you're right, Kenny –"

"Kenneth."

"– Kenneth," Steven conceded with a slight nod. "But let's assume for a moment that you do have a claim to the house...."

Lydia's skin crawled and she shifted in her chair.

Steven folded his fingers together. "What sort of relief are you anticipating?"

Kenny blinked.

"What do you want, Kenneth?"

Kenny glanced at his cheat sheet again and pursed his lips, considering. "By rights, the whole house is mine." He shrugged. "But seeing as how I'm just going to sell it anyway. They can buy it from me if they like."

As he moved his finger down the smudged cheat sheet, his lips moved. Not until his finger touched the bottom of the page did he look up. "Had an acquaintance of mine run some numbers for me." He moved his finger from the page and pointed it at Steven. "Now I'm being generous here, I want you to know that. I'd be willing to agree to some concessions if we wrap this up quickly."

Steven pressed his temples with his fingertips. "What did you have in mind, Kenneth?"

Lydia's water bottle crinkled as her grip on it tightened, but Kenny appeared not to notice.

"Well, for instance, I'm willing to take off the agent's commission if they agree to my price. They seem to be pretty attached to it; they're already fixing it up." He laughed, a bark ending in a dry cracking cough.

Lydia hoped he would choke.

When he recovered, he wiped his mouth with the back of his hand. "See, not notifying me that my dear grandfather passed makes the whole sale void. Technically, you don't own the property at all. I do. Selling it to them is my right."

"Do you have representation?" Steven swallowed and stared so intently at Kenny that Lydia wondered if he was purposely avoiding Tyra, because even from across the room, Lydia could feel the fury radiating from her.

"Could have. But I'm willing to work this out on my own for now. I see that we all want a quick resolution to this. I'll either take a check – cashier's check, if you don't mind – or the house." He shrugged. "You can have three days to decide."

Maureen gasped softly and Kenny smiled.

"I didn't even deduct anything for the damage they did tearing down the improvements I added – downstairs bedrooms and so forth." He waved his hand through the air to demonstrate his generosity.

Pushing his chair from the desk Steven rose and offered his hand to Kenny. "I understand, Kenneth. I'd like to confer with my clients now."

Kenny blinked.

"You can go now, Kenneth."

"What about my house?"

"Did you think you were going to walk out with the keys?" Steven raised his eyebrows. "We aren't even close to that, Kenneth."

Steven walked around the desk and Kenny rose from his chair, clearly confused. "We'll be in touch, Kenneth."

"Well, you better hurry. That property is mine by rights, and you only have three days to decide: check or keys."

"We appreciate your indulgence, Kenneth." Steven guided Kenny down the hall.

***

Steven entered the room talking, a trick Lydia had seen attorneys use many times when they had no real argument. "His claim against us isn't without merit, but it's not strong. I can fix this."

Lydia leaned forward in her chair. "All three of us are on the deed, Steven. There should be nothing to fix."

In the stillness that followed, a drip from the coffeemaker hissed on the hot plate and the space heater in the corner clicked on.

Tyra's voice broke the silence. "You didn't give him notice, did you, Steven?"

Steven rubbed his hands on pants and looked directly at Tyra, his eyes pleading for understanding. "This was my first case. I finally passed the bar, and I bought this practice to celebrate – you were my first official client."

The sisters were silent, so Steven cleared his throat and started again. "The property you wanted had been vacant for years but was languishing in probate."

He looked at Maureen and then at Lydia, and finding no sympathy with either, looked only at his hands folded on the top of his desk. "Lloyd's will specifically said that Kenny was to get nothing." He shrugged. "I thought it would be okay...." His voice trailed off as he reached for a pen, twirling it between his fingers.

Lydia saw Tyra purse her lips together, her face white She leaned forward in her chair and glared at Steven, her voice menacing. "As lawyer for the estate, you were supposed to find and notify every one of Lloyd's heirs – including grandchildren – of his death, even if they weren't specifically named in the will. Isn't that right, Steven?"

Steven nodded. "Yes." Putting his pen aside, he looked up, his face haggard and defeated. "But –"

Tyra swept her hand in the air, cutting off his explanation. Lydia felt goosebumps rise on her arms as Tyra spoke, her words clipped and angry. "So Kenny's claim is very real."

Steven refused to meet Tyra's eyes; his reply spoken into his desktop. "His grievance that he wasn't notified is valid. He could argue that he wasn't given a chance to contest Lloyd's will, but it would take years – and several appeals – before a judge would award him the house."

Lydia watched her sister rise from her chair, place both hands on Steven's desk and stare him down. "Let me get this straight: we have two choices. We can pay Kenny what he wants or we can look forward to a very long and costly legal battle."

Steven slumped in his chair and buried his face in his hands. "I'm so sorry."

But Tyra wasn't finished. Lydia glanced at Maureen to see if they should intervene, but Maureen shook her head slightly. As Tyra towered over Steven, the words shot from her mouth in a volley of accusation. "You knew what I was trying to do – you saw me do it – all the while knowing this whole thing might come crashing down." She slapped the desktop so hard Steven pushed his chair back from his desk. "Do you have any idea how many years it took me to save for this house? You took my cash. You helped me open the repair account and linked it to the property!"

Tyra paused and drew a great breath of air; her hands were shaking as the color in her face drained. She finished in a whisper of disbelief. "And the whole time you charged me for your services, knowing the foundation for them was worthless?"

Steven's head snapped up, his eyes wide. "Now wait a minute –"

"I've lost everything." Tyra dropped to her chair and her lip trembled. Maureen pulled off her jacket and covered her with it, and led Tyra from the office.

Lydia stood and faced Steven, whose chair was pushed back nearly to the wall. "You will retrieve Tyra's file, and all relevant probate information, and you will bring it to me. Now."

Steven held his hand up. "I can help."

Lydia leaned over the desk just to watch him flinch. "You've helped enough. Do it."

Steven shuffled to his filing cabinet, pulled files and papers, stacked them in his arms, and delivered them to Lydia.

"Is this everything?"

Steven nodded, miserable.

"I will be back." Lydia spit the words at him. "I don't know exactly what you did, Steven, but I will find out. And when I do, you will be very sorry."

Clutching the pile of folders to her chest, Lydia strode from the office to find her sisters, but not before she heard Steven's reply.

"I'm already sorry."

***

Maureen guided Tyra out of Steven's office and Lydia followed shortly after, her arms loaded with files. If it was the last thing she ever did, she would untangle this mess.

"Tyra doesn't seem well; we might want to think about

261

getting her to a doctor." Maureen adjusted the fleece tighter around Tyra's shoulders.

"I'm fine." Tyra's voice was flat, muffled under layers of fabric. "I'm fine, just tired."

The glass door to the vet clinic opened and Colleen stuck her head out. "Bring her in here." She held the door as they entered. "Sit her right down here. I've got tea all ready."

Shutting the door behind them, she flipped the closed sign. A tea service was laid across her desk, a steaming pot, four teacups, plenty of sugar and a small bottle of brandy. Four chairs dragged from the waiting room circled her desk. Maureen guided Tyra to one of them and sat next to her.

Lydia went to Colleen's chair behind the reception desk and pulled it back to begin work. Setting the files in front of her, she opened the first one and just as she started to read, Tyra spoke. Her voice was dull, tired.

"I have something to tell you. Before you leave town, before we lose this house for good, I have something to say." She leaned against the padding and closed her eyes. "The Jensens aren't relatives. I bought this house – the whole property – from their estate and hired Steven to tell you we inherited it."

Maureen and Colleen exchanged looks, then both looked at Lydia, but no one spoke.

After a moment, Tyra opened her eyes and looked at her sisters. "Did you hear me? I lied to you – all of you. I bought this house myself and presented it as an inheritance."

Maureen gaped at Tyra. "Why would you do that? We haven't spoken in years. I barely recognized you when I saw you."

Tyra put her hands in her lap and pressed them together. "I wanted to change the ending."

Colleen reached across the small gap between their chairs and put her hand on Tyra's. "Tell them what you did, honey. The whole of it. This is your chance."

Tyra shook her head. "It's not important anymore."

Colleen squeezed Tyra's hand. "It is."

Tyra looked at her hands, her voice faint. "Bringing us back together was one of three things I decided to do to repair the damage I caused, years ago." She took a breath, and her voice got stronger. "The first was to visit the family of the boy who died because of the tainted drugs. It took years before they agreed to meet with me and longer than that for them to forgive me, but they did." She twisted her hands in her lap. "The second was to meet the second family, the girl who ended up in the hospital because of what I did. The father met with me, eventually, but the mother couldn't. Their daughter spent three months in the hospital and another six in a nursing home without ever coming out of her coma. They never said good bye to her.

I told the father what I wanted to do, and that I'd met the boy's family. And I paid all the medical bills for the girl."

Tyra swallowed and looked into the distance. "After about a year, the mother wrote me a letter, and I still carry it with me. She forgave me and gave me permission not to think of them again." Tyra snorted. "But, of course I do." Her eyes filled with tears, and Colleen scooted her chair closer.

After a moment, Tyra straightened. "Selling those drugs was the stupidest thing I've ever done. I didn't know they were tainted, but that doesn't matter. I was only fourteen years old, but that doesn't matter either. And the reason I did it doesn't matter."

Maureen's eyes glistened with tears. She pulled a tissue from her purse and blew her nose. "Oh, Tyra. I had no idea."

Lydia felt as if she were watching a movie, as if the things happening in front of her had no bearing on her life. She asked the only question she could think of. "Why did you do it? It's not like we were close, Tyra. My life didn't include you."

"Maybe it should have. All I know is that you should have gone to college and made your own mistakes. Your life shouldn't have been ruined because of me."

Lydia shook her head, her heart breaking for her sister's pain. "Oh, Tyra. It wasn't ruined because of you. I did that myself, and it was just convenient to blame you. I'm so sorry."

Lydia looked at her sister, the anguish on her face, and knew she had to make this right. If there were any way to help Tyra, she would find it. She would research the files, call in every favor from Janice, even if that meant telling her everything.

Without a word to anyone, Lydia strode to the desk, gathered the files, and left the clinic.

Chapter Twelve

Maureen was a windstorm of emotion as she left the clinic; there was so much to sort out and she needed time to think. When Tyra's color had returned, Maureen called Joe to come get them. When Lydia flounced off, she took her car, and Tyra wasn't in any condition to walk.

The street was still deserted as Joe drove up, and Maureen was surprised. After everything that happened, it felt much later.

Tyra got in and slid over but Maureen couldn't get in. She needed air and an ocean breeze and time to sort things out.

Stepping back from the truck, she closed the door. "Joe, would you mind just taking Tyra? I'm going to walk along the beach."

Joe's brows furrowed in confusion, but Maureen smiled with what she hoped was reassurance. "I'll meet you there. I need a few minutes."

"Okay. I'll see you up there." Even though he didn't understand, he smiled and pulled away from the curb.

Rubbing her eyes with the heels of her hands, she crossed the empty street and sat for a moment on a bench underneath a trellis. As she picked at the events of the last twenty four hours, she tried to piece together all the details that had to come together for Tyra to have made this happen. It must have taken years. And the only reason she did it was to bring her sisters back together.

And for a time, it worked. No one talked about selling the property anymore, even though it was almost completely restored and time to list it with an agent. Maureen looked forward to bringing her family down for the summer and even hoped she could convince Joe to spend most of the summer here.

A passing car splashed through an errant puddle, and Maureen watched it drive through town, past the bright pink awning of the candy store where Dilly spent every penny she earned from Charlie for collecting nails around the jobsite. Sunday afternoon, after Charlie paid her, she would drag Joey downtown to buy taffy. One week she made her little bag last the entire two-hour drive home, and by Thursday she was asking if she could drive back "to the beach house" because Charlie needed her.

A bit further down the street, near the scraggly pine tree decorated with wooden boat floats was the little theatre where Juliette and her dance troop hoped to perform at the end of the summer. Juliette tracked down the director and pestered that poor man for weeks about donating rehearsal space. She was convinced that he was on the edge of giving in.

And at the end of the street was Declan's, where Joe met with Charlie to drink coffee and swap restaurant stories with Declan and his wife, June. Recently, Joe started bringing Joey with him, and they seemed to be full of energy when they came home.

This house, this community, brought her family closer

together, and Tyra had given them that.

With a sigh, she left her bench and crossed the street to the beach stairs, possibly her favorite part of her walks. Pausing at the top, she watched the activity along the shore. Small clusters of two or three walking along the water's edge, and larger families with children and dogs who ran ahead and barked at the waves. Just three months ago, this beach was deserted, rainy and dark, with only the occasional tourist ahead of the season and not afraid of the drizzle.

Crossing the soft sand up shore, she headed for the hard pack at the water's edge, walking just beyond the foamy reach of the waves. It didn't seem possible that the rest of the summer could be erased so quickly. Dilly just had gotten a library card and talked about learning to boogie board, walking to town by herself. Lydia talked to Charlie about building a hammock on the bluff overlooking the ocean, and Maureen was going to surprise Tyra with three fully-grown chickens that Colleen had promised to help her find. And what would happen to that useless rusted drum lying on sawhorses in the yard? Joe, Gordon, and Joey were absolutely convinced it could still be transformed it into the perfect fire pit.

She stopped. She could not lose this house.

Feeling someone approach, she was surprised to find her vision blurred. Wiping her eyes, she saw Joe clearly, his face full of concern. He'd come back to meet her.

When he slipped something soft around her shoulders, she realized she had been shivering. "Thank you."

"You on your way back?"

When she nodded, he said, "Good, I'll walk with you."

Maureen pulled the blanket closer to her and recognized the pattern: gray paw prints over a field of dark blue fleece, one of three blankets Lydia had washed and brought to Mulligan when she visited. She smiled and looked at Joe. "Where did you get this?"

Joe shrugged. "It was folded on the dryer and I grabbed it on the way out."

Maureen laughed – the first real laugh since Kenny had driven up two days ago. "This isn't our blanket. It's Mulligan's."

Joe smiled and pulled her closer. "That explains the paw prints." He shrugged. "Everyone's stuff pretty much blends together anyway now, doesn't it?"

They walked together in silence for a while, past the stack of rocks offshore that marked the halfway point to the house. As they watched the sandpipers outrunning the reaching waves, Joe sighed. "Colleen called. She filled me in."

Maureen nodded but couldn't find anything to say.

As they approached the switchback that led to the house, Joe led Maureen to the driftwood log and sat down. "I've been doing some thinking, Maureen. I know how much you love it here, and I think finding a way to stay should be our priority." He shrugged. "It's kind of grown on me, too."

Putting his palms on his knees, he continued. "While you and your sisters were at Steven's, I thought something serious might be up, so I ran some numbers. If we don't touch any of the kids' college funds, or our retirement, we can contribute two hundred thousand dollars toward keeping this house. If you need it."

"The restaurant money."

Joe nodded.

"What about the second location?"

Joe shrugged. "That was more about something to do, anyway. There's a lot to do around here. The kids are involved, you're happy, and Joey and I are working on something together."

Maureen pushed a strand of hair away from her face. "Kenny wanted the whole thing, but maybe we can offer him that and pay him monthly, like a mortgage."

Joe ran his hand through his hair. "That's all we've got, Maureen. Your sisters need to contribute an equal share and I'm not sure they have it. I know Lydia doesn't have a job and Tyra spent so much already."

"It's a start, Joe. It's a start."

Pulling his arm around her shoulders, Maureen leaned into her husband, and together they watched the tide come in.

***

Lydia made her way to the edge of the property to the overlook where she knew she wouldn't be disturbed. She needed the ocean air to clear her head, and nestled between two ragged pine trees was an old wooden bench, sheltered from the rain and mist blowing from the ocean, the perfect place to think.

Three hours of combing through Steven's legal files in the dim light of her room, with her laptop and shoddy internet connection had given Lydia a pounding headache. Kenny's case was good, maybe even stronger than he thought. There were things missing from the files, but from what she could piece together, Steven pulled the property before it had cleared probate and sold it to Tyra. Before he was allowed to sell the property, he was supposed to tell the court that he had notified all of Elizabeth and Lloyd's heirs, including Kenny. But Kenny said Steven hadn't told him, and there was nothing in the file to suggest he had. Also missing from the file was where the money from the sale had gone. Tyra said she had paid cash, and she had a deed but no record what happened to the money.

She sat in the stillness, breathing the fresh pine air and thought about what Tyra had tried to do. She had bought a house with cash, and under the guise of an inheritance, brought the sisters together to share in it equally. Many of the details were brilliant, really. The cash account didn't provide enough money to hire a general contractor to do all the work, forcing them to do much of it together. The little house gave them a place to live while they worked on the house. And the amount of money involved was staggering. If Lydia had anything close to that, she wouldn't have spent it the way Tyra did. All this planned by the same sister Lydia had accused of stealing her college fund and destroying the family.

Pressing back against the slats of the bench, she pulled her legs up and crossed them on the seat. They could hold Kenny off for a while, but a legal fight would be expensive and their position seemed weak. That Tyra had paid for the house wouldn't matter at all to a probate judge, Steven said, and if the judge ruled in Kenny's favor, they would be forced to give him the house. It was unlikely a judgment would be that drastic, but any judgment would come at the end of a legal battle none of them could afford. They were friends now at least, she and her sisters, but before long the restaurant would claim Maureen's attention, Lydia would go wherever she could find a job, and who knew what would happen to Tyra. The bonds they knit over the last three months were tentative still and without attention would melt into occasional phone calls and holiday cards.

"I thought I might find you out here." Charlie's voice startled her.

"Hi, Charlie." Lydia uncrossed her legs and slid across the bench to make room for him.

Charlie adjusted the bill of his cap as he settled onto the bench. "I hear you've looked through Steven's files, and my guess is that you're looking for a way out."

Lydia nodded. "He gave me access to his office, and I'm trying my best, Charlie. But how did you know that?"

"Because you seem like the one who would."

"How is Tyra doing, Charlie?"

"She's okay. That fool Kenny knocked the stuffing out of her, but she'll bounce back. Just need a few days."

Lydia snorted. "I'm not much better than Kenny is, Charlie."

"How's that?"

Leaning forward, she put her elbows on her knees and rested her chin in her palm. "When I got Steven's letter, the first thing I did was look at how much the house was worth. I wanted to sell it, just like Kenny does."

Charlie nodded. "That he does."

"You never liked him, Charlie, even when he was a kid. Why is that?"

Charlie swiped at the gray stubble on his chin with the back of his hand. "Kenny's always been about destroying things rather than building them up. He looks around to see what everyone has, instead of what they need, and he takes what he wants." Charlie looked down and shook his head. "It would have taken very little effort for him to rent this house properly and send Lloyd the money. The extra money would have helped pay for Elizabeth's care, and a nice family would have enjoyed the house. But as it was he got greedy. Destroyed what his grandparents built for nothing more than a few dollars." Charlie snorted. "You get to be my age and you realize a few things; one is that money isn't more important than people."

Charlie's description of Kenny came a little too close to what she had planned, and she squirmed in her seat.

Charlie pursed his lips and considered. "I know you're the one who called Margo at the health department, but you didn't know any better then. The difference is you've changed and Kenny never did."

Had she changed? Her life in New Jersey seemed so far away. Except for the weekends when Joe and the kids came and Maureen moved with them to the almost-finished third floor, all of the sisters had occupied a space roughly the size of her New Jersey garage, but it seemed easier here. There were touches around the house, like sea glass and driftwood casually displayed on a window sill, a braided rug on the floor, and buckets of pink flowered branches next to the front door that made the small space welcoming.

So had she changed? Yes, she had. But it was too late.

Shifting her position on the bench, she raked her fingers through her short hair. "Kenny gave us three days to give him cash or the house, and no one has that kind of money."

Charlie leaned back and rested his arm on the back of the bench. "Ever wonder about the life Kenny leads and why he needs money so fast?"

Charlie's comment hit Lydia like a firecracker. Why *would* Kenny need money so fast? And why did he demand cash? She had been so distracted by the amount he wanted and his claim to the house, that she hadn't wondered about the rush, and everything that Kenny had said in the meeting clicked together like puzzle pieces.

"I expect you have some research to do." Breaking his gaze over the ocean, Charlie turned to her with twinkling eyes. He nodded. "You go on. I'll just sit here for another minute if it's all right with you."

"Thank you, Charlie. For everything."

Waving her off with a flick of his hand, Charlie said, "Go on now, you don't have much time."

As Lydia ran across the damp grass, she saw Tyra pulling weeds from the garden in the courtyard, but she didn't stop. If what she planned worked, there would be plenty of time to help in the garden later.

***

Tyra knelt on the damp slate in the courtyard, ripping the weeds from Elizabeth's garden. The repetitive motion distracted her from thinking about the house and Steven's mistakes. It took a great deal of effort to accept that Kenny had a claim to the house, especially when she knew Jensen's will purposefully excluded him. But he had the law on his side, and the law was unforgiving. If she were still in detention, she would know exactly how to handle Steven, and it would be looked upon as justice.

And maybe she still would.

But at this moment, she was doing something more important: honoring Elizabeth by rebuilding her rosemary garden. Even though she knew Kenny would get the house, Tyra planned to weed, mulch, and restore the whole area. She would unearth the plaque the town had given Elizabeth, scrub it, and reposition it so everyone could see it. Tyra wanted to do this to thank her for giving her sisters back. There was magic in this house; Tyra had known it from the first.

When she finished weeding, she dragged the flat of rosemary across the slate, pulling out containers and spacing them evenly on the soil. After twisting the container to press a circle into the earth, she dug a hole for the plant and tucked it inside before covering it with soil. She had a full flat – thirty-five plants – and would put every one of them into Elizabeth's garden.

The slam of the back door startled her and was immediately followed by the patter of small feet running down the wooden stairs. Straightening, Tyra looked up to see Dilly running toward her, a wide smile beneath a tangle of dark curls.

"Did you find chickens yet, Auntie Tyra?" She'd remembered to put on her jacket but not her shoes; her little toes were pink with the morning chill.

The last time Tyra saw Dilly, she had been painting the chicken coop pink, getting it ready for the girls, but all of that was so far away it didn't seem real anymore. The idea that Kenny would take possession of this house, and with it Dilly's pink coop, embedded in her heart like a shard of glass.

Dilly stood, bare feet on the slate path, and cocked her head, considering Tyra for a long moment. Placing her hands on either side of Tyra's face, Dilly looked deeply into her aunt's eyes. "Are you sad about the chickens?"

Tyra smiled. "Maybe a little. They would have loved their pink house, Dilly."

Looking first at the weed pile and then at the garden shovel near Tyra's knees, she leaned toward Tyra and her voice dropped to a whisper, "Did you get in trouble? Are you pulling weeds for punishment?"

Pressing her lips together to hide a smile, she reached for Dilly's hand. She would miss this girl; holiday visits and phone calls were not the same as spending summers together.

The creak of the back door traveled across the yard, followed by Maureen's voice. "Dilly, do you have your shoes on?"

Dilly looked down at her feet and her eyes widened. She darted past Tyra and up the stairs toward her mother, the door closing softly behind her.

After a minute, Tyra heard the squish of footsteps walking through the damp grass beside the courtyard. Looking up, she saw Maureen wrapped in Joe's fleece, carrying a coffee mug in her hand.

"Is that baker's coffee?"

Maureen offered a weak smile. "No. I only make that when I'm mad at Lydia."

Reaching for the mug, Tyra held it in her hands and let it warm her fingers. "Where is Lydia?"

Maureen looked away and shook her head. "I haven't seen her since the meeting." Maureen reached to rub her ear. "Tyra, there's no easy way to tell you this. We want to help, but Joe and I can't find the money to pay Kenny for the entire house. We can contribute, but we can't pay it all. We don't have it." Exhaling audibly, she continued. "And we think it's time to find another attorney. Maybe we can fight to stay for the summer."

Setting the mug on the brick edging, Tyra shook her head. "That would almost be worse: staying here knowing it was only temporary. And it would take all your savings. I can't let you do that."

Pulling Joe's fleece tight around her, Maureen tried again. "Maybe we find a summer rental and try again?"

Tyra smiled weakly, appreciating her sister's effort, but it wouldn't be the same. After a season or two, regular life would get in the way and coordinating vacation times would get harder, then disappear altogether. "Maybe."

"We're still calculating, but it doesn't look good."

When Tyra couldn't answer, Maureen turned and walked slowly back to the house.

When the last rosemary plant was covered with soil and the nursery pots collected from the courtyard, Tyra stood to admire her work. Black and damp with the ocean mist the garden smelled like the breath of the earth.

***

Maureen leaned through the doorway and yelled down the short hallway of the studio. "Tyra, you almost ready? It's time for us to go."

Joe left earlier, driving home with the kids because they had already missed enough school. Maureen stayed because what she had to do was much more important.

Tonight would decide everything.

After a moment, Tyra's door opened and she appeared, dressed and ready but not happy. Maureen almost wished she hadn't promised to keep tonight a secret.

Maureen pulled a winter scarf from the peg by the door. "I know you're worried, we all are. But we've been looking at spreadsheets and bank accounts most of the day and a break would do us good. We can pick it up in a few hours when we get home."

Looping the scarf around Tyra's neck, she secured it against the night air. Almost immediately, Tyra snatched it away. "I'm not four, Maureen. And you pull too tight."

Maureen arched her eyebrow in warning.

Tyra snorted. "Oh, please. Everyone knows that. Why do you think you can never find any of Dilly's scarves? She hides them."

Maureen's face must have registered her surprise because Tyra snorted again as she loosened the scarf.

When she was finished, she looked at Maureen, her eyes unguarded for the first time. "Is this a surprise party? Because I couldn't stand it if it was. I can't be around all those people tonight just to have to say goodbye to them – in a month or a few weeks – whenever Kenny gets the house."

Maureen shook her head slowly. "No. It's not a surprise party. Just dinner at Charlie's house. Colleen might be there, though. No one else."

Tyra slipped her arms though her jacket sleeves and looked around.

Maureen held her breath for the question she knew was

coming, but when it did she wasn't prepared. "Where's Lydia? Did she leave already?"

Maureen had all afternoon to think of a good answer, ever since Lydia had revealed her plans, but Maureen was so hopeful that Lydia would succeed that she could think of nothing else, and she tripped over her answer. "She's going to meet us there."

But that wasn't the truth and Tyra knew it.

Her face hardened. Folding her collar, she turned to her sister. "Where has she been all day?"

"I don't know."

"Then how do you know she's going to meet us there?"

Maureen's stomach kicked. She should know better than to make anything up on the fly. "I just do. Let's get going."

Chapter Thirteen

The sound of tires spraying gravel across the driveway caught Lydia's attention. She turned in time to see a knife of light circle the driveway, capturing the studio before stopping in front of the plum tree and going dark. The dark sedan parked carelessly in the driveway as if he already owned it.

As if he'd won.

She went to the desk and gathered the things she would need, carefully slipping everything into the folder and placing Steven's release form on top. She left by the back door, locking it behind her and slipping the key into her front pocket.

In the sky beyond the bluff over the ocean, the sun was a watercolor of purples, oranges, and pinks as it sank toward the horizon. The daylight had already gone from the driveway, silhouetting the house and the studio with fading twilight. Locating the cluster of broken sand dollars that marked a spot in the dark gravel, Lydia stood on top of them and turned her body toward the plum tree. She would not move from this position. The flood lights mounted on the eaves of the studio snapped on as she triggered the motion detectors, and Kenny squinted under the sudden bright light.

He wore the same dirty clothes, and Lydia wondered briefly where he had spent the last three days.

As Kenny turned to shut his car door, it closed awkwardly with a hollow thud, and he swaggered toward her, eyes full of greed. "You waited until the last minute, but you managed to catch me before I contacted my attorney."

She knew he didn't have one, but she said nothing.

As he came closer, Lydia arranged her face into a carefully neutral expression, posing as one whose defeat was inevitable. None of this would work if he saw how much she loathed him. Glancing quickly at the lower branches of the plum tree, she spied the red dot of an LED light and was reassured.

"Where is everyone?" Kenny's arms spread wide and his voice had the arrogant loudness of someone looking for an audience to witness his victory.

A smiled played across Lydia's lips; she was going to enjoy this. "They're out, Kenny."

"Kenneth."

"Oh, of course, I forgot. It's Kenneth. Kenneth L. Jensen."

Kenny nodded warily, not understanding Lydia's enthusiasm. She smiled. It was so easy to confuse the stupid, but she couldn't afford to scare him off yet.

Taking a breath, she cocked her head as if she didn't have a thought in it. "I still can't figure this out, Kenneth." She pointed to Kenny's car. "You said your name is Kenneth L. Jensen, but I can see by the Nevada plates on your late model BMW, license plate number ACG3221, that you haven't lived in Inlet Beach for a long time. Have you spent most of your time in Las Vegas?"

Kenny's eyes widened slightly, but he recovered quickly and they narrowed in warning. "Where I've been doesn't concern you."

Lydia nodded. "Oh, of course not. You're just here to collect your money. A very, very large sum of money."

Kenny turned his head and spit on the driveway. Her driveway. "That's right. All I want is my money and you can have the house."

"This is a lot of money, Kenneth. Like, a LOT."

"Yeah..." Kenney's face hardened. "It was supposed to be. You telling me you don't have it?"

"Oh, I absolutely do, Kenny. Every dollar you asked for, all in this big envelope. Which I am going to give to you right now." Lydia spoke slowly, enunciating every word, then showed him the fat envelope.

Almost immediately, the giddy smile Lydia had been holding back bloomed into a broad grin of joy as she looked directly into the plum tree. "I think that should do it."

The branches rustled and Gordon emerged, triumphant and holding a video camera. "Placement was fantastic, Lydia. We got everything."

As Gordon walked across the driveway to stand beside her, Lydia turned to Kenny, holding the folder firmly against her chest. "See here's the thing, Kenny –"

"– Kenneth."

"– Kenny. The internet is filled with information and can tell you just about anything you need to know if you ask the right questions. Background checks, outstanding arrest warrants, anything."

Kenny sputtered, eyeing the envelope and still not understanding but clearly uneasy about Gordon's sudden appearance.

"And one of the questions I asked is, 'Why doesn't Kenny have a bank account?'" Lydia cocked her head. "You see, the amount of money you want is pretty substantial. An amount like that, you'd want to keep safe. An amount like that should be wired directly into an account. But you wanted cash."

The fabric of his cheap jacket crackled as Kenny folded his skinny arms in front of his chest. He lifted his chin and stared at her through narrowed eyes. "What do you care?"

Lydia shrugged. "Not saying I do, Kenny. I just thought it was strange, that's all. So I did a little digging and found out you're a popular guy. In fact, there is one group in particular looking for you, and they sound anxious to find you. Seems you owe them a bit of money, and I bet they'd be happy to know you got some."

Kenny blanched and Lydia smiled. She almost wished Gordon was filming this part so her sisters could see it.

"So here's what we're going to do, Kenny. You're going to sign Steven's paper relinquishing all rights to this property, and you're going to go away and never come back."

Just as Kenny opened his mouth, Lydia held up one finger, silencing him.

"And in return, I won't tell them where to find you." She shook her head slowly. "I don't know what you did to them, Kenny, but they're not happy with you. So you have a choice. And I'll make it a simple one because I know you're not too bright."

Lydia counted off on her fingers. "One: you can sign the paper, releasing yourself from any claim to the house and you are free to slither back under whatever rock you came from without any trouble.

"Two – and this is the tricky one, Kenny, so listen up – two: you can choose not to accept my offer, in which case I will be forced to help the people looking for you. I will send them the video of you accepting a large sum of cash, and all of the information you gave Steven to prove who you were – social security number, photo id – nice picture by the way. They should be able to find you pretty quick with all that."

Kenny's brow furrowed as he pieced everything together. "You never gave me any money!"

Lydia shrugged. "They don't know that."

"You can't do that! It wasn't my fault – I was supposed to win – that table was rigged."

Balling his fists, Kenny took a quick step toward her, but was blinded by a flash of headlights in the driveway. A car door opened and a deep male voice spoke from behind the headlights. "That's not a good idea, Kenny."

Kenny blinked and lowered his arm to his side.

They both turned at the sound of heavy footsteps. Arnold Bushwick, in full dark blue uniform, strode into the spotlight. At Charlie's suggestion, Lydia had called the tiny police office to tell them about the meeting and asked them to drop by sometime after eight fifteen p.m.

"I happened to be on patrol in the neighborhood, Kenny, and it looked to me like you were about to assault this woman. Is that true?" Officer Bushwick paused to tap the handcuffs attached to his belt. "Think about your answer, Kenny. I might have to arrest you for assault or criminal trespass. And then I'd have to hold you while I ran a check for outstanding warrants." He shook his head slowly, and Lydia smiled, watching him enjoy his performance. "Extradition isn't as fun as it sounds, Kenny."

Lydia unfolded the agreement Steven had drawn up and handed it to Kenny. She offered him a pen and pointed to the signature line at the bottom. "Use your best writing, Kenny; this is going to be filed in the courthouse."

His eyes snapped with fury, but he did what she said, scribbling his signature on the paper before dropping the pen to the ground.

Lydia took the paper and locked eyes with him; she spoke in a low whisper so Arnold wouldn't overhear. "Know this, Kenny. If you come within fifty miles of here, I will know. And then the group looking for you will know. I have no trouble breaking the law to protect my sisters." She glanced toward his car. "Now get out."

As Kenny walked toward his car, Officer Bushwick came closer. "You got what you needed?"

Threatening Kenny and forcing him to relinquish any claim on the property was completely illegal. Lydia gaped at the officer.

"The Jensen's Victory Garden fed my family through two of the coldest winters I've ever seen, and I owe them a lot. Relatives or not, your family are the right people to care for this house."

With a final nod, he turned to catch up with Kenny. "Kenny, I'll just follow you on the way out of town. Wouldn't want you to lose your way."

It was only after Kenny's car left the driveway and the taillights disappeared down the hill that Lydia drew her first real breath. Gordon clamped a hand on her shoulder, making her jump. "Lydia, you were awesome. Remind me never to cross you – you're scary."

"Did you get the chance to stick the tin on his car?"

Gordon nodded, flicking the air with his hand. "That was the easy part. We'll be able to track him wherever he goes. How did you know to do that, by the way? The GPS in the waterproof tin is a brilliant idea."

"I don't remember exactly who suggested it. But the bigger question is what should I do with the tracking information once I've got it?"

A slow smile spread across Gordon's face. "You are one scary woman, Lydia."

She shrugged. "Only when someone messes with my family."

Chapter Fourteen

As she waited for her family, Maureen stood at the bluff watching the waves roll toward the shore, feeling the cool morning breeze and the salty mist on her face.

Digging her fingers deeper into the weave of her cardigan, she pulled it closer, settling into its warmth and enjoying the smell of new wool. She didn't drive home after Kenny left, deciding impulsively to spend the ten days until school let out alone with her sisters at the beach house. And every morning she walked the beach in comfortable black knit pants, white keds with only a bit of the toe worn through, and an oversized black fleece jacket. Until the day Lydia woke early and walked with her, horrified at the way Maureen left the house. The very next day, Maureen was presented with a new sweater in exchange for a promise never to wear 'that ratty black fleece' again.

It was a good trade.

The breeze from the ocean still held a bit of night chill, but there were signs that the ocean fog would burn off in time for the kite festival. The last of it huddled between the rocks in crevices and cowered underneath the massive driftwood logs strewn across the upper beach. Overhead, a high wind pushed away the last of the rain clouds, making way for the sun. Colleen might be right after all. She said that everyone attended the kite festival, even the sun.

Cradling her coffee mug in both hands she brought it to her lips and swallowed the last bit. Declan roasted his own beans; his coffee was the best she'd ever tasted, and she hoped Joe would find a way to use Declan's in the restaurant.

The back door burst open, smacking the unpainted siding by the new window. Maureen turned in time to see Dilly and Joey stuck in the doorway, both fighting to squeeze through at the same time. Finally, Dilly went underneath and shot down the stairs and across the yard, her lumpy beach bag bouncing against her thin legs. After regaining his balance for a moment, Joey stumbled through the door and made his way slowly down the stairs, face blurry with sleep and dragging two oversized canvas totes behind him.

Because of the kite festival, the Saturday morning farmer's market had moved their tents to the front of the library, but they were still open, and Joey was delighted to be in charge of the menu for tonight's party until he realized how early he had to wake up to shop at the Saturday market.

The sound of little feet pounding the ground brought a smile to Maureen's lips as she watched Dilly running toward her, dark curls trailing behind her and her beach bag thumping by her side.

"Daddy's late and I beat Joey out the door again." Dilly was breathless.

In the same motion she had used so many times before, Maureen held her arm out, hooked her daughter and pulled her in for a hug. After depositing a raspberry kiss on top of Dilly's head, Maureen let her chin rest there. Dilly smelled like strawberry jam and wood smoke, and it occurred to Maureen that the last time Dilly was near a fire pit had been the night Kenny arrived, more than two weeks ago. She wondered, with a start, how long it had been since her daughter bathed.

"Dilly…."

Dilly looked toward the house and heaved a great sigh as if she couldn't believe everyone was taking this long. "Juliette is still hogging the bathroom. She's putting on mascaaaaara." Fluttering her eyelashes, Dilly drew out the word, and Maureen pursed her lips to keep from smiling.

"Do you have everything you need?"

"Yup." Wiggling out from her mother's hug, Dilly jiggled her bright yellow bag as proof.

Maureen counted off on her fingers, reviewing the plans of the morning. "We are walking across the beach to town, then you're going to meet Preta at Declan's. After lunch Preta's family is going to come for dinner and for the candle kites."

"I know, Mommy. I know. I'm not a baby anymore, I can remember things." Dilly rolled her eyes, a mirror image of Juliette and Maureen's heart tugged for a moment. She wasn't at all prepared for Dilly to grow up yet.

Joey trudged through the yard toward them, wiping the sleep from his eyes with his palm and dragging the market bags in the sand. "When I have a restaurant, I'm not going to make anyone get up this early. I won't even turn on the lights until mid-morning."

Maureen reached to smooth Joey's damp hair. A lanky sixteen, he was taller than his mother by a good six inches and the only time she could kiss the top of his head now, is when he's seated. "That's very generous of you, but I'm afraid you'll miss most of your morning deliveries."

Joey jerked his chin toward the house. "Aunt Lydia said she'd drive Juliette into town when she goes. She's doing something with Juliette in the bathroom." He flapped his hand in the direction of the house, indicating something was happening in there that he had no interest in.

Dilly was indignant. "See. Juliette's hogging the bathroom."

Maureen smoothed her daughter's hair with her palm and turned to Joey. "So we're only waiting for Daddy. Do you have a list for the farmer's market?"

Rolling his eyes, he scoffed. "No one uses a list anymore. I buy what's fresh and create recipes from local ingredients. Everyone does it that way now."

Arching an eyebrow, she fixed her son with a pointed stare. "Really? Is that how it's done now?"

He returned her stare with a smile, and she brushed his cheek with her fingers, a bit surprised to feel stubble.

When Joe finally emerged from the path, they were ready to go. Maureen set her mug on the ledge along with the others. To her dismay, the collection of mugs on the ledge was growing and she made a note to bring them inside when she came back. The flat rock at the top of the trail was a convenient place to put her cup before her morning walk, but she didn't always remember to bring it back into the house.

Joe stopped in front of them with an expectant smile on his face. "Let's go! What are we waiting for?"

Dilly tilted her head up to look at Joe. "We're waiting for you, Daddy."

"Really?" Joe feigned surprise. "I would have been here sooner if I had known you were already here."

But neither Dilly nor Joey waited for their father's answer; both took off, running and surfing the sand of the beach trail. Dilly because she said running down the hill made her feel like she was flying, and Joey because Dilly had called him slow.

Maureen reached for Joe's hand, warm from being inside the house and still slightly calloused at the base of his fingers where his chef's knife rested. She had spent a lifetime holding his hand, and she knew every callous and cut. "So I guess it's just us then?"

He nodded. "Tyra left a note. The city insisted that Gordon plant flowers in his window box and sweep in front of his store, so Tyra's gone to help but had to leave early because Gordon wants to make sure his shop is closed before the festival starts."

Maureen laughed, leaning into Joe. "Gordon wants to close his kite shop before the kite festival? Isn't that bad for business?"

He shrugged. "He seems to be making it work." But his eyes clouded with concern as they neared the steep trail. "You going to be okay?"

"Of course." Maureen kissed him soundly on the cheek. "I've lost a few pounds already, you know, from walking, and my knees feel better."

Joe kissed her back, on the lips. "I knew you could do it. But it wouldn't be any trouble to put stairs here. Charlie and his crew are finished with the house, but you and Tyra feed them so well that I don't think they'd mind coming back for another few days."

Maureen shook her head. "I'm fine Joe, stop fussing. I've been using this trail every day since Kenny left. And the kids seem to love it – I've seen Joey trying to surf the sand all the way down. Plus, I think it might be easier for Mulligan if there were no stairs. "

"Mulligan?" Joe brightened. "So Lydia's decided to keep him?"

Maureen nodded and started down the trail. "Now this house is ours, Lydia can give him a home. She's already moved into the studio because it doesn't have stairs, and Tyra was willing to move to the third floor until he's stronger, but she's pretty attached to the studio and wants to live there."

Joe laughed as they moved down the trail. "That whole giant house – completely refinished – and your sisters are fighting over the studio?"

The middle of the trail was Maureen's favorite part. It narrowed to a switchback and the corner was planted with shrub roses and wild grass, their heads heavy with dew and bent across the trail. The toes of her white keds soaked through as the texture of the sand moved from dry and sugar-fine to coarse and wet from the ocean mist. At the bottom of the trail was a pocket where the scent of the rose flowers combined with the sharpness of the wild thyme, and the heavy smell of low tide. Maureen drew a deep breath and held it, enjoying the stillness of the beach.

In an unexpected show of courtesy, both children waited at the bottom of the trail for their parents, but once Maureen's foot hit the beach, they scampered away like chipmunks.

"I call the sand dollars, Joey." Dilly dropped her bag in the damp sand and raced toward her brother, whose long legs had taken him almost to the water's edge.

Automatically scooping up Dilly's dropped bag, Maureen brushed the sand from the bottom as she kept a watchful eye on her children.

When they got to the edge of the shore, Joey and Dilly stopped to look for treasures hidden in the foam outline of the last high tide.

Despite being the official opening day of the summer tourist season, and the day of the kite festival, the beach was almost deserted this early in the morning.

Falling into step beside him, Maureen slipped her hand beneath the crook of Joe's arm and pointed toward the rock offshore. "Colleen told me a tourist scaled that rock a few years ago. He got stuck halfway up and had to be rescued before the tide came in."

Joe laughed, a deep rumbling in his chest that warmed Maureen's heart. "You have to expect stupid sometimes, I guess."

Further down the beach, near the ocean-front hotels, they passed the only other tourists on the beach, a young couple introducing their dog to the ocean. The dog pranced and barked at the low waves as they broke on shore, biting the foam and shaking his head at the taste. On the far side of the hotel a cluster of white canopies scattered along the upper beach, their trim snapping in the morning breeze. In the grassy courtyard an army of hotel staff set up displays of kites for sale, beach chairs for rent, and rough triangles of firewood for the night's bonfires. On several balconies facing the ocean, sleepy tourists greeted the day, bathrobed, with coffee in hand.

Maureen and Joe walked in comfortable silence until just past the hotels. As they neared the wooden beach steps, Joe stiffened and slowed his pace. Years of walking with this man had taught her that Joe only did that when he had something important to say, so Maureen waited.

He stopped before the bottom step and cleared his throat. "Ben called me a few days ago. He and Zoey want to make an offer for a half partnership at the restaurant. I told him I had to talk to you."

"Interesting." Maureen looked Joe to see if he took their offer seriously, but his expression was carefully blank. "How do they want to share ownership?"

"He doesn't have details; he just wanted to know if we were open to the idea." Joe took a deep breath, holding it a moment before exhaling loudly. He was choosing his words, about to say something he thought Maureen wouldn't like, and she felt herself tense. Joe raked his fingertips across the stubble on this chin. "I think this offer may be worth considering because there's something I want to talk to you about before we get to town."

Maureen glanced at the steps just before the inlet; he didn't have much time.

"Joey doesn't want to go to college."

Maureen's shoulders relaxed immediately. Over the past several months, Joey had spent more time experimenting in the kitchen and learning about sourcing the best ingredients than he had looking at college catalogs that came in the mail. Not that he wouldn't do well in college, making the honor roll seemed almost effortless for him, but academics didn't hold his interest. Not like cooking.

"We left college, too, remember?"

Maureen heard Joe exhale and realized he must have been holding his breath, and she squeezed his arm. She remembered the cavernous lecture hall of an early morning econ class, a required first year class. Joe's assigned seat was next to hers and by December, the only thing they had learned was that college wasn't for them.

"But it might have been easier, in the beginning, to know things. We dove right in, opening the restaurant without knowing anything about accounting or staffing or management. We're lucky we survived the first year, and even luckier we made it work. I want better than that for Joey."

"We both do. The college funds are in case they want to go, not to force them. Joey's got to find his own way. He's a really smart kid, he'll be fine. And we'll be close by if he needs help."

Joe called the kids in from the water's edge and looped his arm around Maureen. When Joey and Dilly arrived, breathless and red-cheeked, they turned to race each other up the beach stairs, and Maureen wondered where they got the energy. When the kids reached the top, they waved and wandered ahead, toward Declan's.

When Joey was out of earshot, Maureen turned to her husband. "What does he want to do instead?"

Joe looked at Maureen, his eyes twinkling with excitement. "It's pretty impressive, really. He wants to start a picnic takeout for tourists –coolers for the beach crowd, backpacks for the hikers, toy packs for kids – and toys for dogs. Locally sourced ingredients and locally made crafts. Maybe a kite from Gordon's or – I don't know, something else –" He circled the air with his hand to indicate the endless possibilities. "But before he starts, he's going to take a basic restaurant management course at the community college – the next session starts in the fall and he can take those classes after school. He's waiting until I talk to you before he registers. Then on the weekends, he's going to train in the restaurant as a sous-chef and shadow Josh when he can. Pretty ingenious really."

Color rose in Joe's cheeks as he spoke, a broad smile sweeping across his face. This is what Joe had been looking for when he proposed buying a second restaurant in Portland: another challenge. His passion was in the planning, the beginning work: developing a business plan, creating recipes, finding vendors, designing the layout, and ordering appliances.

She smiled. "Okay."

Joe stopped, mid-sentence, his brow furrowed in confusion, his mouth agape.

She laughed. Only a few times in her life had she managed to render her husband completely speechless, and she enjoyed it every time. Shrugging, she said. "I think it might be a good idea."

"You do?"

"Absolutely."

Pausing with his foot resting on the bottom tread, Joe said. "He still has a year of school left, we know that." He held his palm out to her as if to stop her objections, but she didn't have any. A restaurant in town for Joey was more than she could ever hope for; he would be close, her husband would be happily occupied, and her family would be together. It felt like she had won the lottery.

Again.

Reaching for the wooden railing, she smiled at him. "I'm sure you boys know what you're doing."

He wasn't following. Maureen turned to see him frozen at the bottom of the stairs. His eyes narrowed as he thought of something else. "We're going to use his college fund to start the business."

Even though she knew she shouldn't be, she was enjoying this. Flashing him an overly bright smile, she said. "Oh, I think you should."

"Okay, now I know you're screwing with me."

At the bench under the arbor, she turned to face Joe, completely serious. "All I ever wanted was to have my whole family together." She let her hand rest on Joe's forearm. "I won't hold Joey back from moving away to college if that's what he wants, but if his dream takes him only a few miles from us, then I'm thrilled. And if this project involves you in some way, then even better." She shrugged. "If it takes his entire college fund, it's still worth it."

As Joe leaned in to kiss her, he whispered in her ear. "You should have told me this; it would have saved me a lot of aggravation."

Maureen reached for Joe's hand and walked the street toward town. Joey had already made his way to the farmer's market and reached for a carton of fresh chicken eggs. Maureen thought about the pink coop waiting for them at home and smiled, imagining how surprised Dilly would be when Colleen arrived later tonight with three real chickens. Maureen scanned the thinly crowded street and spotted Dilly running toward her friends at Declan's, absolutely positive that Declan had saved the biggest cinnamon roll just for her.

Leaning into Joe, she put her head on his shoulder.

Her heart was full.

***

Tyra slipped the last trailing geranium plant into the window box, brushed the dirt from her hands and stepped back to admire her work. The original window boxes had rotted through when Gordon finally attempted to fill them, and he panicked and called Tyra, offering to build new boxes if she would select the flowers and help him plant them. Lydia laughed when she heard, calling it the oldest trick in the book and wondering why Gordon didn't ask her outright for a date. Joe told her that Gordon was the least helpless man he'd ever seen and refused to believe he'd panic. Tyra helped him anyway.

As she swept the potting soil from the bricked path, Gordon emerged from inside his shop, a smile of appreciation on his face. "This looks really stellar, thank you."

Leaning the broom against the gray siding of Gordon's shop, Tyra bent to stack the plastic nursery containers so he wouldn't see her blush. She was still uneasy around him, not sure how to act. They didn't teach this kind of thing at the group home.

He reached for the pots, brushing her fingers with his. "Really, Tyra. Come see how good it looks." He pointed down the alley to the riot of early summer flowers spilling from the windows boxes along the path.

They walked to the end and looked down the main shopping street. It was a beautiful sight. Red summer geraniums and purple spikey flowers filled white painted boxes that lined both sides of the sidewalk.

Tyra waved to Maureen and Joe, and watched the kids join the crowd in front of Declan's.

Turning back to face Gordon, he did not look pleased. Tyra followed his gaze to see a brightly painted sign at the edge of the alley pointing the way to his shop.

He shook his head sadly. "This is going to be a problem."

Twisting the sign so it pointed the other way, he ducked back down the alley toward his shop. For the start of tourist season, the city insisted he make his shop more presentable. The wooden sign, once a splintered pink was now newly sanded and freshly painted a vibrant purple. The picture window, boarded and draped with heavy fabric for almost a year was bright and open, with two brightly colored box kites displayed prominently.

Tyra pointed to the stencil on the plate glass door, a picture of a triangle kite blowing in the wind, its tail spelling out his shop name, "Above Your Head" and smiled. "I didn't know you had a logo."

"Lydia did that."

"What?"

"That's right." Gordon brightened. "Very soon I won't have to worry about talking to customers at all because Lydia's going to build a website for me and all I'll have to do is pack the orders. She found a college kid to wait on customers in the front of the shop while I build kites in the back and made me hire him. She said she worked with him at the jobsite and that I'd like him. I did. He solos this morning, in fact. " He brushed his arm across the air as a joyful smile spread across his face. "If everything goes according to plan, I could go *weeks* without talking to anyone."

"You're a strange man, Gordon Warnick."

A squeal from the top of the alley caught their attention and both turned to look. "Oooooh – let's see what's down here." A large woman wearing white capris and a billowing flowered shirt squinted down the path. When her eyes adjusted to the filtered light, she started down the bricked path, immediately followed by a man in oversized cargo shorts, strapped sandals, and an enormous beer belly.

Gordon snatched the broom from the side of his building and threw it behind the bushes. Seconds later the plastic nursery pots clattered behind, followed by the fluttering cardboard box Tyra used for the plants. Tyra suppressed a giggle just as the couple approached.

"What's this one?" The woman pointed to Gordon's shop and the man, wearing a long-suffering expression of resignation mumbled something incoherent.

"You think it's open?" The woman tugged at the front doorknob, rattling the frame, and Gordon's eyes grew to saucers. No wonder he didn't like tourists.

"I heard they went out of business." Tyra said solemnly, clearing her throat to drown out the guffaw from Gordon.

The woman placed her palm on her throat and dropped her chin in a dramatic show of concern. "Now isn't that tragic, I bet they could have used the business, especially today. They sell kites in there, don't they? I don't know a thing about kites and

I don't have need of one, but it would have been nice to browse."
The woman brought her hand to her forehead and squinted
through the picture window.

Tyra bit her lip and refused to look at Gordon.

"Well, maybe it's for the best." She tugged the arm of her
companion. "Come on dear, there's more to see. I hear this whole
shopping area is filled with secret alleyways."

The woman disappeared down the brick path, her
companion lumbering behind, but as he passed Tyra, he tilted
his head and gave her a quick wink and a smile.

"Okay, let's get out of here before someone else shows up."
Gordon clapped his hands together to show he meant business.

Tyra jerked her chin toward the young man walking down
the alley. Wearing a blue oxford and a serious expression, he
smiled tentatively as he approached Gordon. "I'm ready for the
keys."

Tyra smiled. "I know you. You pulled rotten drywall with
Lydia and you volunteered on Kitchen Day, didn't you?"

He nodded. "I did. And I'd do it again just for the pleasure
of working with Charlie Gimball."

Gordon handed his new employee a key to the shop tied with
a red bow. "Your very own key, you've earned it. I'll be back in
two hours – call me if you need me before then."

Tyra and Gordon went back to the house to help get ready
for the party. Maureen told them to expect fifty to sixty people,
most just dropping by at dusk to see the launch of the candle
kites.

After that was dinner and Joey was in charge of the menu.
Everyone else had a support job. Juliette and Dilly set the

buffet, Lydia was kitchen help, Tyra was in charge of seating and Maureen supervised.

Although Tyra was pretty sure Joe and Gordon were asked to do something else, she saw them sneaking around the blackberry vines, poking at the rusted drum. As she set up the rental chairs, she listened to them whisper about it.

"This fire pit is going to be awesome." Gordon bent to lift it, while Joe hung back, still looking dubious.

Finally, grabbing the jagged edge of the drum with gloved hands, Joe murmured something unintelligible. Tyra watched them pick their way through the blackberry thicket until she couldn't stand another second.

Tyra snorted. "You guys have been trying to put it together for almost a month. You might want to wave the white flag on this one."

Gordon slapped his palm over his heart in mock horror. "Nonsense. It will be the best fire pit for miles."

The back screen door slapped shut, Maureen strode around the corner, and everyone scattered.

***

Lydia slid her car along the curb in front of the vet clinic until she was almost parallel to the front door and parked, intentionally ignoring the No Parking sign. Before getting out of the car, she turned around to check the back seat, running the checklist in her mind:– seats laid flat, the space behind circled with quilts.

Check and check. Everything was ready.

As she turned back around, she glimpsed her reflection in the rearview mirror and barely recognized herself. She was smiling. In fact, she'd been smiling since she woke up this morning; her cheeks ached with it. Getting out of her car, she moved the No Parking sign to the side to give herself more room and walked inside.

"Well, good morning, honey. You're getting an early start today." Colleen slipped off her green reading glasses and smiled in welcome.

Lydia smiled back and reached to squeeze Colleen's hand. Lydia had been to visit Mulligan and Colleen at least a dozen times since she found him that day under the beach stairs and she'd grown very fond of both of them. "I wanted to get him settled in the house before things get crazy out there." Lydia pointed toward the door. "You're not staying open during the festival, are you?"

Colleen shook her head. "Oh no, I'm just finishing a few things up." She wiggled her eyebrows; her brown eyes sparkled with mischief. "I've got a dinner party to go to, I can't waste my time around here."

Lydia smiled. "I'm glad you're coming. She caught Colleen's gaze and held it. "And you're sure you're okay with me taking him?"

Colleen's eyes filled, but she waved Lydia away with a flick of her fingers. "I'm not going to lie, honey, I'm going to miss that sweet baby, but he's always been yours, ever since you found and brought him here to be fixed up. He would have gone home with you sooner, but you had that mess with Kenny to deal with – I just looked after him for you." She nodded firmly to convince herself, though the tears in her eyes threatened to spill. "He's a sweet boy and he needs to run with a young family, not spend his days behind the counter with an old woman like me." She clapped her hands together. "Let's go find him. I think Rebecca's taken him outside one last time."

They found Rebecca and Mulligan in the side yard, Mulligan loping after an old tennis ball, and Rebecca happily watching. As soon as Mulligan recognized Lydia, he trotted up to greet her, bringing his precious tennis ball with him.

Rebecca stroked his head. "It's hard to believe this is the same dog you brought in four months ago."

Colleen put her hand lightly on Mulligan's back. "We are going to miss this little angel." After a moment, she looked at Lydia. "Remember now, he likes his chicken boiled until it's tender, and he prefers dark meat."

Lydia bit her lip to hide her smile. "Really? I didn't know that."

"Oh, honey, don't you remember? We've gone over this –" Understanding spread across Colleen's face, and she swatted at Lydia's arm. "Smartass."

A scrape across the concrete sidewalk out front drew their attention; vendors had starting to set up tables for the street fair. Shop owners were unfurling their awnings and opening their doors to the earliest customers.

Lydia faced Rebecca and Colleen, not sure how to thank them for all they'd done. She began with, "Thank you," but stumbled on the rest, and it was Colleen who made it okay. "Oh, honey, you're just up the hill. It's not like you're moving away."

That feeling bloomed in Lydia, and she sat with it for a moment, letting it grow, then smiled. "No, I'm not moving away."

"And I need to see Mulligan in a few weeks anyway, just to check his progress." Rebecca handed the leash to her. "You better get going. Local or not, Albert will ticket you if you block his beloved street fair."

As they walked through the waiting room to her car, Colleen pointed to Mulligan's bed, tucked behind her reception desk. "I suppose you'll want to take that with you." Her voice trailed off.

"Actually, I've been meaning to talk to you about something." Lydia turned. "I didn't think now is the right time, because I don't have any details yet. But I was going to ask you if you wanted to watch him a day or two during the week –"

"Oh, honey – that would be wonderful." Colleen's eyes lit as she nodded. "Yes, I would love that."

"Good. I'll tell you more when I know. And thank you. Thank you both."

Lydia led the way to her car. Behind her, Dr. Brinkley laughed, pointing at the No-Parking sandwich boards stacked beside the curb. "Did you move those?"

"Of course."

"And you parked in front of the fire hydrant?"

"It was the closest spot to the front door."

Rebecca laughed harder and shook her head. "I will not worry another moment about Mulligan, he's in good hands."

After asking again if there were any last minute thing they could bring to the kite party, they waited until Lydia got in her car before waving and walking back inside.

As she made her way to the end of the main street toward the crowd spilling out of Declan's, she waved to Joe and

Maureen, who must be just finishing their morning walk. Maureen wore her new cardigan, and Lydia hoped never to see the ratty black fleece jacket again.

Joe was only too happy to grab the barricade that blocked the street and move it, allowing her to pass. Lydia waved her thanks and made her way up the hill.

The drive was short, and Mulligan slept all the way, snug in his quilt bed, apparently tired from chasing the tennis ball. Before settling him into the studio, she brought him with her to the kitchen in the house to check the job assignments for the kite party tonight. Maureen practically vibrated with excitement for this party, reminding them several times that they all had jobs and woe be to the person who neglected theirs.

Lydia wandered around back, entering through the storm porch, framed but not yet finished. The studs reached from the floor to the ceiling and without windows, the room looked a little like a pumpkin's smile. Joe and Gordon claimed the project of installing windows as their own, even though both Tyra and Maureen had tried their best to talk them out of it.

Opening the door to the kitchen, Lydia was greeted with the smells of someone who knew their way around a kitchen. Onions and butter and garlic sautéed in an oversized frying pan, a stock pot bubbled on a back burner, and the counter was strewn with bundles of asparagus, spinach, and cartons of strawberries. Joey, at the counter, was confidently in charge of it all.

"Hi, Aunt Lydia." He glanced from his work long enough to smile at her.

"Hiya, kiddo. What have –"

"Mulligan! You brought Mulligan." Joey put his knife safely

away and kneeled down to pat the dog's head.

Mulligan rested his head on Joey's knee with a deep sigh. This was the same dog who not twenty minutes ago had chased a tennis ball around the yard. Lydia was beginning to think she had an actor on her hands.

"I have chicken and rice for him." Joey glanced up, his face glowing. "I kept it warm and mixed in some steamed sweet potato and carrot."

Lydia was about to tell Joey that Mulligan should be transitioning to regular dog food at some point, but stopped and nodded instead. Mulligan would be spoiled living here, but he deserved it. "Sure. Thank you, Joey."

As Joey grabbed a spoon and lifted a pot off the stove. As he scooped up stew for Mulligan, he pointed to the far counter with his chin. "I almost forgot – some mail came for you, Aunt Lydia. It's over there."

Sifting through the stack, she found two envelopes addressed to her. The first, oversized from an attorney's office in Virginia. She opened that one right away. Gregg's attorney explained that it had taken longer than he expected to find her, and divorce proceedings were well under way. She could help speed the process by signing the no-contest waiver and returning it at her earliest convenience. Once she did, she could consider herself divorced. There were no assets, nothing to divide, and Greg proposed no spousal support.

Snatching a pen from the cup by the phone, she signed the last page of the agreement and considered herself lucky. Pushing the waiver back in the envelope, she would personally deliver it to the post office before they closed and celebrate at the party tonight.

When she saw the return address on the second envelope, her heart skipped a beat and she squeaked.

"You okay, Aunt Lydia?" Joey glanced up distractedly.

"Yup, I'm okay."

She didn't think she'd get in, but she had. The state's university had a small coastal campus about an hour away. Tyra found it and helped her with the application, and they accepted her as a part-time student for the fall. Before her classes officially started, she would take one professional development class in web design. When she was certified, she could work from home and use the money she earned to pay her tuition.

Gordon would be her first client. Joey's new restaurant would be her second, and she planned to donate time to the vet clinic and the community center.

Holding the letter to her chest, she looked out at the kitchen in the house she wanted so badly to sell and closed her eyes. She was surrounded by family, she was going to have her own business, and she was finally going to college.

Opening her eyes, she watched Joey choose a soft bit of chicken from the pot and offer it to Mulligan. And she watched Mulligan gently take it.

Lydia smiled.

Her heart was full.

***

Dilly skipped across the driveway toward the little house and slid to a stop at the edge of the plum tree garden. With all the cars in the driveway and people in the yard, she knew the fairies inside would definitely be scared so she went inside the little house, wrote a note in her best writing, and left it by the tree. After that, she gathered three unbroken oyster shells from the driveway and lined each of them with a blanket of spongy moss in case the fairies needed extra beds to watch the candle kite launch. By the time she finished, she'd forgotten what she had been sent for and was on her way back to ask.

She liked this big beach house and was glad they were spending the summer here all together. She could go to the beach anytime she wanted, as long as a grown-up was with her, and she liked sliding down the steep hill to get there. Most of the time Aunt Tyra went with her, to look for sea glass and driftwood and later today she and her friend Zachary were going down to poke jellyfish with sticks before the tide took them away.

Her shadow was long on the driveway when Dilly ran toward the house to find her mother. As soon as the sun went completely down, they were going to launch candle kites, and Dilly had her wish in her mind for two days.

Someone lit the twinkle lights that Mommy and the aunts had strung in the big tree, and Dilly ran toward it to get a closer look. Every branch was wrapped with tiny white lights as far as Charlie's big ladder could reach and from the lower branches hung red paper lanterns. Scattered around the base were wooden picnic tables, each covered with a different colored tablecloth. The flowers and beach grass she and Juliette and Aunt Lydia collected earlier that morning were on the table, grouped together in different sized vases. Straight down the middle of each table was line of fat white candles in tall hurricane glass, but they weren't lit yet.

Closer to the house, the screen door slammed as people streamed in and out of the house, bringing platters of food to the table or folding chairs to the firepit. Daddy was there with Gordon and Joey, watching the fire and congratulating themselves on winning the bet with Mommy that it would be finished before the party. She waved to them as she ran past, on her way to find Zachary.

She circled once around the house running as fast as she could, looking for Zachary while keeping one eye on the sun setting over the bluff. Gordon told her if they released the candle kites at sunset, the wishes they whispered into the bags would come true. And Dilly had been holding her wish inside for too long already. She wanted the whole summer to be like this, with everyone together at the big house.

Everyone seemed happier here. Even the blurry lady who watched them from the upstairs window smiled now.

As she rounded the corner of the house, she found Zachary in the sandpit, shaking hands with Gordon. She ran toward them, hooking her arm around her daddy's leg so she could slingshot like she always did, but Daddy scooped her up before she really got going.

He put his finger over his lips. "Shh, Dilly. Gordon's talking to Zachary now."

Gordon's face was very serious. "You must be Zachary. My name's Gordon, and I've been waiting for you."

Zachary stiffened, probably hoping he wasn't about to get in trouble. His mother and her boyfriend yelled at him a lot at home, that's why he spent the summer with Charlie.

"You have?"

Gordon nodded, and Dilly wished he wasn't so serious. Zachary didn't like serious, it scared him. Anyone could see that. "Absolutely. I have candle kites that need to be launched and no one to help me. I need an assistant, and I believe you are the right man for the job."

Zachary twisted his fingers together, something he only did when he was nervous. Dilly squirmed out of Daddy's arms to stand next to her friend as Gordon explained things.

"The candle kites need to launch as close to sunset as we can, because that's when you make your wish and let it go. I could really use someone to keep track of the time and remind me when it's time to launch. You think you can do that?"

Zachary bit his bottom lip and nodded. He waited as Gordon slipped his watch on Zachary's wrist. As he tightened the band, he explained. "We need to start at eight forty-five. Do you know what that time looks like?"

"Time is my best thing." Zachary stood up straight, smiling for real and Dilly was glad. Before the party, she heard some of the grown-ups talking about Zachary, and she didn't like what they said about what happened to him when he was with his mother. She was glad he had come to Inlet Beach, glad he could live with Mr. Gimball. She would watch out for him.

"Good, I'm counting on you." Gordon shook Zachary's hand and let him go.

The rest of the party was a blur.

As soon as Dilly realized no one was watching her, she could do what she wanted. Zipping around the party, she pulled root beers from the ice bucket, handfuls of marshmallows from the s'mores basket, brownies from the dessert table, and shared everything with Zachary. They were asked to join a soccer game, but Zachary was afraid he would forget to check Gordon's watch; so they watched instead, and Dilly made sure they played far enough away from the guest house so Mulligan wouldn't bark. Aunt Lydia told her so many people might scare Mulligan, so he was in the little house by himself. Dilly wasn't allowed to go inside to check on him, but she was supposed to tell Aunt Lydia if he started to bark.

Finally, when the big hand was on the six and the little hand was just past the eight, Zachary showed her the watch. "It's time to look for that man now."

Dilly scrambled to her feet. "That's easy. All we have to do is find Aunt Tyra and he'll be close by. Just look for her black and purple hair."

Dilly wanted purple hair, just like Aunt Tyra, but Mommy said not yet, which was almost as good as a yes.

As they crossed the driveway, Dilly crushed the oyster shells with her sneakers, listening to them crack. Zachary was careful of his new sneakers, avoiding every fun thing that might scuff them. Mr. Gimball bought them for Zachary yesterday, as soon as his mother had dropped him off, along with new summer clothes. He told Dilly that he liked his sneakers best, that he could run faster in them, so Dilly wished she had a pair, too.

Dilly pointed toward the fire pit. "Over there."

Gordon had his arm hooked around Aunt Tyra's shoulders, and they laughed at something Joey said. Dilly grabbed Zachary's arm and ran toward them, eager to hear the joke.

Gordon saw them coming and nodded. It was a good thing

Zachary was in charge of the time because Gordon looked surprised, as if he had forgotten. "Is it time?"

Gordon could sometimes look scary if you didn't know him, and Dilly knew it would take a minute for Zachary to answer.

Zachary showed him the time and mumbled something. Gordon smiled and clapped a hand on his shoulder. "Thanks, little dude. I might have forgotten if you hadn't reminded me."

As Gordon climbed onto one of the tree stumps circling the firepit and called everyone around, Dilly sneaked a look at Zachary. His cheeks reddened as he smiled, and Dilly was glad to see it.

"Could everyone gather around please?" Gordon's deep voice echoed around the party, and he waited as people wandered toward him.

Dilly listened as he asked everyone to take a box of matches from the big basket on their way down the trail to the beach. She thought it would be a good time to circle back to the dessert table and grab some more cookies for later, but Zachary wouldn't let her.

He took her hand and led her toward the trail.

"This is important," he said. "I have an important wish." He sounded so serious that Dilly didn't even slide down the sandy trail. She walked as slowly as if they were going to library time in school.

They weren't the first ones on the beach, although Dilly would have liked to be. Aunt Tyra and Aunt Lydia were already there, and Mommy joined them with her arm around Juliette's shoulders. Mommy didn't know about the boy Juliette met at the community center and liked enough to invite to the party.

Dilly would have to tell her later.

Aunt Tyra asked everyone to gather around and thanked them all for coming. She thanked Mr. Gimball and said they wouldn't have a home without him. Mr. Gimball looked away, but Dilly saw him smile.

They talked so long that Dilly and Zachary turned their attention to the candle kites to see how it worked. It was a bag, a thin, colored bag not much bigger than a lunch sack, and it didn't come with a string to launch it from the ground or a tail to rudder the wind. The only bit of string was wedged in a triangle of wood just inside the bag. Dilly hoped it would fly because she didn't want Gordon to be embarrassed if his kites didn't work.

Finally, when they were ready to launch, Gordon called for Zachary to come to the front. Dilly pushed her hands into the pocket of her shorts; she knew what was going to happen and she wasn't the tiniest bit jealous. She was excited for her friend.

"This is a perfect night for a launch. The breeze is with us." Gordon clamped his hand on Zachary's shoulder. "It's customary for the youngest member of the group to launch the kites. And since Zachary just finished first grade, he's the youngest." He paused to whisper something into Zachary's ear. When Zachary nodded, Gordon straightened.

"Before Zachary starts the countdown, I'll just remind you how the kites work. Unfold the paper and pull down the wick. After you've whispered your wish inside the bag, you strike the match and light the wick. The air inside will warm and it will lift the kite into the air. Don't throw it or try to launch it; the kite will do all the work."

He looked out over the crowd and smiled as he caught Dilly's eye. "If you don't have matches, or aren't yet allowed to use them, you can share a kite or find someone to light yours."

Dilly realized she wasn't allowed to use matches, so she found Mommy, who helped her unfold the kite and pull down the wick. Dilly whispered her wish into the bag just as Zachary started his countdown.

In the loudest voice Dilly ever heard him use – the one even recess aides at school would shush – Zachary counted back from five.

When he said three, Gordon told everyone to strike the matches.

When he said two, Gordon told everyone to light the wicks,

When he reached the last number, Dilly's kite felt lighter in her hands and lifted into the air to join the others.

As the sky purpled with the setting sun and the sky darkened, the kites floated into the air and rode the evening breeze toward the ocean, filling the darkness with pinpricks of light.

Every one of them carrying a wish.

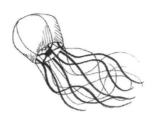

Epilogue

Charlie and Colleen were the last to arrive for the Harvest Dinner, turning in just as the sun started its descent behind the bluff. He was on time to pick her up, but Colleen's cornbread wasn't quite ready and he didn't mind waiting.

As he pulled his truck into the driveway, instead of the usual crunch under his tires, he hit hard-pack dirt. He slowed the truck to peer through his windshield. All the coarse gray construction gravel and all the oyster shells had been scraped away and it was a bit jarring to see a change to Elizabeth's house that he hadn't overseen.

Colleen reached to touch his arm. "Charlie, isn't it wonderful that Gordon and Joe plan to restore even the driveway? The firepit project went so well that they've decided to tackle something bigger. I hear Joey talked them into reclaiming oyster shells from restaurants." One hand steadied her basket as the other waved in the air as if the details eluded her. "They want the whole thing done by next summer, but all they've done so far is clear the driveway. Either way," her voice dropped to a whisper even though it was just the two of them in the cab, "it gives Gordon an excuse to come by, and I think that's good. Tyra lives here full-time now. In the guest house."

Charlie was glad Tyra had found a place where she belonged,

glad they all had. He parked his truck where he always did, just behind the little house by the plum tree. And like he always did, he walked around his truck, opened the door for Colleen, and offered his arm.

Together they looked at Elizabeth's house.

"It almost looks like she's still there, doesn't it?" If he closed his eyes, he could imagine Elizabeth bustling in the kitchen, and Lloyd out back shucking oysters or cleaning fish. And the house, finally, had come to life.

A single candle was placed in the deep sill of every window in the house, casting a warm glow in the half-light of the winter afternoon. From their place on the driveway, they could see the storm porch was finished, glassed and decorated with twinkle lights and beach grass wreaths. The table was laid in that room, a change from Elizabeth's time, but one she would have approved

He felt Colleen nod beside him. "I believe she would be happy her house is in such good hands."

And it was.

Thank You

There are a number of people whose help made writing this book easier and I would like to thank them for their time.

To the PNWA, especially Pam Binder, Gerri Russell, and Terry Persun: thank you for graciously answering all my questions (and there were many).

Thank you to my critique group, who are so not afraid to tell me when something isn't working and who celebrate with me when something does: Sandy Esene, Liz Vissner, Ann Reckner, Laurie Rockenbeck, and Bridget Norquist. All amazing writers.

A special thank you to Sandy Esene (again), Mitch Patterson, Barb Lutz, Colleen Broddus, Debra Patterson who read an early draft of my novel and didn't laugh (much).

Thank you Nancy Leson, who answered all of food and restaurant related questions, and to Dave Berkey who answered email from a stranger and then gave me two hours of his time to sift through estate law.

And finally, to my own sister, Heather Furfari, who is nothing like any of the characters in my book.

ABOUT THE AUTHOR

Heidi adores making up stories and firmly believes it's a great tragedy that people put such emphasis on telling the truth. While truth does have its place, a good story is far more entertaining. Her favorites involve strong characters, unique circumstances, a strong family dynamic and a splash of humor. If they take place at the beach, all the better.

Heidi currently lives in the Pacific Northwest with her family and visits the beach every chance she gets. This is her first novel.

To connect with Heidi, please visit her website at HeidiHostetter.com or visit her on FaceBook. She welcomes your comments.

Made in the USA
San Bernardino, CA
27 October 2017